# HEMIOLA

## THE MOORE FAMILY SERIES BOOK 1

## MADISON BAILEY

*For my Momma,*

*For loving me, for believing in me, for making me the woman I am today.*

*I love you.*

# 1

## MICAH

I'M the son of Andrew Moore, one of Hollywood's most renowned directors and screenwriters. I'm famous now too, but I'm not sure I want to be.

Growing up, the movie set was my playground. I don't remember making a conscious choice to pursue acting, it was just something that always fired me up, something I always felt called to do.

I had only small roles growing up; an uncredited extra in a film, a guest-star on a Disney Channel series, a model for a children's clothing line at Target. I was good with these small roles. I didn't want to be one of those child stars who burned out before they were even 12 years old and ended up in a "Where are they now?" puff-piece on Buzzfeed.

When I was 15, my dad decided if I really wanted to do this, it was time to hire an agent and start looking for bigger roles. I didn't have the be the lead yet, but I had to take some more serious parts. I thought my dad could just pull some strings or call in a few favors, but he insisted I go the traditional route. Paying my dues, he called it. He wanted me to build my own success, not ride on the back of his. We found Winston, and he hit it out of the park by finding me a role as one of the leads in a family-friendly feel-good flick. I celebrated my 16th birthday on the set of that movie, and after a year of post-production, the movie premiered and was a bigger hit than we all expected. I mean, I knew it was a great movie when I took the part, but I was in no way prepared for the fame it launched me into.

I used to believe change wasn't a bad thing. It's just a part of life, and the sooner I learned to embrace and adapt to the inevitability of change, the easier life would be. But what am I supposed to do when I'm suddenly a huge success and still trying to figure myself out while the world watches. Was such a drastic change all that good when suddenly I didn't recognize myself in the mirror anymore?

At only 17 years old, everyone knew me. Or, at least, they thought they did. Tabloids with half-baked truths popped up about me weekly, and I was getting more auditions than ever before. I started wearing sunglasses and a baseball cap wherever I went and took to pulling the collar of my jackets up around my face to avoid being recognized.

I turned it into a game, to see how long I could be out, or how many places I could go, without people discovering who I was. Pretty soon, my best friends, Logan and Olivia, and I grew tired of that game, and so we upped the stakes. With some of my earnings from the movie, I bought the three of us the most legitimate fake IDs I could find and we spent our summer sneaking into bars all over Hollywood.

I patted my back pocket to make sure I had my wallet, adjusted the hat over my dark hair and slid a pair of sunglasses over my eyes even though it was 11:30 pm. I looked in the full-length mirror that hung on the back of my bedroom door, checking my appearance one last time.

My phone pinged with a message. *Hey bro, I'm parked around the corner from your house. Ready whenever you are.*

I slipped on my black leather jacket and slowly opened my bedroom door. I knew if I opened it too far, it would squeak and alert my twin sister, Melanie, and my parents, to the fact I was trying to sneak out. With barely enough room to fit through, I slipped out of the cracked door. I turned to shut it quietly when someone cleared her throat behind me.

"Crap," I sighed, leaning my forehead against my bedroom door in defeat before turning to face my sister.

"What do you think you're doing?" she asked, crossing her arms in front of her and raising an eyebrow.

"Shhh," I whispered, closing the distance between us and grabbing her shoulders. "Mom and dad will kill me if they hear us."

Usually, when I planned to go out with friends, I would walk through the house without caring how much noise I made, take my keys off the second to last hook by the door, and stroll down the row of my dad's extensive high-end car collection in our 14-car garage to my cherry-red Lamborghini. It was a 16th birthday present from my parents and it was always parked next to a 1965 classic baby-blue mustang, which had been Melanie's birthday gift.

But tonight I was reduced to sneaking out because I was in major trouble with my dad. A few nights ago, I'd called Melanie to pick me up from a party. When I'd gotten in the car with an almost full bottle of beer, she promptly took it from me, poured it out the window, and tossed the empty bottle in the back seat.

She told me she would throw it away, but forgot, and our dad found it. Given it was in our black Audi, the family stealth car, it could have been anyone's bottle, but my parents don't drink cheap beer, and they know Melanie doesn't drink, nor would she dream of disobeying them. It didn't take Sherlock Holmes to figure out it was mine.

My dad is usually a pretty chill person, but when he found out I had been drinking, he was furious. It could have been thanks to the acoustics in the garage, but I've never heard him yell so loud. He gave me a lecture about throwing away my life to horrible addictions and then grounded me for six whole weeks, saying I could only go to events with him so he could ensure that the most exciting thing I'd be drinking would be a cranberry Sprite.

So here I was, begging my sister not to give me away.

"I'm just going out with Logan and Olivia, no biggie," I continued in hushed tones.

"Micah, you've seriously got to stop this." Thankfully, she'd started whispering now, too. "You are in so much trouble with dad. If you mess up again, he's going to make good on his threat to send you away. And think about your career, and that great part Winston found for you today. Don't you want to see if that pans out?"

She was referring to a meeting I'd had earlier that day. Winston had been in touch with some of his contacts in Europe and found me an audition for a French movie. Both he and my dad thought it would be a great move for my career to find roles in international markets and diversify my experiences. The film was a small-market, independent project, and I was excited to potentially be a part of it.

"You finally made it big," Melanie continued, "you finally

have the chance to make your mark on the world, and you are spending your time getting wasted with good for nothing friends."

"Logan and Olivia are not good for nothing," I whisper-shouted, taking my hands off her shoulders and folding my arms. "They are the only people left in my life, besides you and mom and dad, who knew me before I was anybody. They are the only true friends I have left."

I knew Melanie meant well. We had always been close. She is sweet, yet fierce. No one loved, supported, or celebrated me more than she did. With great expectations, however, came great disappointments, and I knew I'd disappointed her more than I'd lived up to her expectations this summer.

Here's the thing: I loved Melanie more than anyone in the world, more than life itself, but I was trying to figure myself out. Who was I supposed to be in light of such great success? Who was I supposed to be now that I wasn't Micah Moore, the son of a great director and screenwriter, and I was finally Micah Moore, a talented actor in his own right?

"If they were true friends, they wouldn't let you do this to yourself. Come on, you're better than this."

I knew she was right. Melanie was always right.

"Can I just go, please?"

"You don't need my permission. But don't call me to sneak your drunk butt home past mom and dad." She pointed a finger at me accusingly. "I'm done doing that. Get an Uber." She turned and went back to her room.

"Fine," I huffed, resuming my stealthy walk down the stairs.

I held my breath and took extra time getting past my parents' bedroom, placing one tiny tip-toe down at a time and waiting between each one to make sure they hadn't heard me.

My heart raced with each step I took. If they heard me and came out of their room, it would be hard to explain my way out of even more trouble. After all, I clearly wasn't in my pajamas, so I couldn't play it off as just heading to get some water before bed.

Four steps later, I was past their room, and sneaking into the dining room. I went to the window and jimmied it up. This would have been so much easier if I could just use the front door like a normal person, but our house had an alarm system that dinged every time someone opened any outside door.

With the window pushed up as far as it would go, I bent over and stuck my right leg through the opening, stepping into my mother's pristine flower beds. After I was steady on one foot, I slowly moved the rest of my body through the window and pulled it almost all the way shut. I had to leave it cracked if I was going to get back in without setting off the alarm.

Finally free, I ran around the corner to Logan's car and climbed in the front seat.

"Took you long enough," he greeted me, shifting the car into drive and speeding away.

"Sorry, Mel caught me. Had to make sure she wasn't going to give me away to our parents." I twisted around, surprised to see the backseat empty. "Where's Olivia?"

"She's already there. We'd better hurry, or the game will be over before we even get a chance to play."

Once we figured out that our fake IDs were good enough to get us into any bar we wanted, we had to raise the stakes again. It was never enough for us to just play it safe and enjoy a night of drinks and dancing. That's when we came up with another game, the Kissing Game. It was silly really, but it gave us all something to do. The point was to zero in on someone and get them to initiate a kiss before we called it a night. Olivia won most nights, probably because most guys were eager to kiss her as soon as possible, and Logan won the nights Olivia didn't. I hadn't won a single time, which was ridiculous because I was the celebrity here. The losers had to split the bill, and Olivia always ordered these outrageously priced girly martinis. But she'd have to pay for her expensive liquor tonight because I was still high on adrenaline from sneaking out of the house and determined for a victory.

It shouldn't have been that hard for me. Most girls were eager to spend time with me, but for some reason, none of them made any moves to kiss me. Olivia said it was because I tried too hard to get to know the girl and that I just needed to make it clear it was all about the physical. It wasn't like I was afraid of kissing, and the point of the game wasn't even about finding someone I could actually have a relationship with. "Kiss it and quit it" was the motto of our little game, but it was hard for me to not feel like a huge jerk. To me, kissing meant more.

When we got to the entrance, I handed my ID to the bouncer. He looked between me and the card in his hand. The first few times we used our fake IDs, I would hold my breath in anticipation as the bouncer checked us out, but after fooling enough people into letting us in, I felt invincible. Very few doors were ever shut in my face. Whether that was because of the fame or the fact that my fake ID was just *that* good, I didn't know. After a few seconds, he nodded, handing back the card as I stepped inside. The whoosh of air conditioning hit me, sweet relief from the humid California summer outside. Live musicians played on a stage in the far corner, and the bass boomed through my whole body like a heartbeat.

Once Logan made it in, we went to the bar, ordering our

usuals; me, a bottle of Bud Light, and Logan, vodka on the rocks. I turned around, leaning my elbows on the bar, and lifted the bottle to my mouth, savoring that sweet, almost fruity smell before the fizzy liquid hit my tongue. I surveyed the dance floor for Olivia and scoped out a target for tonight. My gaze landed on many possibilities, mostly brunettes. I found them the most attractive. It always seemed like they had some dark, mysterious quality to them and I was intrigued.

One was sitting by the window at the front of the bar, sipping some sort of pink drink. The way the technicolor lights shined in her long curly hair made me want to run my fingers through it. She sat up straight, allowing her form-fitting white dress to compliment all her curves, and she crossed her long legs, her foot bouncing to the rhythm. She was with three other girls, so it was safe to say she wasn't here with a date. I would never go after someone who was already spoken for. I didn't want to get into a fight with someone's angry boyfriend, I was just trying to get my drinks paid for.

"What about her," I turned to Logan and tilted my head towards the front of the bar, "the one by the window?"

He took a quick glance in that direction and nodded. "Nice. Looks like she checks all your boxes. Dark hair, long legs, no man in sight."

Another possible conquest danced at the edge of the floor not far from where I was standing with Logan. Her dark, straight hair was cut in a short bob, and she ran her fingers through it as she swayed her hips seductively to the beat. She was hot and she knew it. Pretty soon, a guy joined her, wrapping his hands around her waist. She threw her arms around his shoulders and gave him a long, slow kiss before they moved

8

towards the middle of the dance floor. She was obviously off the table.

We finally found Olivia dancing near the far side of the wall. Making our way over to her was slow going as we were jostled and shoved by sweaty dancing bodies. Despite the AC, it was considerably muggier in the middle of the dance floor. Logan peeled off, going after a leggy blonde with a pixie cut before we even made it to Olivia.

"Hey," I yelled over the beat when I finally reached her.

"Have you found your target yet?" Olivia turned her back against mine, speaking over her shoulder directly into my ear so I could hear her over the deafening music.

"Not yet, but I've got a few ideas."

"Looks like Logan has. He's going to close before you. Better get on it."

"Have you found yours?" I turned to face her, putting my hands on her hips as we moved together.

"I'm thinking that red-head over there." She tilted her head sideways towards the bar and I turned to see a tall guy facing the dance floor. He stared right at Olivia, swirling the ice in his empty glass around absentmindedly. "Get your hands off me," she teased. "He's not going to think I'm available."

"You can do better than that," I said as I let go of Olivia.

With vibrant red hair and round brown eyes, she could get any boy in the bar. All she had to do was tuck a piece of hair behind her ear and look up at them through her long thick lashes, and they melted. I must admit I'd almost fallen for her a few times too, but Olivia, as great a friend as she was, wasn't relationship material. She flitted from boy to boy, and I believe her longest relationship lasted about 10 days. I may not have looked like it, as I was playing a game of no commitment kisses, but I was a hopeless romantic. I wanted the long term girl-friend, wife material, even though I was only 17 and probably wouldn't get married for years. I knew that successful relationships were rare in my line of work, but my parents, who had been together for nearly 25 years, were proof that it could happen.

I looked over Olivia's shoulder and zeroed in on Logan, checking to see if he'd made any noticeable progress with the blonde. He was dancing with his arms wrapped around her waist, their heads close together in conversation. He must have said something funny because she threw her head back laughing.

"Well, better find someone," Olivia said before she sauntered through the crowded dance floor and over to the red-head. She put her hand on his arm and looked up at him, before turning and saying something to the bartender.

Now that she had contact, the game could potentially be over in seconds. That's how it always happened. I had to buy myself more time if I didn't want to foot the bill for whatever drink Olivia was about to order.

To throw a wrench in her endgame, I followed her to the bar, leaning in close with my arm around her waist. "I'll be winning tonight," I whispered in her ear.

She turned to face me, her eyebrows raised in annoyance. "Micah, what are you doing?" I kept my arm around her just a little bit longer, took a long swig of my beer and then set it down on the bar.

"I told you, winning." I gave Olivia a little peck on the cheek and turned back to the dance floor. That ought to deter the redhead. Now it was go time.

I decided the girl by the window I'd seen earlier was my target, but when I looked towards her table, it was empty.

"Shoot," I muttered under my breath as I moved back onto the dance floor. Could I find her again?

I jumped up and down, dancing to the beat while I kept my eyes peeled for either the girl I saw before or someone else I thought could give me an easy win. Maybe a girl who was dancing alone, or someone who made eye contact with me. Finally, after turning and surveying all the possibilities one more time, I found the girl from the table.

I strutted towards her with purpose, passing Logan and his current conquest on the way. He winked at me. It was his MO. It meant he was close. Even after deterring Olivia, I didn't have much time.

The song changed as I reached her back, putting my hands on her hips. The beat of this one was much more seductive, perfect for what I was trying to do here, get a quick kiss and win. "Care to dance," I whispered in her ear.

She spun around to face me. At first, her expression looked tired, like she was used to unwanted advances and she was going to tell me to beat it, but her eyes widened when she saw who I was.

"Sure." She gave me a sly smile and lowered her eyes, but didn't stop dancing. Her voice was hoarse and I wondered if she had been screaming, or if it was always like that. I hoped for the latter. It was hot. Not that I'd ever see her again, that was the point of the game. Kiss it and quit it, right?

We moved together for a few more songs before she pulled me into an ill-lit booth near the back of the bar. I'd never personally sat in the booths before. Everyone knew what couples did back here, and that was not part of the game.

She slid in first, never letting go of my hand. Without the multicolored strobe lights changing her face, I could see now that she had icy grey eyes and bright red lipstick. It was off-putting and magnetic, and I couldn't decide whether to abandon the game and take the loss or move closer. I froze.

"Can I take a selfie with you?" she asked, opening the camera on her phone and holding it up.

"Sure," I nodded as she pulled me closer, pressing the side of her forehead to my cheek.

She snapped the picture, checked to make sure she looked good in it, then placed the phone face-down on the table.

"So why me?" She placed her hand on my forearm seductively and leaned into me.

"What?" My eyes flicked between her eyes and her lips. Olivia said I had to stare at her mouth if I wanted girls to get the hint, but suddenly, I was unsure if I wanted this at all.

Truthfully, even though I tried to come off as having a lot of romantic experience, I'd only ever kissed one girl before. Margot. We met on the set of our movie and dated for a few months after filming wrapped. She was a good friend, and fun to be with, but there wasn't that undeniable chemistry with her. It definitely wasn't love.

"Why did Micah Moore choose to dance with me tonight?"

I cleared my throat, trying to recover some of my charm. "What's your name?" I asked instead of answering her question. Surely she wouldn't take well to the real reason I was paying attention to her.

"Sarah." She moved closer, lowering her eyes, moving her hands to my chest.

"Oh." I swallowed. My heart raced, and I blushed because I was sure she could feel it, but it wasn't what she thought it was.

She moved the rest of the way to my mouth, closing her rose-colored lips around mine. And when she kissed me and I knew I had won, all I felt was empty.

Was I supposed to kiss back? Was I supposed to get lost in butterflies, tangle my fingers in her hair, never let her go?

Before I even had a chance to do more, she pulled her mouth away from mine. "We should take this back to my place," she whispered in that raspy voice, tracing a long finger down my torso.

Panicked, I scooted away. Not only was this not part of the game, but something about Sarah and her icy eyes and that empty kiss made me sick inside.

"I don't even know you." I had lost all charm now, and all I wanted to do was get out of the booth and run.

"But I know you." She slid closer and I slid away, trying to put as much distance as possible between us.

"You don't know me."

"Your name is Micah Moore. You were born July 16, you have one sister, your twin. Although you've had small roles up to this point, your first big break was this summer. You live in Malibu with your family, your father's a famed director and screenwriter, your mom also writes screenplays. Your favorite color is orange. You love pasta and can't stand seafood. See, I know plenty."

I shook my head, unnerved by how much this complete stranger knew about me. "This was a mistake."

"Excuse me?"

"I've got to go."

I didn't look back, and she didn't follow me. I pushed my way back through the crowded dance floor to the bar. I considered ordering another beer, but I needed something stronger. I decided on a shot of tequila. I watched the bartender slide a shot glass in front of me, pour the gold liquid and set a lime on a napkin next to the glass. I took the shot in one quick swig, almost choking as the liquor burned my throat. I bit into the lime and lifted my arm to check the time. My eyes struggled to focus in on the glow-in-the-dark hands of my watch and although I couldn't see what time it was, I knew one thing was for sure: I was wasted.

Logan came up behind me, slapping my back. "Dude, I totally struck out. She and her friends ended up leaving before I got a kiss. What about you? Any luck?"

I smiled and tried to pretend that I wasn't feeling complete humiliation after what happened in the back of the bar with Sarah. "Yeah, man, you're looking at the face of victory."

"No way," Logan grabbed my shoulders and jostled me against the bar. "Your first win, way to go."

"Pay up." I slapped the bar and laughed, but even to me it sounded forced. "You ready to call it a night?"

"Go tell Olivia we've got a bill to split. Let's have one more shot, a toast to your victory."

I rubbed my head, already feeling a headache start to set in. "Alright, one more drink won't hurt."

Back on the dance floor, I shimmied over to Olivia, lifting her hand off the redhead's shoulder. "Mind if I interrupt," I yelled, making my headache worse. "I won."

"Seriously?" Olivia looked at me with wide eyes. "Way to go," she said, jumping up and down to the beat.

"Come on, we're having victory shots at the bar."

"Okay, I'll be over in a sec."

I went back to Logan and Olivia joined us a minute later.

"To Micah's first win," she shouted, raising her glass.

Logan and I lifted our glasses too, and were about to drink before Olivia said, "No, keep them raised." She took out her phone and angled it towards our trio of shots, snapping a picture. "For the 'gram." she winked. "Okay, we can drink now."

We all threw our heads back to drink the tart tequila, immediately chasing it with the lime. Logan settled the tab, and Olivia Venmoed him her share before we made our way towards the door.

"Well, it's been a great night," I lied. "Let's call an Uber."

"No need, man, I'm fine driving." Logan shook his head as we walked outside.

Before I could protest and insist we find someone else to drive us home, a thousand flashes hit me like lightning, almost knocking me over, and blinding me before my eyes could adjust to all the light. Instinctively, I raised my hands to cover my face and ran. I knew if the photos showed up on some gossip site later, I would hear an earful from my parents, my sister, and my agent. All I could think about was getting away before they got a usable picture of me.

"Get in the car," Logan shouted. "Let's get out of here."

When we reached Logan's car, I pulled open the passenger door and almost lost my balance as I stepped in one foot at a time. Slamming the door shut, I ducked down below the window. Logan started the car and put it in drive.

"Are you sure we shouldn't get an Uber?"

"No, man, we gotta get you out of here."

Logan flipped on the headlights. They seemed unnaturally bright, and it took my eyes a minute to adjust to the new light. He pulled out of the parking lot, swerving a bit before he centered the car in his lane.

He picked up speed, and I closed my eyes. Why hadn't I

insisted we stop, why was I letting him do this? I opened my eyes again, ready to tell him to pull over, when suddenly, the road ahead of us curved, but Logan wasn't turning.

"Logan," I yelled as we lost control.

Panicking, he turned the steering wheel, trying to stay on the road, but he over-corrected. The car spun in terrifying circles. My stomach lurched. I was going to throw up. Cars around us honked and Logan screamed. Maybe those screams were mine too. My whole body tensed, anticipating a collision. I covered my head, terrified this was the end.

Finally, I heard glass shatter, the shards flying into the car and slicing my hands and the side of my face. Warm, sticky blood ran down my cheek, and everything went black.

# 2

## NAVY

"Is this for your college portfolio?" Becca stood over me at my drafting table as I sketched the gables of the house I'd designed.

"It sure is," I put the pencil down, looking up at her.

"You know, we're only juniors. You probably don't need to worry about this yet."

"I know, but I like planning ahead. Notre Dame doesn't accept just anyone. This portfolio needs to be the absolute best thing I've ever done."

"It's stunning," Becca gushed, picking up the sheet and holding it out in front of her. "You are so talented. They would be crazy not to accept you."

Heat rose in my cheeks. I was never sure how to react to praise, even a simple compliment from my best friend.

"Thanks," I looked down, pushing a strand of dark hair behind my ear.

"So, are you so excited for tonight?" She set the blueprint down in front of me again.

"I'm mostly just excited because it will be over and my dad can stop stressing."

"But Brock will be there." Becca took my dress for the city council fundraiser gala off the back of the closet door where it was hanging and held it up to her body, spinning around. "He'll dance with you, and tonight will be the night he finally falls back in love with you."

"Do you really think so?" I picked up the pencil and resumed shading the gables, but couldn't ignore the butterflies in my stomach.

I was trying to go into tonight without any expectations, but a part of me hoped my tea-length black dress with a high neck and a full skirt would finally catch Brock's eye and something just might happen. Maybe tonight he would see me in a different way, and realize I was more than just the girl across the street. Perhaps I could be his first relationship that lasted longer than just a few weeks and he would finally see something in me that made me unforgettable.

"Oh my goodness." Becca stopped twirling and stood in front of the window. "Navy, don't look now."

I jumped up from the drafting table and leaped two steps to my bedroom window to see what made Becca stop.

My stomach dropped. Across the street, on his driveway, Brock was kissing Bethany Trottweiler, the student body president. He had her pressed up against her old red Corolla, with his hands tangled in her perfectly straight, smooth blonde hair, cradling her face. Bethany's arms were wrapped around his waist, pulling him against her body. Even with my distanced view from my bedroom window, I could tell this kiss was passionate and hotter than the beautiful summer day outside.

Becca reached over and pulled the blinds shut, dimming my bedroom and any hope I'd had for tonight.

"Navy," Becca looked at me like she was about to cry. "Are you okay?"

"Yeah," I said, looking down at my hands, trying to keep the desperation out of my voice.

"It's okay, you can cry. It's just me."

I looked up at her and smiled. "You know I don't cry about these kinds of things."

"Still. You've been in love with the kid for seven years."

"I wouldn't say I've been in *love* with him. Just a massive crush."

"No, crushes last a month, maybe two or three. This is love."

How could it be love? We'd merely admitted to having a crush on each other four years ago, and nothing had happened since.

"Navy, don't look out the window!" Max, my older brother, rushed into my room, breathing heavily.

"She's already seen." Becca turned to him matter-of-factly, laying my dress back on my bed.

"Are you okay?" Max looked at me, his face falling.

"Guys, I'm fine." In reality, I was finding it hard to stay standing up.

I knew Brock was a player, and I knew he dated, *a lot*, but knowing that he was kissing other girls, and actually seeing him kiss them were two different things, and I'd never felt so defeated.

Becca sat down at my drafting table and pulled out her phone. "Let's see how long this has been going on."

I looked over her shoulder as she pulled up her Instagram feed and searched through both Bethany's and Brock's profile. There were a few pictures, one of them at the lake, another at a drive-in movie, and, the most romantic one, a silhouette shot of them kissing during a beautiful melted orange sunset. I turned away, not wanting to read the captions. It would just be twisting the knife to see them gushing over each other. I picked my dress up off the bed and hung it on the closet door again, smoothing out wrinkles in the skirt that weren't there just to keep my mind and my hands busy.

"Well," Becca said, looking up from her phone. "At least you have a smoking hot revenge dress."

"I think that's only for when you break up with a guy you were actually with," I said, rolling my eyes.

"I don't care. You're still going to be stunning."

"Agreed," Max said, checking his phone. "And speaking of the gala, mom just texted. She wants us to meet her and dad there at 6."

"That's my cue to leave," Becca said, scooping up her purse and dropping her phone in it.

I walked Becca to the door, and we peeked out the front window to make sure Brock and Bethany weren't still locking lips across the street.

"Promise me you'll call if anything happens at the gala," Becca said, wrapping me in a hug.

"I promise," I said, smiling before I shut the door.

I knew I needed to go upstairs and get ready, but I rested my forehead on the door and let out a sigh. I'd never cried over a boy. I thought it was trivial. But here I was, blinking away the tears that stung the back of my eyes. I moved to the front window again, peeking out at Brock's house.

Brock's family moved in across the street when I was 10. I was sitting in this exact spot, looking out this window when a giant orange moving truck pulled into the driveway, and a sandy-haired boy hopped out of the cab. I believed it was love at first sight, and thus began my infatuation with the boy across the street.

My eyes went to the top right window of the house. I knew it was Brock's room because he and Max used to use my bedroom window to pass Morse code messages back and forth with a flashlight. They'd learned it at a summer camp they'd been to and thought they were going to grow up to be secret agents one day.

"Navy, do you want the shower first?" Max called down the stairs, shaking me out of my thoughts.

"Yeah, do you mind?" I said, walking back upstairs.

"Not at all, just let me know when you're out."

I took a quick shower and wrapped myself in a fluffy robe before I went back to my room.

As I sat at my vanity doing my makeup, I thought about eighth grade. That was the year that kept me holding on to all of this. Max and Brock were in ninth grade, and they were best friends. Brock was over at our house nearly every day, and whenever I stole little glances, he was looking at me too. My go-to hairstyle at the time was a ponytail with a ribbon to match whatever I was wearing. I'd be sitting at the counter doing homework, or standing by the closet getting a board game out, or looking for something in the refrigerator, and Brock would walk by, pull the bow loose, and give me a little wink. I would try to scowl, but I loved when he pulled the ribbons, and my smile gave me away.

On Valentine's Day that year, someone left a single red rose on the doorstep with a new ribbon for my hair tied around it, and a card that simply said, "Navy." I had my hopes, of course, but they were confirmed about a month later when Max accidentally let it slip that it was Brock who'd left the flower. At this point, I was almost certain Brock had a crush on me too.

During Spring Break, we were on a hike together with a big group of friends. We were at the top of this mountain, and I was standing a little bit away from everyone else, overlooking the beautiful lush green valley and breathing in the woody mountain air. Brock walked over and said, "You know Navy, this is beautiful, but not as beautiful as you."

I was so surprised, elated, and filled with butterflies that I said, "You know I have the biggest crush on you, right?"

Brock just looked over at me, gave me one of those little winks, and said, "I have a crush on you too."

I had to keep my cool on the way down the mountain, but when we were home, my mom, Becca, and I squealed and danced around the kitchen. I thought it was the beginning of our love story, but it was the end. Max and Brock grew apart, he was at our house less and less, and pretty soon all I had were glances out my bedroom window. One would think that it would have been easier to get over him when he wasn't hanging out with my brother all the time, but no.

I shook my head to clear the memory of the mountain and jammed the curling iron plug into the outlet with a little more force than was necessary. I clicked it on and ramped up the heat. While I waited for it to warm up, I looked out the window again.

I'd seen a lot of girls come and go from Brock's house from this view, and they were all like Bethany. Popular, tall, with long tan legs, shiny blonde hair, and big blue eyes. I was the complete opposite of the girls Brock seemed to go for, not only in appearance, with my dark hair and green eyes, but in personality too. I was shy and studious. I wasn't the Student Body President, like Bethany, or a cheerleader, like some of the other girls he'd dated.

I looked back to the mirror and picked up the hot iron, wrapping a piece of hair around the barrel. I couldn't get the image of Brock kissing Bethany out of my head, and I felt silly for wishing it had been me he was kissing on the driveway instead. I had always hoped that one day, Brock would rush over and admit he still had feelings for me, that he would realize I was different, and everything he wanted. But where had hope gotten me? Brokenhearted and humiliated. Maybe it was time to give up and move on.

I ran my fingers through my freshly curled hair, spritzed it with hairspray, and stood up, facing my black dress again. I must admit that I had originally bought the dress hoping Brock would ask me to dance at the city council fundraiser gala, but maybe now it was my revenge dress after all. I slipped out of my bathrobe and stepped carefully into it, zipping it as far as I could before I walked across the hall to Max's room.

"Will you zip me up?" I asked, turning around and holding up my hair.

"Sure thing." Max pulled the zipper the rest of the way up. "You look beautiful."

"Thank you," I smiled, turning to face him and letting my hair drop. "You are quite handsome yourself."

"You ready to go?"

"Almost, I just need to grab my clutch." I ran back across the hall into my bedroom, grabbing the little black bag. I saw a tube of red lipstick sitting on my nightstand, and I picked it up, rolling it in my hands. The deep shade was bolder than the usual subtle pink I wore, but I wanted to be bold tonight. I leaned in close to the mirror, uncapped it and filled in my lips carefully. I straightened back up, my hands on my hips. Max was right. I was stunning. Thank goodness for black dresses and red lipstick.

"Navy, you coming," Max said, walking into my bedroom.

"Yup, let's go." I tossed my phone and lipstick into my clutch and stepped into my glittery gold high-heels.

We walked to the garage together and Max opened my door, always the perfect gentleman. I slid in the passenger seat, arranging my dress so it wouldn't get caught in the door.

The spacious hotel ballroom took my breath away. Every year since my dad had been on the city council, we'd come to these galas, but I had never been to one so beautiful. The lights were dim, but the crystal chandeliers still sparkled. Large round tables with black tablecloths and tall glass vases with fresh white peonies were set up in clusters around the edge of the ballroom. In the middle of the room, the marble dance floor had been polished so much it looked like water, reflecting the lights above it. The string quartet was setting up on the far side of the room, looking like chess pieces in their black floor-length dresses. Behind them, the floor-to-ceiling windows and heavy velvet black drapes framed the indigo mountain view outside. Waiters in crisp white shirts and black slacks were already wandering around, balancing silver trays of bubbling champagne in their outstretched hands. Looking around the room, I couldn't decide if I wanted to throw out my arms and twirl around like a little girl who got to play princess for the night, or if I should stand up even straighter, talk with a British accent and sip my drink with one pinky out. Leave it to my parents to plan the classiest fundraiser anyone had ever seen.

We found them talking to the Event Coordinator.

"You look absolutely stunning," Mom put her hands on my shoulders, holding me at arm's length to get a good look at my dress before pulling me in for a hug.

"Do I look like Audrey Hepburn?"

"Absolutely."

"Do you guys need help with anything?" Max spoke up.

"Nope," Dad said, taking two champagne flutes as a waiter walked by and passing one to Mom. "All that's left to do is enjoy the night."

"Everything is beautiful, Dad," I said, looking around the room again.

Before he could reply, Brock and his parents walked up to greet mine. As our parents swapped pleasantries, I gripped my clutch in front of me, looking at the ground. When I finally dared to look up, I saw Brock looking at me. He flashed me a heart-melting smile as our eyes met. I smiled back but resumed looking at the floor to keep myself from staring at his mouth and remembering what it had been doing just hours before. I only looked up again when Brock's mom complimented my dress, and Brock only spoke when my dad asked him something about football. Max and Brock would usually talk, but an awkward silence hung between us while our parents finished their conversation. I wished I could walk away, but I didn't know where I would go.

Max and I spent another twenty minutes following our parents as they greeted and introduced us to all the other city council members. By the time we sat down to eat dinner, I was seriously regretting my choice of footwear, and I kicked off my high heels under the table.

I sat up straight, arranging the cloth napkin on my lap before a waiter placed a plate of steaming pot roast, buttery mashed potatoes, and crispy asparagus in front of me. My mouth immediately watered, and I tapped my foot impatiently, waiting for the rest of the table to get their food so I could eat mine.

The second I finished my last bite of creamy mashed potatoes, I felt a light tap on my shoulder. I turned, surprised to find Brock leaning down, his hand extended towards me.

"Do you want to dance?"

"Sure," I answered breathlessly.

I took his hand and he pulled me up and led me to the dance floor. I was prepared to keep some distance between us, but he pulled me to him, keeping me close with his hand on the small of my back. Any thoughts I'd had earlier about moving on fluttered away.

"You look beautiful tonight."

"Thank you," I said, almost sure the smile on my face was big enough to give away the butterflies in my stomach. Maybe my revenge dress was working after all.

"So how has your summer been?" he asked.

"Really good. I've spent a lot of time working on my senior architecture portfolio."

"But you're only a junior," Brock raised his eyebrows, his eyes wide.

"I know, but I want plenty of time to make it my absolute best. Notre Dame won't accept just anyone."

"Would you show me your plans sometime?"

"Yeah, absolutely. Do you know where you want to go to college?"

Before Brock could reply, I felt another tap on my shoulder. This time it was Max.

"Can I steal my sister for a dance?" he asked.

"Absolutely. Thanks for the dance, Navy."

I nodded, trying to ignore the sinking feeling in my stomach. "Yeah, you too."

"What are you doing?" I asked, annoyed, as Max and I started dancing.

"Saving you from yourself. Look, Navy, I know you don't want to hear this, but I think it's time you really try to move on. How are you supposed to get over him when he's got you dancing that close to him?"

"It was fine. We were just talking about summer. He wants to see my portfolio."

"Did you forget what he was doing this afternoon? You know that's what he does, makes whoever he's talking to feel like the center of the universe. It's how he's kept you trapped in this vicious cycle for seven years."

"What vicious cycle?"

"You know he's dating someone, and you say you're going to move on, and then the next time you guys talk, you're into him again. You think that this year will be different, that this will be the year you finally get a chance. This is not the year. Move on, cut him out."

My heart stung because I knew he was right. "I can't just ignore him. He lives across the street, I have to be nice."

"Of course, be nice. But be strong. You deserve better."

People always told me that, but it was hard for me to believe them when I'd never so much as kissed a boy, much less known of one who was interested in me. High school was hopeless.

"Do you believe me?" Max prompted me when I didn't reply.

I nodded. "I do. And—" I paused, taking a deep breath, not sure I could admit what I was about to say. "And I know you're right, I know I need to move on."

"Now, enjoy the night. You're gorgeous. Dance with every guy here and show Brock what he's missing."

I raised an eyebrow teasingly. "He doesn't want it, remember?"

Max gave me a smile. "His loss."

After the gala, I hung my dress back on the closet door and climbed in bed, facing it, trying to shake the rejection I felt. Max knocked lightly on my door, pushing it open with his foot.

"Are you in the mood for hot chocolate and a movie?" he asked, walking over and setting a steaming mug on my nightstand.

"Sure," I smiled, scooting over so he could crawl in bed with me. "What movie?"

"I was thinking *The Proposal.*"

"Really?"

"Of course. I know you've had a rough day, and it's your favorite. I thought it might cheer you up," he said, settling down next to me. He opened the laptop and I saw he already had the movie cued up.

"Thanks, Max," I said, arranging the pillows and blankets around me. "You always know exactly how to make me feel better."

"That's what brothers are for. And don't worry, Navy, everything will look better in the morning."

Where were all the boys like Max? I loved that my brother made me hot chocolate and was willing to watch my favorite chick flick with me to cheer me up, but part of me wished I was snuggling up with a boyfriend. I glanced out my window at Brock's house and the conversation Max and I had during our dance ran through my mind. I knew he was right, it was time to move on, but I just didn't know how I was going to do that.

# 3

## MICAH

WHEN I CAME TO AGAIN, I was laying in a hospital room that smelled so sterile it made me nauseous. The lights cast a greenish glow over the whole room. An IV dripped in my peripheral and monitors beeped around me. I turned my head, looking out the window. The sky outside was clear and grey, so it must have been early in the morning, just before sunrise. Melanie gripped my hand, dozing off in a chair next to my bed. I squeezed her hand to wake her up.

"Mel, what's going on? Where's Logan?"

She jerked awake, standing up when she saw I was conscious. "Why didn't you call me, you idiot?"

"Gee, I love you too."

"No, I'm serious. You could have died. What were you thinking? I need you, Micah."

"I know, I'm sorry. It was a stupid decision. The paparazzi surprised us coming out of the bar and Logan was just trying to help me get away."

"Never, *never,* do that again, do you understand?" She was starting to sound more like a mother than a sister, but I didn't need her to convince me not to get in the car with a drunk driver again. I knew I was lucky to be waking up.

"I won't Mel, I promise. Where's Logan? Is he okay?" I asked again.

She sat back down, still not letting go of my hand. "He's a few doors down. He woke up about an hour ago, and aside from a concussion and a few broken bones, he'll be fine. How are you feeling?"

"Sore. I have a huge headache. How long was I out?"

"A few hours. It was a pretty bad crash."

"Did I die? Did they have to revive me? Did we hit anyone else?"

Melanie looked at me, raising an eyebrow. "No, you didn't die. And thankfully all you hit was a cement barrier blocking off a construction zone."

"Oh good." I shifted my position in the bed, but immediately stopped as a shattering pain shot up my leg.

"Oh yeah, and you broke your leg."

"Yeah, I noticed." I dug my head into my pillow, clenching my teeth until the pain died down a bit, but it never completely went away. "Where are mom and dad?"

"They're walking Winston out. They should be back any minute."

"Is Dad mad?"

"You snuck out while you were grounded, got drunk even though you're only 17 and got in a car accident that could have killed you. Mad is an understatement. He's grateful you're still alive though."

My parents walked in, and my mom rushed over, holding

my face. "Oh Micah, I'm so glad you're awake. How do you feel?"

"Okay. My head hurts, and I moved my leg, so now that hurts too."

"Don't you ever drive drunk again, and don't you ever drink again. Do you understand?"

I nodded. "I'm sorry, mom."

She touched my hair, teary-eyed. "I'm just glad you're okay. It's a miracle you escaped with just a broken leg."

My dad stood silently behind my mom. I looked over her shoulder, "Dad, I'm so sorry. I really am. I was stupid."

He didn't say anything for a while, he just paced in front of my bed pinching the bridge of his nose. Finally, he stopped, leaning over and gripping the footboard. "Micah, how could you be so foolish? I understand you are going to make mistakes, I do. But these kinds of mistakes are unacceptable. You could have killed yourself, or someone else. Something has got to change."

"I know. It will." And I meant it. Those few, out-of-control seconds before I was knocked unconscious had been some of the scariest of my life. It was the wake-up call I needed to realize I was on a dangerous path, and that this wouldn't be the last time I'd wake up in a hospital room if I didn't stop.

"I just don't trust you. You say you're going to change, but I fear that once you're better, you'll forget that you could have died tonight. I'm not willing to let that happen again, and I think it's time for a little reality check. I'm sending you to live with my sister in Utah for your senior year. No more drinking, no more partying, no more girls."

"What?" I tried to sit up. Suddenly the room was spinning. My mom eased me gently back. "But my life is here."

"And how, exactly, is that going for you?"

"Dad, please don't send him away," Melanie spoke up for the first time since our parents had come back.

"You're going too."

"I'm sorry, what?" This was as close to back-talking our father as Melanie had ever gotten.

"Yes."

"But why? Like Micah said, my life is here."

"I'm sending you as a precautionary measure. I realize that you are not leading the life your brother is," Dad turned to me and raised an eyebrow before going on, "but things change, and I think that a year away will be good for *both* of you."

"But—" Melanie tried her hand at back-talking again.

"No buts." Dad cut her off.

"Mom," I turned my head. "What do you think?"

She looked from me to Melanie, to Dad, and back to me. She slipped her hand in mine. "I don't want either of you to leave—"

"Then say we can stay."

"But, I agree with your dad. We couldn't bear to lose you, Micah, and we're afraid we might if you keep living like this. It's clear grounding you isn't going to be punishment enough. I think a year away will be a good thing."

"I'll be better, though. I won't go out without your permission. I'll stop drinking. I'll make better decisions," I pleaded.

"Please, try to understand." Mom's eyes were glossy with unshed tears.

"What if Winston finds me another role, and I can't take it because you've shipped me off to the middle of nowhere?" I said in a last-ditch effort to convince my parents to let us stay.

"That could be detrimental to my career." Even as I said it, I knew their minds were already made up

"You actions have consequences, son," my dad said, "and that just might have to be one of them."

I clenched my jaw, turning away from my parents. The logical side of me did understand, but the angry teenager in me refused to admit it. Did my parents really expect me to put my whole life on hold for a year? My life, my family, my friends were all here in California. There couldn't possibly be anything for me in Utah. Nothing I wanted, anyway.

A week later, we landed at a little municipal airport surrounded by purple mountains. I took a deep breath as I stepped out of the plane and smelled pine needles and wood. It reminded me of the Christmas candles my mom burned during the holidays. Pangs of homesickness hit me as I took in my new surroundings, and I felt trapped in this new life and an unfamiliar landscape.

Mountains—the first reason I hated Kimball Junction.

My Aunt Juliet waved as we stepped off the plane, and we made quick work of loading our luggage into her car. Her little tan Camry was a far cry from the Lambo I drove in California. Would I even have a car while I was here? I knew that after my accident, Dad was hesitant for me to drive, but surely he didn't expect me to rely on rides from my aunt, or public transportation, to get me places.

Tan Camry, no car, public transportation—the list continued to grow.

Once the car was loaded, I turned to my parents. My mom

had been weepy on the flight, but I was too angry with my dad to care. I gave her an awkward hug, still clutching my crutches, trying my best not to take my anger out on her.

When it came to saying goodbye to my dad, I simply stood in front of him, fuming.

"Be good, Micah," he said, putting a hand on my shoulder.

I shrugged it off. "Okay."

Melanie's goodbyes took longer. She gave each of my parents a hug, told them she loved them countless times and promised that she would call and text often. I still didn't understand why Dad roped her into this too. Guilt swirled in my stomach.

I doubted that I would ever be able to love Kimball Junction. I'd had no choice in coming here, and no matter what happened here, Utah would always remind me of my mistakes, and my dad's lack of trust that I could make better decisions on my own at home. It was a step above being sent to a juvenile detention center. Everything about my lavish life was about to change, and this was just one fresh start I was not ready for.

Once goodbyes were said, my parents reboarded the jet. We watched as it taxied back to the runway and took off. I had a mini panic attack as I watched my parents, and life as I knew it, fly away.

This was real. I was stuck in Kimball Junction.

"Well loves, should we get some dinner?" Aunt Juliet's cheery voice got on my nerves. How could she be happy at a time like this? Didn't she know that everything was falling apart?

I rolled my eyes and tapped my crutch against the back tire of the car. I could understand why Aunt Juliet was fine.

Compared to Melanie and me, her life was only changing a little bit.

"Yes," Melanie said, equally cheery, equally maddening. "I'm starving."

Once we were all in the car with our seatbelts on, Aunt Juliet pulled out of the airport and we drove for about twenty minutes through what looked like miles and miles of empty land. I'll admit, the mountainous landscape had a certain beauty, but it still didn't make me feel any better about my new situation.

"Look, I want to be the cool aunt," Aunt Juliet said after we'd driven in silence for a little while, "but given the circumstances, I think we need to lay down some ground rules." She looked at me through the rearview mirror, making eye contact to make sure I was listening.

"First of all, there will be no sneaking out. Of course, you can go out with friends, but I want to know where you guys are at all times. Just let me know when you're leaving, or shoot me a text so I know where you're going. Curfew is 10 o'clock on school nights and 11 on the weekends, don't be late. Also, you won't be allowed to go out until your homework is done. I don't want you falling behind in school."

Mel nodded, "Sounds great."

"Micah?" My aunt looked at me through the rearview mirror again.

"I understand," I said, resisting the urge to roll my eyes.

"Good. Second, under absolutely no circumstances will you be allowed to drink. There won't be alcohol in the house, and I trust you didn't bring your fake ID."

"No, my dad took it and cut it up," I looked out the window. We were coming into Park City now, and we drove by a few hotels, a grocery store, a Starbucks and a little store that sold skis and snowboards. All the buildings were wood and rock, and the whole town look like it was made up of cozy log cabins.

"Excellent. You guys are good kids, and I know you know what's right. Just behave, and make good decisions and we'll be golden."

"We will," Melanie said, turning around in the front seat to face me. "Right, Micah?"

"Yes, I promise, I'll be good." I raised my right hand as if making an oath. I knew Aunt Juliet was making all of these rules specifically for me because Melanie certainly didn't need to be reminded to get all her schoolwork done, be in by curfew, and abstain from alcohol, but I appreciated that at least she addressed both of us.

Finally, we pulled onto a street crowded with colorful shop fronts and equally colorful people. This was the first glimpse of life I had seen in Utah. Aunt Juliet drove slowly, cautiously up the street, (Main Street, I learned it was called,) allowing me to get distinct looks at almost everybody we passed. Everyone looked so happy and carefree. There were men in tank tops and shorts, with man buns or dreads, and women in sundresses or halter tops, who had their hair tied up in bandanas or blowing free in the soft summer breeze. I saw families meandering up the street, stopping to look at the window displays. Siblings teased each other, and I watched as a little boy with a chocolate ice cream cone and a sticky face pulled on his mom's pants to get her attention. We passed a post office, restaurants, bars, stores that sold little trinkets and souvenir tee-shirts, and art galleries that displayed beautiful paintings in their windows.

Near the top of Main Street, my aunt parallel parked and

ushered us into a cramped little café. I slipped on sunglasses and pulled my hood on to avoid recognition.

"Welcome to Red Banjo Pizza," someone behind the bar yelled as we walked in.

The pizza parlor had a mess of mismatching chairs assembled around tables of all shapes and sizes. Every table was covered in a classic red and white checkered tablecloth.

"This place has the best pizza and root beer ever," Aunt Juliet said as we made our way to a little table in the back. "You're going to love it."

As I hobbled on crutches between the tables filled with families, friends, and couples, I looked at the crazy decorations that adorned the walls. Banjos of every shape, size, and color hung on the wall in no clear formation. There was a corkboard with currency from all over the world tacked on it. Some of the bills had been written on, others were folded into origami people or birds or boats, some just hung there, fluttering each time a waitress whisked past with a tray full of pizza. Black and white pictures of an ancient Park City were displayed on the back wall.

A waitress bustled over to us, smiling as she flipped to a new page in her notepad and gripped her pen, ready to take our order. "Welcome to Red Banjo, have you had a chance to look over the menu? Is there anything I can get started for you?"

"We'll just have a pitcher of root beer and a large pepperoni pizza, please," Aunt Juliet ordered and passed the menu back to the waitress.

She nodded, wrote down our order, and said, "Coming right up," as she hurried away.

The little café, as crowded and loud and crazily decorated as it was, was homey, and for a split second, I started to believe that perhaps this town wasn't as bad as I thought it was.

But then, Aunt Juliet started talking about school, and I felt a new wave of anxiety.

"Tomorrow we will go and get you both registered. You may have to take some placement tests, but those shouldn't be too hard. And you'll both be taking theater, right?"

Aunt Juliet was the new theater teacher at Park City High School, where we would be completing our single year of public school. She and my dad were a lot like Melanie and me. While I preferred big roles and lots of attention, Melanie had preferred small supporting roles and hid from the spotlight. Similarly, my dad preferred to take his love of movies to the big screen, while Aunt Juliet had channeled her love of acting into teaching teenagers to love it too.

The thought of taking a class with a bunch of people who thought they could act seemed horrendous to me, but Melanie perked right up, saying she would love it. Eventually, I agreed to take theater too, because as long as I was stuck here, I might as well get to do something I love.

"What show are you doing this year?" Melanie asked.

"*Beauty and the Beast*," Aunt Juliet said, smiling as she rested her elbows on the table and laced her fingers together. "It's my favorite, so of course that has to be the first show I direct at Park City High School."

"That is so exciting," Melanie said. "I'd love a part in the chorus if there is one."

"You'll have to audition," Aunt Juliet winked, "I've got to make sure you can act. Micah, do you want to be in the show too?"

I shrugged, still not jazzed about being demoted to high

school theater, but figuring there were worse ways to spend time here. "Why not?"

The pizza and root beer arrived and we all pulled pieces onto our plates. Aunt Juliet was right. This was arguably the most delicious pizza I had ever eaten. The Red Banjo Pizza Parlor was the first thing I added to the list of things I didn't hate about Utah.

After the pizza was gone and we had all sipped the last drops of root beer, we made the ride through nowhere back to my aunt's house, which was now my house too.

Aunt Juliet led us upstairs and flipped on the lights. "I didn't have much time to do up the bedrooms, but we can do that tomorrow. Micah, I thought you could stay in this one."

I limped into a tiny room, which was furnished with a queen-size bed, a nightstand, and a desk. Gone was my luxurious king-size, my walk-in closet, my own bathroom, my balcony. All I had out my window were more mountains.

"I know it's not quite what you're used to, but tomorrow we can work on making it a little more homey for you."

"Yeah," I said, looking at the bare walls. "It's different."

My aunt walked out, and I heard her showing Melanie her room. Melanie seemed much more content with hers.

"So do you guys want some ice cream?" Aunt Juliet asked, coming back into my room.

"Absolutely," Melanie said, walking in behind her.

"Actually, I'm really tired. I'm going to go to bed."

"All right," Aunt Juliet said, turning to leave. "Just let me know if you need anything."

"Yeah, okay," I said, shutting the door as they walked back downstairs.

I lugged my suitcase over to the wall and stripped off my

clothes, jamming my legs into sweatpants, which took longer than it used to with my leg in this stupid cast. I fell backward onto the bed and fell asleep angrier than ever.

The next morning, there was a loud knock on my bedroom door. I stumbled out of bed, hopped over to the door on one foot and pulled it open.

"Good morning," Aunt Juliet smiled at me, already dressed and ready for the day.

"What time is it?" I asked, rubbing my eyes.

"It's 7, and we have a busy day ahead of us." She knocked on Melanie's bedroom door while she talked. "Time to get ready."

Melanie opened her door, leaning on the doorframe. We watched our chipper aunt walk downstairs. "Breakfast will be ready in half an hour."

I let out a long sigh, hobbling towards the bathroom.

"And so it begins." Melanie seemed much less peeved by the fact that we were awake at 7 AM.

PARK CITY HIGH school was a new, modern building that stood out against the rustic former mining town.

Aunt Juliet had already scheduled an appointment for Melanie and me to meet with school counselors. The counselor I met with was a ridiculous woman named Mrs. Bisk. She was far too excited to sign me up for my classes, and her happy manner and passion for public education did nothing but plunge me further into disdain for this whole situation. It wasn't like I didn't enjoy learning, and I was sure public school had its merits, but I wasn't interested in taking random classes teaching me things I would never use again. Up to this point, my education had consisted of my mom homeschooling Mel and me when we were in elementary school, and then private tutors who catered our lessons to things that I wanted to learn. This whole school thing was just another change in my new life I didn't want to make.

"Mr. Moore, you have so many interesting classes to choose from. Let's first get your generals scheduled," she turned her computer screen towards me. "Which science class seems most interesting to you?"

I skimmed over the page: chemistry, physics, biology, zoology, astronomy, and more. Nothing looked even the slightest bit interesting to me.

"Chemistry is fine," I said without much enthusiasm, slumping back in my chair.

"Now on to math," Mrs. Bisk brought up another page with more classes. "What looks good?"

"Mrs. Bisk, I don't really care," I said, leaning forward and resting my arm on her desk.

"Excuse me?"

"I don't care. I don't care what classes I take, I don't care to be here. I just want a diploma by next June."

"But don't you want to enjoy your time here? Don't you want to choose classes that are fun and interesting for you?"

"No, I really don't. I would just like you to make a schedule for me."

"Hmm." Mrs. Bisk just looked at me. "Okay."

She turned the screen back to her and I watched as she clicked and typed, and, about five minutes later, printed out a single piece of paper and handed it to me. "Good luck, Mr. Moore."

"Thanks," I said, taking the paper and folding it into my back pocket without even looking at it.

Aunt Juliet and Melanie were waiting for me when I left Mrs. Bisk's office.

"I talked to Principal Friedman about added security measures for you both while you're at school. There will be security guards at the doors to ensure the paparazzi and the media can't get in, and he'll make an announcement on the first day outlining some rules for the students. Primarily, to respect your privacy and not post pictures of you at school. We both want to try to make this experience as normal as possible for you. Do you guys want to go find your classes?" Aunt Juliet asked.

"Yes," Melanie answered immediately.

"I'll just find my way on Monday when school starts," I said.

"Suit yourself. At least walk the halls with us."

Melanie and my aunt walked ahead of me, discussing where each classroom was and which route would be best to take to and from each class. Meanwhile, I lagged behind, observing the brick walls of the building. Bright banners shouted "Welcome Back" and shiny blue lockers lined the walls, waiting to be filled with books and bags and a school year's worth of garbage.

After Melanie finished finding her classes, we stopped at Bed, Bath and Beyond. I was dragged through a totally new level of miserable while Melanie and our aunt contemplated new bed sets and decorations for our bedrooms. I couldn't have cared less for chevron versus stripes because I honestly saw no difference, and it didn't matter to me what color the bath towels were so long as they got the job done. In the end, after they insisted I give input on a new bed set at least, I chose a navy and green plaid down comforter and blue sheets. It was similar to what I had at home.

After stopping at Walmart for school supplies and a few groceries, we finally made it home from the longest morning of my life. It was only the early afternoon, but I was exhausted. I went straight to my room, dropped my crutches, and fell spread-eagle on my bed, letting out a long sigh.

Aunt Juliet came in and plopped the bag full of my bed set on top of me.

"You didn't need to buy me new bedding," I said, pushing it off of me as I rolled over. "I'm fine with the stuff you already have on this bed."

"I know," she said, sitting down on the bed. "But don't you want to make this space your own? After all, this is going to be your home for at least the next nine months."

"No." I sat up. "This is not my home."

"Fine," Aunt Juliet said, turning to leave. "Use the new bed set, don't use it. It doesn't matter to me. I'll be helping Melanie if you need anything."

I gathered the bags in my arms and stuffed them into the closet. I slammed the doors shut, and moved my suitcase in front of them.

No need to unpack, no need to make this room mine. I'd only be here a little while anyway. Did I have a plan to get myself out of this mess? Not yet, but I knew I needed to come up with one fast.

# 4

## NAVY

IT DIDN'T REGISTER to me that the blaring siren wasn't a part of my dream for a good five minutes, and by that time, Max was shaking my shoulders, telling me it was time to get up. I groped blindly around my nightstand for my buzzing phone, and tapped the screen lazily, trying to get the alarm to turn off. When the phone was finally quiet, I dropped it and snuggled into my blankets again.

"I don't want to get up," I said into my pillow.

"You better have not hit snooze. We can't be late today," Max said as he walked out of my room.

I finally forced myself out of bed and went into the bathroom, blinking as my eyes adjusted to the light. I ran through my routine on autopilot, still waiting to feel alert and get energy for the first day of school. When my makeup and hair were done, I changed into my favorite dark skinny jeans, a pale pink blouse, and a white cardigan. I slung my bag over my shoulder, walking downstairs.

Max sat at the bar, finishing up a bowl of cereal. My mom, already in her workout clothes, sat at the table, reading the newspaper and sipping green juice. Dad must have already left for work.

I grabbed a banana from the fruit bowl on the counter, and Max and I kissed our mom goodbye.

When we got to school, a crowd swarmed the front of the building. Some of them were dressed in pencil skirts and slacks, with microphones and huge cameras. They drew most of the attention. Others were subtler, dressed all in dark clothing simply with phones or smaller, point-and-shoot cameras.

"Did someone die?" Max asked, looking wide-eyed at the commotion.

"I have no idea. We should probably go through the music hall."

Max agreed as we headed the opposite direction, and let ourselves in through one of the school's side doors.

"I thought you said you talked to the principal about security measures," a deep voice floated around the corner. It was strangely familiar, but I couldn't put my finger on where I had heard it before.

"I did, but nothing is stopping the media from waiting outside the school building." That voice definitely belonged to the theater teacher, Miss Moore.

We rounded the corner and met a trio of people standing just outside the auditorium doors. I suddenly realized why the voice had sounded so familiar. Micah Moore leaned against the wall with a couldn't-be-bothered air, a grey crutch under his arm and a black cast on his leg, while a pretty girl with her dark hair tied up in a ponytail and Miss Moore stood facing him. He straightened up when we came around the corner.

"Hi, Navy," Miss Moore smiled when she saw us.

"Good morning," I said, adjusting my bag on my shoulder.

"This is my niece and nephew. This is Melanie," she gestured to the girl, "and Micah."

"Good to meet you both. I'm Navy." I turned to Max, assuming he'd introduce himself, but he was staring stupidly at Melanie and didn't seem to hear any of the conversation going on around him. "and this—" I rolled my eyes as I put a hand on Max's arm, trying to shake him out of his trance, "is my brother, Max."

"Oh, yeah," Max said, finally joining us back in the music hall. "Nice to meet you."

"Navy." I was surprised at how beautiful my name sounded when Micah's deep, honey-coated voice said it. "Like navy blue?"

"No, just Navy." I moved my eyes from Max to Micah's, mesmerized by how icy blue they were. The camera hadn't done them justice. He was much better looking in real life.

A bell echoed in the empty music hall to let us know we had five minutes until classes started.

"That's the bell to go," Miss Moore turned back to Micah and Melanie. "What do you guys have first hour?"

"World History," Melanie said, looking down at the crisp piece of paper in her hands.

"Do you know where it is?" Max spoke up. "I'd be happy to show you."

"Yeah, we found it last week, but I wouldn't mind the company if you're going that way," Melanie said, smiling at Max and looking at him bashfully through her lashes.

"I'll go with you guys," I said, moving around Miss Moore and Micah and joining my brother and Melanie as they made their way up the music hall.

"Navy Blue, wait," Micah called to me.

"That's not my name," I turned around, crossing my arms in front of my chest. I couldn't decide if I liked my new nick-name. Was Micah Moore flirting with me? We'd only known each other for a few minutes, but I couldn't deny there was something magnetic about him. I blinked a few times, clearing my thoughts. Yes, I'd just met a celebrity in the music hall of my high school, but I needed to keep a level head. It wouldn't be wise to go falling in love with him. I was already trying to get over one unrequited crush.

"My first class is AP Chemistry, Mr. Thompson, room 108. Can you help me find it?"

"Are you kidding me?"

"Um, no?" he answered, raising an eyebrow, his eyes flicking between mine.

"I'm going there too. Follow me." I turned around and resumed walking to class.

I listened to the click-clack of his crutches as he limped over. When he fell into step next to me, I could smell something clean, like mint and musk.

"So," Micah said as he crumpled his schedule and shoved it into his pocket. "How are you?"

"I'm fine. How are you?" Given Micah's crutches, getting to class was slow going.

As we walked down the hall, students parted around us and stared. "Is that Micah Moore?" I heard one girl whisper. Another guy pointed before turning to his friend and saying something with his hand cupped around his mouth. Other students had their phones out and were holding them up, snapping pictures. I ducked my face down, self-conscious of being photographed. No doubt those photos would end up all over Instagram. I worried that at any minute, the crowd would stop giving us space and swarm us instead.

I looked at Micah out of the corner of my eye to see how he was reacting to the whispers and pictures, but he didn't seem to notice.

"I've been better, honestly," he said.

"Well, welcome to high school."

"You mean I'll feel like this all the time?"

"If you choose to. Look, if you want to be miserable, you'll be miserable. But if you want to enjoy your time, you'll discover high school isn't always as bad as it seems," I said, lifting my shoulders in a shrug. "This is it." I pulled open the heavy wood door, relieved we were finally to our classroom. "After you?"

"Oh no, ladies first. Always," Micah said, sticking one of his crutches out to catch the door.

I was about to walk in when someone called to me from the opposite direction.

"Navy, hey," Brock yelled, jogging towards us, dodging around students making their way to class.

"Hey," I smiled, trying to suppress the butterflies fluttering in my stomach. I was supposed to be getting over him, but everything around Brock seemed to blur as I watched him.

"I know we've got to get to class, but I was wondering if you want to go to Homecoming with me?"

Oh my goodness, Brock was finally asking me on a date! Maybe Max had been wrong, maybe this was the year after all. Wait, hadn't he been kissing Bethany, like, a week ago? Suddenly, the butterflies died and that humiliating feeling was back. Here I was, finally being asked to a dance by a guy I'd been infatuated with for seven years, and all I could think about was watching him kiss Bethany on the driveway. Even if I wanted to think I was different, that something about me would suddenly make him want to be in a relationship longer than a few weeks, I had known Brock long enough to know that he was, and always would be, a player. But standing here, face-to-face with him in the hall, with his tousled caramel hair and those hazel eyes, made me want to ignore everything I knew and just take the leap.

"Wait, aren't you dating Bethany?" I couldn't help asking as my eyes lingered perhaps a little too long on his mouth.

Brock furrowed his brow. "Bethany? No, we had a fling for a couple of weeks in the summer, but it's over now."

"Oh, I see," I nodded.

Out of the corner of my eye, I saw a girl walk up to Micah, and ask if she could take a picture with them. I watched her put her arm around his neck, and Micah held out the phone to snap a selfie. I wanted to roll my eyes, annoyed that a moment I'd waited practically my whole life for was being interrupted by this movie star taking pictures with a fan.

"Yeah, and to be honest, I'm still kind of trying to get over her," Brock moved closer to me, putting his hand on my arm and pulling me back into the moment. Warmth spread all over my body and I wanted to collapse into him and give him a hug. "I would love to just enjoy this dance with a good friend, so will you go with me?"

So that's all I was, a friend. My excitement was no longer a raging fire. It had dwindled to a tiny flame, barely enough to light a candle. But it was still there, Brock was still standing in front of me, asking me on a date. What would it hurt if I held on for just a few weeks longer? I didn't have to extinguish my hope yet.

"Of course I will," I smiled. "I'd love to go with you."

"Sweet, I'm excited. I'll get you more information as it gets closer. Talk to you later, Navy," he said, taking off down the hall again.

As I watched him go, I should have felt exhilarated, and while a part of me did, I felt a little brokenhearted too. I'd imagined the moment Brock would ask me out on a date for so long, and I always thought it would be because he had feelings for me again. It dawned on me that this was how all of my interactions with Brock were. I always hoped for something great, and it was always tainted with disappointment.

The annoying fangirl had left, but Micah was still there, holding the classroom door open for me.

"You have a crush on him," he said. It wasn't a question, it was a statement of fact.

My goodness, was I that transparent?

"No," I said, perhaps a little too forcefully, walking into the classroom. "You heard him. We're just friends."

"I don't know about you, but my voice doesn't light up like that when I'm talking to someone who's just a friend."

The classroom was so full there were only a few empty desks. All eyes were on us as we quickly slid into seats in the back.

"My voice didn't light up, whatever that means," I continued our conversation in a whisper.

"The second you saw him, you smiled, you stood up straighter, your eyes were moving between his mouth and his eyes the whole time you were talking. Your body language said it all."

"Micah, I mean it, we're just friends. He lives across the street from me."

"Oh, you may be just friends, but you definitely want more."

"I don't think so."

"Whatever, Navy Blue, deny it all you want."

"That is *not* my name, and I am not denying anything."

Before Micah could make any more witty comments, the bell rang, and Mr. Thompson started handing out course disclosures and going over the curriculum for his class.

I pulled out my phone and cradled it in my lap as I typed out a text message to Becca.

*Brock just asked me to Homecoming.*

Seconds later, my phone vibrated with her reply.

*WHAT! Navy that's the best news! Why wasn't that last message in all caps with a thousand exclamation points? Mere glances from him have elicited more excited text messages!*

I looked up, making sure Mr. Thompson wasn't on to me. I'd heard he was a stickler about students using phones during his class.

*He told me he's still trying to get over Bethany and that he wanted to go to Homecoming with a friend, so I'm trying not to get my hopes up. I'm just a friend.*

*Why not get your hopes up? HE ASKED YOU TO HOMECOMING!!! He may think you're just a friend now, but things can change.*

And that's the thing. My hopes *were* up. Not even walking a celebrity to class this morning fired me up like Brock did.

*Let's talk more at lunch!*

I signed my last text message with a heart emoji, slipped my phone back into my book bag and turned my attention back to Mr. Thompson, where it should have been all along.

I spent the rest of chemistry thinking about Homecoming

and had almost forgotten that a movie star was sitting next to me.

"Navy Blue," he said as the bell rang and we shuffled out of the classroom, "I don't know where I'm going next." He sounded slightly panicked.

"Look," I said, pointing to the classroom numbers on the crumpled schedule he was holding. "If the classroom number starts with a 1, it's downstairs. If it starts with a 2, it's upstairs. The numbers after that are in numerical order. It's pretty self-explanatory. You're a smart boy. You'll figure it out. See you later."

I turned the other direction and walked to my next class before he could reply. I was sure that aside from a few glances and nods now and then, this morning would be the last of the personal interactions I ever had with Micah Moore.

At lunch, Becca and I sat in my car, eating our sack lunches. I sat with my legs pulled up to my chest, facing her, while she sat forward in the passenger seat, her long legs kicked up on the dashboard.

"So, how did he ask you?" Becca asked, her eyes lighting up as she took a bite of her sandwich.

I relayed the story of walking to chemistry and being intercepted. "And then Micah Moore was like, 'You totally like him.' Can you believe that? Am I that easy to read?"

Becca sat up, almost choking on the food in her mouth. "Micah Moore? The movie star? Is that why all those cameras were going crazy out front this morning?"

"Oh yeah. I met him when Max and I went in the back by the music hall so we wouldn't have to go through all those reporters. I thought you would have heard by now."

"Nope, you failed to mention that."

"Sorry." I gave her an apologetic look and popped a potato chip into my mouth. "I was just so caught up in Brock asking me to Homecoming, I guess everything else slipped my mind."

"Forget Brock, tell me about Micah Moore." Becca turned to face me, bracing herself with one hand on the dashboard and the other on the seat, "Is he hot? Is he charming? Do you know what he's doing here?"

I laughed. "Oh, he's even better looking in person than he is in the movies. I suppose he's charming. He did hold the door open for me," I lifted my shoulders in a shrug. "He's Miss Moore's nephew, but I don't know why he's here, we didn't get to talk a whole bunch. Oh, and get this, he insists on calling me Navy Blue. How annoying is that?"

"Navy," Becca slapped the dashboard in excitement, startling me. "You walked to class with Micah Moore, and he's already given you a flirty nickname. Remind me why you're still hung up on Brock?"

I rolled my eyes. "He asked me to Homecoming. This could be the beginning of the love story I've been waiting for."

"No, no." Becca shook her head. "Brock told you he was asking you as a friend, and come on, we know his MO. He's not love story material. Not when Micah-Freaking-Moore is in the picture."

I had a feeling this is how Becca would react. In her mind, falling at the feet of a celebrity was a foregone conclusion. And while one could argue I was insane for falling for Brock all these years, I could keep my head on straight regarding Micah Moore.

"This morning you were telling me to get my hopes up, what changed?" I asked, biting down on another crunchy potato chip.

"That was before a celebrity called you Navy Blue and asked you to walk him to class. Isn't the thought of a fresh start with someone new exciting?"

"Maybe if that someone new wasn't an unattainable movie star." I rolled my eyes.

"Micah Moore isn't unattainable if he's here, if you have a class with him, and if you've already talked to him." Becca ticked each of her points off on her fingers.

"Yeah, but I like Brock."

"And Micah Moore might be the perfect opportunity to finally get over him."

"What if Micah is just like Brock?"

What good would it do me to go from one unrequited crush to another? The way I saw it, it was all hopeless.

"And what if he's the exact opposite?" Becca leaned on the center console, resting her face on her fist with a dreamy look in her eyes.

"I don't know," I said, shaking my head.

I didn't want to think about that electric feeling I had when I looked at Micah's stormy eyes for the first time, or the little butterflies I'd gotten when he said my name, and I definitely didn't want to admit that I kind of liked my new nickname, because all of those feelings evaporated when Brock asked me to Homecoming, even if he'd made it clear we were going as friends.

"Fine, if you're not going for him, I will. Does he have a date for Homecoming? How do I get him to ask me?" Becca wiggled her eyebrows up and down mischievously as she popped the last bite of sandwich into her mouth.

"Be my guest," I laughed. "I'll put in a good word for you next time I see him in Chemistry."

"So, when are we going dress shopping? Tonight?"

"I can't tonight, I have to play for musical auditions."

"Oh, that's right." Becca bit into her apple thoughtfully. "I can't this weekend because we're going away for Labor Day, but maybe next week?"

"Sounds like a plan."

We spent the rest of lunch looking at dresses on Pinterest to get inspiration. I couldn't believe I was going to a dance with Brock. I had to look perfect. After all these years of watching out my window and crushing on him from a distance, we were finally be going on a date. Excited, thrilled, ecstatic were all understatements. This was my dream come true. Maybe I just needed to hold on a bit longer. Maybe I wasn't supposed to move on just yet. Maybe this could be the year that changed everything.

After school, I met Max at the auditorium.

"Max." I gripped his shoulders, excited to tell him about Brock and Homecoming. I hadn't texted him because I wanted to see his face when I told him. "Brock asked me to Homecoming."

"You're kidding me." He did look surprised, but not as excited as I hoped he would be.

"No. Micah and I were walking to chemistry, and he stopped me in the hall and asked me to go with him."

"What did you say?"

"I said yes, obviously."

"Are you sure that's a good idea?" He scrunched his eyebrows together and tilted his head in that annoying way that meant he thought he knew better than me.

"I've been waiting for this for *seven years*. And finally, we're going to go on a real date. Aren't you excited for me?"

"You're supposed to be moving on, remember? Who's to say this is going to turn into anything but a single dance and your hopes dashed yet again?"

"Who's to say it's not?" I took my hands off his shoulders and folded my arms. He was my brother and my best friend; he was supposed to be excited for me. I didn't need him playing protector of my heart. I was a big girl.

"I'm just saying that we know his dating record. He dates a girl for two weeks, three tops, and then he moves on. What if he's going to do that to you? What if you're just another girl in his ever-growing, ever-changing portfolio of conquests."

"Yeah, but what if this is different. What if I'm different?"

"Navy, it's never different, not with guys like Brock."

"Why can't you just be happy for me? I've pined over this kid since fifth grade, and now we're finally going on a date. Can you blame me for getting my hopes up?"

"I just want you to be smart."

"I'm a big girl, Max," I said, adjusting my bookbag on my shoulder. "I can make my own decisions."

"I know, I'm just saying—"

"Look, be happy for me, don't be happy for me, it doesn't matter to me. I'm going to Homecoming with Brock regardless. Now I've got to go play for auditions. See you later."

"Navy, wait," Max called behind me, but I didn't turn around.

I stalked all the way through the dark auditorium and up to the stage, practically throwing my bag down at my feet as I slid onto the piano bench and began playing scales to warm up my fingers and keep my mind off of my frustrating conversation with Max. I knew he meant well, but I still wanted him to understand how big this was for me, how excited I was, and I wanted him to be excited for me. This was the first time in four years, since that day on the mountain, that I had reason to hope I was more to Brock than just the girl across the street.

"You already know I can act, why do I have to audition?" I stopped playing as I heard Micah and Miss Moore walk on stage.

"Yes, but everyone has to try out. You're not in Hollywood anymore, here you are just like everybody else."

"Fine." He let out a sigh. I rolled my eyes before turning to face them.

"Hi, Navy," Miss Moore said. "How are you?"

"I'm good," I said. "Micah, did you find the rest of your classes okay?"

He walked over to the piano, leaning on it. "I did, thanks for your help."

"Navy, could you play the audition number for us? Micah, I thought we could get your audition out of the way right now."

"Micah sings?" I directed the question more to Miss Moore than I did to Micah.

"I don't want to," Micah said, standing up straight again. "But as long as I'm here I might as well act a little bit, and the school musical seems the least painful way to do that, so I'm singing."

"Ah, I see," I said as I turned my attention back to the piano and started playing.

I was surprised at how beautiful and smooth Micah's voice was, and was suddenly self-conscious of my playing, as if the scratched, old upright piano couldn't play music lovely enough to match Micah's voice. It gave me goosebumps.

"How did I do?" Micah asked when the song was over.

I thought he was talking to Miss Moore, so I kept my eyes

steadily focused on the music in front of me, rubbing my arms to rid them of goosebumps and feigning deep interest in the fingering for the chorus of "Be Our Guest."

"Navy Blue?"

My eyes snapped up to meet his and the goosebumps returned. "Oh, you're asking me?"

"Yeah, what did you think?"

I debated lying and telling him I'd heard better. After all, this dude's ego did not need to be plumped even more than it already was. But something about those captivating blue eyes made me open my mouth and say, "I think you are very talented and have a beautiful voice."

"Thank you," he winked at me before jumping down off the stage and joining his aunt in the front row of vibrant purple auditorium seats.

Before I had time to react, students began filing in and auditions were in full swing. After playing "Be Our Guest" for three hours, and not once hearing a voice as beautiful as Micah's was, I was right on the edge of insanity. Finally, the last student walked off the stage, and Miss Moore stood up, stretching her arms above her head, and announcing we were finally done for the day.

"I'm gonna head back to my classroom and finish up a few things. Navy, you're welcome to stay. Micah, we'll leave soon. Will you go find Melanie?"

I watched Miss Moore leave through the backstage door and waited until Micah walked up to the back of the auditorium and I heard the heavy door swing shut behind him before pulling out my phone. I had a single message from my brother.

*Got a ride home with Becca. See you at home.*

I'd almost forgotten our little disagreement from before

auditions, and it was hard to tell if Max was still upset. I guess I'd find out when I got home, but for now, I was going to enjoy the empty auditorium and do something no one, not even my brother, knew I could do: sing.

I ran my fingers over the dull black and white keys and then started playing my favorite song. The stage around me melted away as I lost myself in the lyrical genius of the song, and wondered if I'd ever feel love as extraordinary as the one I was currently singing about.

"Navy Blue sings?" Micah walked on the stage, clapping slowly.

I jumped, startled as Micah's voice snapped me back to reality. "Micah, what are you still doing here? I thought I was alone."

"I forgot my backpack. That was really amazing. Why don't you try out for the musical?" Was that a hint of admiration I'd heard in his voice?

"I don't sing," I said, folding my arms defiantly.

"Clearly, you do." He leaned on the piano.

"Listen, no one knows I can sing, and no one will ever know, do you understand?" I asked, standing up and motioning between us. "This is between you and me."

"Fine, it's our little secret," he said, jumping off the stage and scooping his bag onto his shoulder. "But you should seriously consider trying out for the musical."

"No, I think I'll stay in the pit."

"Micah, we're leaving." Miss Moore poked her head through the doors.

"Coming," he called over his shoulder before turning back to me, running his long fingers through his thick, dark hair. "Are you happy there? Really?"

"Yes," I answered on instinct, not really taking a second to consider if it was true.

I belonged behind the piano, not up on the stage. I was not born to be under the spotlight. Besides, who was Micah Moore to waltz in here and make me question my life choices? I didn't owe him any explanations.

"Fine." Micah looked at me as if he knew something I didn't. "Goodnight, Navy Blue."

"That's not my name."

# 5

## MICAH

ON TUESDAY MORNING, the second day of school, I walked into Creative Writing and slid quickly into an empty seat. More and more students filed in and eventually filled the classroom. Seconds before the bell rang, Navy walked in. She took a quick survey of the room, noticed that the only free seat was right behind me, and made her way over. We smiled at each other as she slid into the desk.

Miss Akekian handed out the syllabus for her class and went through it with us, just like we'd done in all of our classes yesterday.

"Now, your first assignment," Miss Akekian perched herself on a stool in front of the class, crossing her legs and leaning her elbow on her knee, "is to choose a word, any word, that you want to represent this particular year of your life and write a one-page essay about why that word is important."

The class scrambled to pull out paper and write down the assignment.

"Next Tuesday, we'll share our words with the rest of the class, and your essays will be due. Any questions?"

When no one raised their hands, Miss Akekian stood up, moved her stool to the side of the whiteboard, picked up a marker, and started her lecture.

I heard Navy shift in her seat behind me. I was painfully aware of every move she made throughout the rest of the class. Since I'd met her yesterday morning, I'd barely been able to stop thinking about her. She was beautiful, but not in the way most girls in Hollywood were. She had big doe eyes that looked like a stained glass window had been shattered and then all of the different green pieces had been pushed back together. Her long wavy hair complemented her fair complexion, and her clothes were simple, classy. And what intrigued me the most was that she couldn't care less about me. In our brief interactions the day before, she'd come off kind enough, but she was guarded and distant. Something funny swirled in my stomach as I thought about that guy asking her to homecoming before we'd gone into chemistry, and how much happier she seemed to be talking to him. It couldn't be jealousy; I'd only met her yesterday.

I reminded myself that I could never have a relationship with Navy, for many reasons. No girls had been one of the rules Dad laid out when he sent me here, and while I may not have been one for following rules, I wasn't going to give him any more reasons to keep me from coming home as soon as possible. And if I could get out early for good behavior, and go home before the school year was over, I wouldn't have time to develop a relationship anyway.

Navy was beautiful and intriguing, yes, but our lives would never fit together. Sure we were in the same place now, but this small town wasn't my life. I was just playing pretend. It was best I viewed Navy like I did the girls I played the Kissing Game with, merely something to pass the time.

The rest of the week passed as monotonously as the first two days, and school wasn't getting any more interesting. By Friday, I was exhausted, but had one good thing to look forward to: I was getting my cast off. Aunt Juliet drove me to my doctor's appointment, where I got the all-clear to walk again. I was overjoyed until we got home and I saw the mountain of homework I had to do before we went back next week. I cursed Mrs. Bisk every day for the heavy class load she'd set me up with.

I walked up to my room and dumped the contents of my backpack out onto my bed. Organization was had never been one of my strengths, but I knew I had to make sense of all these syllabi, assignments and notes. Discouraged, and not wanting to deal with the upwards of fifty sheets of paper splayed across my bed, I pushed it all onto the floor and collapsed. Surely I would feel better after a nap.

I was wrong.

I'm not sure how long I slept, but I woke up to Melanie shaking my shoulder gently. I heard my parents' voices and was confused about where I was. Hadn't I fallen asleep in Kimball Junction?

"Micah, Mom and Dad want to say hi and see how your doctor's appointment went today." Melanie held up her phone and I saw my parents squished together on the small screen. A small part of me missed them and was happy to see their faces, but a bigger part of me was still upset.

"I don't want to talk to them."

"Micah," Melanie said in the voice that meant she was about to launch into a reprimand.

"Don't say my name like that. You're not my mom."

"No, your mom is right here," she pointed to the phone, "and wants to say hi. They miss you."

"Well, they should have thought of that before they sent us away." I rolled over and stuffed my face in the pillow, hoping that would be enough to let Melanie know I wasn't going to talk to my parents.

"Can I call you back?" Melanie said to her phone.

My parents told her they loved her and that they'd talk to her soon, and then I heard the three little beeps to signal they were gone and it was just Melanie in the room with me.

"You're a jerk."

"Excuse me?" I turned over and sat up.

"You think I'm happy to be here? You think I love that our life was uprooted because you made stupid decisions?" She crossed her arms, raising an eyebrow.

I stared at her, not sure what to say. She sure seemed to be handling the move better than I was, but I don't think I'd actually asked her how she felt about being shipped off with me.

When I didn't answer, she moved closer, leaning forward slightly and pointing a finger at my chest. "No. I miss California. I miss mom and dad. But you know what, I'm trying to make the best of it. So buck up, Micah. This sucks just as much for me as it does for you."

I was still speechless, and that uncomfortable guilty feeling I'd felt watching Melanie say goodbye at the airport was settling in my stomach.

Melanie turned and walked to the bedroom door. "Oh yeah, dinner's ready."

I slumped down the stairs, and slid into my chair at the dinner table, keeping my eyes down.

"Thanks," I mumbled when Aunt Juliet set a plate of steaming chicken Alfredo in front of me. It smelled divine, the fresh homemade cheese sauce and garlic chicken, but I'd lost my appetite.

For a while, we all ate in silence. I kept glancing at Melanie. She stared at her plate, stabbing her fork into her pasta before each bite.

"Alright, what's up with you two?" Aunt Juliet asked after one of Melanie's more forceful stabs made a particularly horrible screeching noise as the metal utensil scraped the glass plate.

"Melanie is mad at me," I said to my aunt before looking over at my sister. "Mel, I'm sorry, okay."

"Sorry isn't going to cut it, Micah," she replied, slamming her fork down. "Sorry isn't going to get us back home."

"Why aren't you mad at dad? He's the one who made you come for no other reason than a 'precautionary measure,'" I lifted my fingers, putting the last words in air-quotes, "whatever that's supposed to mean. He should know by now you'd never break the rules like I do."

"I'm not mad at dad because he's just doing what he thinks is best for his children. I'm mad that because of you, what he thinks is best is sending us away. I'm mad that he can't seem to trust either of us because you made some bonehead decisions that forced him to take extreme measures. But most of all, Micah," she stood up, her chair scraping against the tile floor, and planted her hands on the table, "I'm mad because we've been here a week and you think you're the only one who's having a hard time. You're so busy wallowing in your own pathetic pity party that you forgot I didn't ask for this either." She jabbed finger in my direction. "This whole week, I've felt so alone because the only other person who really understands what I'm feeling during this huge change is too wrapped up in himself to see he's not the only one who's struggling."

With that, Melanie stormed up the stairs and slammed her bedroom door. I stood up, about to follow her, to apologize for being such a horrible brother and tell her I'd find a way to make it better, to get us back home, but my aunt stopped me before I'd even put one foot on the first step.

"Hold up," she said, walking over to the fridge and pulling out a plastic container with eggs in it. "She needs a minute to calm down. And our neighbors just texted, they need these eggs, so you're going to take them."

I sighed, looking up the stairs at Melanie's bedroom door and wishing I could just go make things right with her. But my aunt was probably right, Mel needed some time to herself. "Alright. Who am I taking these to?"

"The Monroes. They live three houses down."

I took the eggs and went outside. The sun was setting, turning the sky my favorite color of melted orange. The contrast between the sky and the vivid purple mountains was stunning and made me believe that perhaps Kimball Junction wasn't as bad as I thought it was. As I walked, I kicked a rock up the sidewalk and thought about what my sister said. Melanie had always been so good at going with the flow and taking things in stride, and that's what she'd been doing this whole time. She was making the most of a hard situation, but that didn't mean she didn't have her own struggles with the curveball that had been thrown at her. I should be more like her, looking for the bright side in this new opportunity. I knew what I needed to do to make it right with her after I delivered the eggs.

Three doors down was a little white house with a yellow door. I hoped this was the right house and that my aunt hadn't been mistaken about which neighbors needed the eggs, or how far they actually lived from our house.

I knocked twice and waited, swaying back and forth between my heels and the balls of my feet. The door swung open and a tall dark-haired woman stood in front of me, wearing a flour-covered apron, a dishtowel slung over her shoulder. She looked like an older version of Navy, and I blinked a couple of times to clear the image. I needed to stop thinking so much about her.

"Hi, my aunt said you needed eggs," I said, handing her the plastic container.

"Yes, thank you so much for bringing these over." Her voice was soft and bright.

"Yeah, no problem." I turned to walk back down the steps.

"Wait. You should come meet my daughter. We saw your movie this past summer and loved it. It's become one of our favorites."

Great. A meddling mother who wants to set me up with her daughter.

I turned to face her again, prepared to respectfully decline. I closed my mouth, reconsidering. What did I have to lose? It wasn't like I was doing anything else tonight, and it had only been a few minutes since Mel's meltdown, I'm sure she needed more time.

"Okay, sure."

She led me through the house, setting the eggs on the counter before ushering me through the back doors into a spacious backyard. Tall trees and perfectly manicured flower beds outlined luscious green grass. A sweet floral scent floated around me each time the soft breeze picked up.

"She's just in her treehouse."

I hadn't noticed it at first, but tucked back in the far right corner of the yard, perched in the biggest tree, was an idyllic little treehouse. It wasn't very big, with a single opening for a door, and a little window to the left of it.

"Navy," Mrs. Monroe called up. I almost choked on my own spit. This was Navy's house? I should have known when I saw how much this woman looked like her. I thought back over the week and realized I'd never found out what Navy's actual last name was, I just called her Navy Blue.

"Yeah," Navy poked her head out, her dark hair falling around her face as she looked down at us. "Micah?" she said when she saw me.

"Navy?" I said back, equally surprised. "I didn't know you lived so close to my aunt."

"You two know each other?" Her mom looked back and forth between Navy and me.

"Yeah, we have a couple classes together at school," Navy answered.

"Can I come up?" I smiled. "I've never been in a real tree-house before."

Navy pursed her lips and it looked like she was about to say no, but her mom spoke before she could. "Absolutely. I'm making cookies. I'll let you know when they're done."

"Thanks," I said before climbing up the ladder and pulling myself into the treehouse.

It was much smaller than it looked, and even as Navy moved to the very back to make room for me, our knees still touched as we sat cross-legged, facing each other. Butterflies erupted in my stomach at this simple, innocent contact. I leaned forward, fighting the urge to trace imaginary doodles over Navy's legs where they touched mine just so I could feel more of her skin on mine. I watched Navy carefully, wondering if she would make any attempt to shift so we weren't touching. I suppose it may have been because the treehouse didn't give her much space to do anything, but she didn't move, and I'd like to think it was because she liked our closeness too.

"Did you understand anything that was going on in Chemistry today?" She asked, twirling the ends of her hair around her fingers.

"I don't want to talk about chemistry."

"Oh? What do you want to talk about?"

"You."

"Me?" She leaned back against the wall of the treehouse, her eyes wide.

"You are the most intriguing person I've ever met," I leaned my elbow on my knee, resting my face in my hand.

"Oh come on," she rolled her eyes. "The most intriguing person you've ever met? I'm sure that's not true."

"You think I'm lying?" I leaned back, putting a hand over my chest in mock offense.

"No, I just think you're really good at flattering girls."

"I'm not a player, if that's what you're implying." I suppose that depended on who you asked. I mean, yes, I'd only had one steady girlfriend in my life, and when I was with her I didn't go around flirting with anyone else. If you counted the Kissing Game, I guess you could say I'd become a little bit of a player. I didn't count the Kissing Game, though, because I'd only won once.

"I'm not implying anything, I'm just saying I know what you

do for a living and surely you've met more interesting people than me."

"No, I stand by what I said. I want to know more." I couldn't explain it, but there was something magnetic about Navy. It was refreshing for someone to treat me so normally, like I was just another boy from school. I knew I was supposed to be viewing her like a target for the Kissing Game, and not get too attached. Maybe I should have jumped out of the treehouse and ran home, but I couldn't bring myself to leave.

"Alright, ask me anything. I'm an open book." She spread her hands out in front of her, her palms up. I looked at them and resisted the urge to slip my fingers through hers.

"Tell me about the Brock kid who asked you to Homecoming and your obvious crush on him."

"Oh no, no, no," she leaned back, folding her arms. "I'm not about to talk about that with you."

"So you admit you do like him? I recall you saying you were just friends earlier this week." I leaned forward. The setting sun cast a warm orange glow over us, intensifying the pink blush that appeared on Navy's cheeks at the mention of Brock.

"Ask something else." Navy leaned forward too, almost like she was challenging me.

"Alright," I said, deciding to take it back to surface level, "What's your favorite color?"

"Blue," she let out a small laugh. "Yes, navy blue, but that's still not my name."

"My favorite color is orange, but not like pumpkins, or Halloween orange. This orange." I pointed out the door of the treehouse to the sky.

"It is a beautiful color," Navy nodded, looking out the little window. "Utah has some beautiful views. Just look at how stunning the indigo mountains and the orange sunset are together." Navy let out a little sigh, and I could tell she really loved where she lived. I studied Navy's profile, her long lashes, her small rounded nose, and her lips with that perfectly feminine bow in the middle. I wondered if she would ever look at me the way she was looking at the sky, like it was the most beautiful thing she'd ever seen. I thought maybe that's how she looked at Brock, and this time I knew I was feeling jealous. I know I'd only known her for a week, but I didn't want to be just surface-level with Navy.

"So let's talk about earlier this week, on the stage, when I heard you singing."

"Please, Micah," Navy shook her head. "Not that."

"You said you were an open book, and you've only answered one of my three questions," I teased, raising an eyebrow.

She filled her cheeks with air and then let out a long slow breath. "You're right. Okay. Fine. What do you want to know about it?"

I wanted to pump my fist in the air in celebration. It was a small achievement, I know, but I was excited that Navy was going to open up a little bit more to me.

"You said no one knew you could sing. Why?"

"I don't know. It's just something I'd like to think I can do."

"Navy, you do realize you have an amazing voice, right?"

"Thank you, but not like yours."

"Yeah, actually, I think our voices would blend together beautifully. We'll have to try it out sometime."

"I think not."

She was so stubborn. I knew our time in the treehouse was probably limited and I wanted to know more, so I decided to move on. "So what else do you like to do?"

"Well, I don't have much time for anything else but school, homework, getting ready to take the ACT and the SAT, stuff like that."

"Do you know what you want to study when you get to college? Music?"

"No, architecture actually."

I raised my eyebrows, surprised. "Really. That's super cool. Why?"

Navy smiled. "Do you realize how much you ask 'Why?'"

"Yeah, I want to know more than just surface-level facts."

"Why?" The sun had gone down now, but even in the dark, I could tell Navy was giving me a strange look, tilting her head to one side.

"Look who's asking why now," I teased.

"Okay," Navy laughed, scrunching up her petite nose. It was the first time I'd heard an actual laugh out of her. It was light and sounded like a fizzy drink tasted. I felt it through my whole body, and it made me want to reach across the small space in the treehouse and wrap her in a hug. "I asked once. You've asked at least five times in this conversation, which means I get four more chances to ask why after this one. So tell me, why are you so interested in getting to know me?"

"Because you treat me so differently than everyone else here. Almost like you don't care who I am."

Navy's eyebrows scrunched together. "It's not that I don't care who you are. It's just that I don't find myself incredibly remarkable."

I opened my mouth to protest, but she put up a hand, stopping me.

"I didn't say that to dig for compliments. It's true. I'm just an ordinary Utah girl. So I guess when I met you that day in the music hall and we walked to class together, I thought that would be the last time you gave me the time of day. Surely you would fall for one of the cheerleaders, or perhaps another popular girl. You'd run with the popular crowd, and I'd do what I do best: remain invisible."

"You deserve more than to be invisible. I know you say you're nothing special, but I've been around *a lot* of girls, and believe me when I tell you you're the most impressive girl I've ever met." The summer breeze picked up again, bringing the floral scent from the yard into the treehouse. This time it was mixed with something else, something sweet like vanilla. A strand of hair blew across Navy's face, and I wanted to reach out and tuck it behind her ear, but she beat me to it.

"How can you say that? You hardly know me. Most guys don't pay any attention to me. They know I'm just ordinary." She tilted her head again and gave me another one of those looks like she didn't understand me. I decided I liked being looked at this way.

"Perhaps we've only had a few conversations, yes, but on Monday, at auditions, instead of playing the same song over and over, you'd add little things each time, sometimes rolling chords, or adding a little trill. That tells me you're a wicked talented piano player. Then I heard you sing. Again, wicked talented."

"You're sweet to say that, but—"

Now I lifted my hand, cutting her off. "I'm not finished. I watch you take rigorous notes in Chemistry, and the comments you make on the things we read in Creative Writing are deep, like you understand the text way more than the rest of us. And then I learn that you want to be an architect, and I'm sure one day you'll be responsible for the eighth wonder of the world because based on what I've seen of you this week, you probably design crazy beautiful buildings too."

She leaned forward, her green eyes flicking between mine. The strange look she'd been giving me faded, and it was replaced by a soft one, like I'd finally broken down a wall.

"What?" I asked softly when she didn't say anything.

"I don't know." She shook her head, smiling. "That was seriously one of the sweetest things anyone has ever said to me."

I leaned forward too, placing a hand on her knee. "See, Navy. You are remarkable. Why don't you take a chance? Try out for Belle." I knew there was a good chance I would be the Beast, and the musical would be a great excuse to be close to her.

"Micah, I just told you. I'm better in the pit, I'm better with my head down, working hard."

"Why?"

"Because I have goals, and none of them are to be the lead in the school musical."

"Alright, what are they then?"

"First, get through high school with as much college credit as I can."

"That explains the mountain of AP classes you're taking."

She nodded. "Design a stunning portfolio so I can make it into Notre Dame's architecture program. That's where playing the piano for the musical comes in, to diversify my resume and college application. This comes later of course, but once I get my acceptance letter next year, I'll have to apply for scholarships and then keep my GPA up to show that I qualify for them."

"Those are all great, but you forgot one thing."

Navy raised her eyebrows, her look accusing me, like who

was I to question the plan she'd obviously put a lot of thought into. "And what is that?"

"You've forgotten to make sure you have fun. You only get to be a teenager once. After this, life gets real."

"Exactly. My whole life rides on decisions I make now. Perhaps your life is handed to you on a silver platter, and you have time for fun, but I've got to work to do."

Now I was the one to give her an accusing look. She hardly knew me, and here she was assuming that my life was handed to me like I was some bum who couldn't work hard for the things I wanted. "My life is *not* handed to me on a silver platter."

"You've already got an established career, don't you? It doesn't matter what you do this year because when you go back to Hollywood, or wherever it was you came from—"

"Malibu," I interjected.

"Well, when you go back to Malibu, I'm sure directors will be banging down your door for you to be in their movies. I've seen you act, and now I've heard you sing too, and you are, as you would say, wicked talented."

"But that doesn't mean I didn't have to work for it. Yes, I've had little supporting roles since I was a kid, but when was the first time you saw me in a lead?"

Navy thought for a moment.

"This summer," I answered for her. "I've been acting for ten years and this was the first time I got a lead. So yes, my career has started, but I still have to work really hard for it."

Navy looked at me for a second and then dropped her eyes to where her hands rested in her lap. "I'm sorry," she said. "I was wrong to assume that about you. Can I ask another one of my 'Why?' questions?"

"Yes," I grinned. "I think you have a few left." To be honest, I'd lost track, but I wanted to keep talking.

Navy shifted her position, leaning against the back wall of the treehouse, and pulling her legs up to her chest. Now we weren't touching at all and I wanted that warm buzzing feeling in my body again. I moved too, so I was sitting next to her and my legs were stretched out the door in front of me. That sweet vanilla smell intensified now that I was closer to Navy. I took a deep breath, enjoying how subtle and feminine and beautiful she smelled.

She looked over at me, resting her head against the wall. "Why did you come to Utah? Was it for another role?"

"Ah, no, that's a bit of a long story." I looked down at my hands, worried that if I told Navy why I was really here, it would ruin any chance I would ever have with her. But what chance was that, honestly? I thought about Melanie and what she said at dinner. And even if this time in Navy's treehouse made me feel like Utah wasn't all that bad, I had to remind myself that I had one goal, and that was to get home. Besides, Navy wasn't interested in me. She had a thing for Brock, and as much as I wished she didn't, he was probably a better fit for her anyway.

"I don't mind long stories," she said softly.

"Well," I took a deep breath before beginning, "this summer, after my movie came out, I was kind of launched unexpectedly into a lot of fame and recognition, and I wasn't always sure how to handle it, so my friends and I started drinking."

I decided to leave out the little details about the Kissing Game.

"And when my dad found out, I was in big trouble, obviously, and I got grounded. But I was stupid and snuck out to be with my friends anyway. We were hanging out at this bar, and when it was time to leave, there were all these paparazzi outside, so my friend Logan and I hid in his car. We were so worried about getting out of there because if I showed up in the tabloids leaving a bar when I was supposed to be home, I was going to get in even more trouble. So even though Logan and I were both drunk, Logan started driving, and we crashed."

"Ohhh," Navy scrunched her nose up. "That's not good."

"Yeah, no kidding. That's how I broke my leg."

"Ah, I was wondering how that happened." She nodded.

"Yeah, so anyway, I woke up in the hospital and my dad said he was sending me and Melanie away because obviously grounding me wasn't going to do anything. He had to stop me from making more stupid decisions, even though that crash really shook me up. I knew I needed to change."

"So now that you're here, do you still drink?"

"No," I shook my head vigorously. "My aunt has strict rules. No alcohol in the house."

"But what if she did have alcohol at home? Would you drink it? What happens when you go back? Are you going to start drinking again?"

I stopped for a minute before answering her. I thought about this week, and what I might be doing if I was still at home. No doubt I'd be with Logan and Olivia, but would I go back to drinking? Memories of the crash, and those seconds before we hit the cement barrier, swirled in my mind and that raw fear filled my stomach again. I may not have had a lot of temptation with alcohol or partying living in Utah with my aunt, but I knew I had to make a decision for when I would inevitably be surrounded by it again.

"No," I said confidently. This was my decision. This was me figuring out my life and who I was in all this fame. "That car accident terrified me. I thought I was going to die. I know I've got to find a better way to spend my time and a healthier coping mechanism for my newfound success. I think that's what my dad hopes I figure out here."

Navy didn't say anything, and I was trying to gauge how she felt about what I'd just told her, but the treehouse was almost pitch black now, and I couldn't read her face.

"The cookies are done," I heard Mrs. Monroe's voice below us.

"Thanks, mom," Navy called back, "we'll be right down."

I climbed out first, and Navy followed close behind. When we got inside, Mrs. Monroe motioned for us to sit at the bar, and set a plate of warm cookies and two glasses of milk in front of us. "Have as many as you want," she said, smiling.

My mouth watered as I took a gooey cookie off the plate, setting it on the napkin in front of me. I broke off a piece and dipped it in the cold milk before popping it in my mouth, the warm melted chocolate chips coating my tongue as I chewed slowly, enjoying the sweet treat.

"Mmm, these are amazing," I said after I swallowed. "Thank you so much, Mrs. Monroe."

Navy was quiet while we ate our cookies, and I worried it was because of what I'd told her in the treehouse. I wanted to know what she was thinking, and assure her I was a good person, but I didn't feel like I could do that with her mom in the kitchen with us.

After enjoying my last bite, and finishing off my milk, I stood up. "I'd better get home. Thanks again for the cookies," I told Mrs. Monroe.

"I'll walk you to the door," Navy said, pushing back her barstool and standing.

When we got to the door, I stopped, putting my hand on her arm. "I'm not a bad person, Navy."

"Of course not," Navy shook her head. "Why would you say that?"

"I don't know," I looked down, taking my hand off her arm. "I guess I'm just a little worried about what I told you in the treehouse. I want to be friends."

"Me too," Navy said, pulling open the front door.

I looked up to find her smiling at me, and it felt like another small victory. "Goodnight, Navy Blue. Thanks for the chat."

"How many times do I have to tell you that's not my name?" she rolled her eyes but kept smiling.

I walked back up the street to my aunt's house feeling slightly giddy thinking about the time I'd just spent with Navy in the treehouse. I was determined to show her that: one, I was not the entitled movie star she believed me to be, and two, you could still work hard and have fun. I wanted to spend all the time I could with her.

But the light feeling from the treehouse quickly became heavy. When I remembered Navy was interested in someone else, I knew she probably viewed our night in the treehouse as two people getting to know each other, even though I hoped I gave her giddy feelings too. At least Navy and Brock weren't actually dating, which meant there was every possibility that Navy's feelings could change, and she could fall for me. But what did it matter, because when I remembered the fight I'd had with Melanie before I was sent to deliver eggs, I knew I needed to focus on one very important thing: going home. It was more than a selfish, defiant desire now. It was about

Melanie and getting back what she shouldn't have lost in the first place.

Before I reached the front door, my phone vibrated. I pulled it out to find a text from Winston.

*Not sure if I'm supposed to have contact with you while you're away, but just heard back about the part in France. The director wants to see you read some lines. I've emailed you the script. If you still want to be considered for the part, make an audition tape of the scene I sent and send it back to me. Maybe Melanie can help.*

This was it. This was my chance to fix everything. But as I stood on the front porch, in the dull gleam coming from the light above me, I felt bittersweet. I looked down the street at Navy's house and thought maybe Kimball Junction wasn't so bad. Maybe I could make good, real friends here. Maybe I could even fall in love. I was well on my way after tonight. But when I looked back at Aunt Juliet's red-painted front door, I knew I had to do everything I could to make it up to Melanie, and surely if I got this part, Dad would let us come home.

I pushed open the door and walked upstairs, knocking softly on Melanie's bedroom door before opening it. She was on her bed, her back propped up against the headboard. She had headphones in and was typing something on her laptop.

She looked up when I bounced down on the bed. She pulled out her earbuds and looked at me. "What?"

"I know you're mad, and I'm so sorry," I leaned forward, putting my hands on her shoulders, wanting her to know I truly meant it. "I'm sorry I was selfish, and that I wasn't there for you when you were struggling. I'm sorry I was stupid, and the whole reason we're here in the first place."

Melanie's gaze softened and she closed the distance

between us, wrapping her arms around her neck. "It's okay, Micah."

"I've been such an idiot."

"Maybe a little," she pushed away from me, smiling. "But you know, it's not all bad here." She laid back on her bed, her legs dangling over the side. "We've met some good people, and Max Monroe has been a pleasant surprise."

I laid down next to her, putting my hands on my stomach. "Oh, so you've got a crush on Max now, huh?"

She giggled. "Just a small one."

"They live down the street, you know. I just took eggs to their mom."

"Yeah, he mentioned that earlier this week."

"You're right, it's not all bad here, but I think I've found a way we can get home sooner. I need your help."

She propped herself up on her elbow and raised one eyebrow, curious. "What is it?"

"I just heard from Winston, and he emailed me a script because the director in France wants me to read some lines. I need someone to read the scene with, so if we can nail this and wow the French director, I'll get the part and we could go home."

Mel hesitated for a minute, looking around her room, and twisting a loose string from her comforter around her finger. I was about to speak up, ask her what she was thinking about and remind her that even if I got the part, we probably wouldn't start filming for at least another four or five months. It would mean we would still have some time here, but less time than if I didn't get the part and we stayed the whole school year. Before I could say anything, she pushed herself off the bed, standing in front of me, her hands on her hips. "Alright, let's do it."

We walked into Aunt Juliet's home office to print out the pages and found her working on casting decisions for the musical. I filled her in on Winston's text and what we needed to do, and she agreed to run the camera for us. All I had was my phone, but it would have to do.

"Let's set this up in the living room," Aunt Juliet said, grabbing the paper from the printer and handing me the warm pages.

Melanie and I sat on the couch and read our parts aloud a few times. After a few read-throughs, I sat in silence, thinking about how I wanted to uniquely portray this character, how I could step into his head, bring him to life, and make him relatable. Before we filmed the scene, Mel and I stood in front of the fireplace and talked about how we would act it all out. Aunt Juliet gave us some pointers, and we practiced a few more times before she called "Action!" and tapped the screen to start recording. Melanie and I made it through exactly seven lines before we messed up and called cut.

It took as a surprising amount of takes to finally make it through the scene without forgetting a line or laughing and breaking character, but I finally felt the tension between my sister and me lifting. We were having fun, and I never wanted to stop. We went through the script over and over, sometimes switching up where we were standing, the way we delivered a certain line, or our use of body language. Aunt Juliet would step in with direction after every few takes.

Even with the memory in Navy's treehouse fresh in my mind, I knew that acting was what I was meant to do. It was the perfect balance of work and play for me. Even just in front of the fireplace at my aunt's house being filmed on an iPhone fired me up, inspiring me to take this seriously and do the best I could in this moment so I could get the part and get back on set. This audition tape was more than getting out of Utah, it was about doing what I loved.

Finally, after two hours of running the scene and flirting with the edge of delusion because we were so tired, we ran the scene one last time. Aunt Juliet and Melanie went to bed, but I sat up, editing the best of each take together to make a nearly perfect scene. Around two in the morning, I wrote an email to Winston and attached the final video. My mouse lingered over the send button, and I held my breath as I hit it, hoping it would be enough to score me the part.

# 6

## NAVY

ON SATURDAY MORNING, I sat at my drafting table sketching more buildings. I should have been working on my homework, but I couldn't focus, not after last night. Knowing I could sing, and climbing into my treehouse, Micah Moore had just weaseled his way into some of the most special and private places in my life...and I wasn't mad. In fact, I liked it. That free-falling feeling in my stomach I got when I stuck my head out of my treehouse and saw Micah standing with my mom had surprised me. Even the news that he was here because of his underage drinking and bad decisions didn't deter me like I thought it would. I didn't think those choices were who he really was, and I hadn't been lying last night when I told him I thought he was a good person. There was something about him, not just the fact that he was a movie star, that made me want to know more.

My phone buzzed, causing the pencils next to it to vibrate and roll off the table. I checked the phone. It was a number I didn't recognize. I slid my thumb across the bottom of the screen and held it up to my ear.

"Hello?"

"Navy Blue, it's Micah." A fluttering feeling danced in my stomach at the sound of his voice.

"How did you get my number?" I asked.

"My aunt gave it to me. Hey, I need help with my word assignment for Creative Writing."

"Yeah? How can I help?" I straightened out the blueprint to keep my hands busy.

"I just need to talk through some thoughts. I can't seem to settle on a single word that I want to represent my year at public school."

"I'm surprised you're taking this so seriously," I laughed.

"Hey," Micah said in mock offense. "I take school very seriously."

I sensed he was teasing me about last night, and I smiled at the memory.

"Alright, what are you thinking?"

"What does love mean to you?" he asked as I leaned down to scoop up the pencils.

"What?" I straightened up too quickly, hitting the back of my head on the drafting table. "What does that have to do with your word?" I rubbed the sore spot, almost certain it was going to leave a bump.

"I just think that love has a lot of different meanings. There's puppy love, there's loving food, and loving the place you live. When you think about it, they're all different. You love puppies because they're adorable, you love your favorite food because it makes you feel a certain way, you love the place you live because it makes you feel safe. Are all those feelings really love, or do we just lack the right words to describe it? What is love, at its core?"

I thought for a minute. What did love mean to me? As much as I did love puppies, and food, and the place I lived, that's not what immediately came to mind when I thought of love. So far, love meant a lot of empty feelings. But I shouldn't be so cynical. Yes, perhaps romance hadn't worked out for me yet, but I'd felt love in lots of different ways. My parents, for example, had been happily married for almost twenty years. Their romance gave me hope that at the right time, in the right place, with the right person, I would finally get that whirlwind romance I'd always hoped for. Familial love was another thing. Max and I knew, without a doubt, that our parents loved us, we loved them, and Max and I loved each other. We were a really tight-knit family, the four of us. So to answer Micah's question, I really would need a novel, but instead, I cleared my throat and summed up my feelings the best I could.

"Love is change and stability. I think you know by now that I like routines, I like certainty. I'm grateful for the stability my parents' love has given me, but at the same time, I wonder what a whirlwind romance would do to me? Would it change my life like all the books say it will?"

"You have a real sunny outlook on love," he said.

I laughed. "I actually feel pretty confused about it right this moment."

"Why?"

Oh, I don't know, because the boy I've liked for seven years finally asks me on a date, but a movie star walks in and shakes everything up, and makes me question everything I thought I wanted. But I was not about to tell Micah any of this, and I worried I'd already said too much.

"I don't know," I finally replied. "Romance has just never been my strong suit."

"We're in high school," Micah laughed. "Is it anybody's?"

"I guess not."

Micah sucked in a big breath on the other side of the phone. "Navy, you've just given me the greatest idea. Thank you. Talk to you later."

He hung up before I could reply. I smiled, shaking my head. Micah Moore was something else.

ON TUESDAY MORNING, I sat in English, anxious because we had to present our words to the whole class. I never liked being the center of attention.

Miss Akekian stood in front of the class, asking for volunteers to go first. Micah's hand shot up the second she asked. Figures. He was probably craving some attention.

"Alright, Micah. What have you got?" Miss Akekian moved her little stool to the side of the classroom and perched herself on it, ready to listen to what Micah and the rest of the students had to say.

Micah slid out of his seat in front of me and walked to the front of the classroom, gripping a flawless sheet of paper. I leaned forward, curious as to what in our phone conversation on Saturday morning had sparked such a good idea.

"My word," he cleared his throat, "is *hemiola.*"

He looked at me, giving me a small smile before looking back at his paper and going on.

"Hemiola is when a song is being played in two-four time, but two groups of three beats are replaced by three groups of two beats, so it sounds like it's being played in three-four time, or vice versa. To me, it means that even though the song is the same, it experiences a little change. Now, it may seem obvious why I chose a musical term for change to represent my senior year. After all, coming to Utah was a big and unexpected change for me. But it's a little deeper than that."

He cleared his throat again, as if he was nervous to go on and share why hemiola had more meaning to him.

"All of the changes I've experienced this past year were because I am loved a lot of different ways. The movie in which I got my first leading role came out earlier this year, made possible only by the love and support of my parents, my sister, and my agent. All of a sudden, people knew who I was. I had become a celebrity. People loved me because of my movie, and it all went to my head. I started making incredibly stupid decisions. And while I was making those stupid decisions, my sister was constantly telling me I needed to change, to give up the bad habits I'd developed. The only reason she gave a crap about what I was doing was because she loved me. When my dad found out about these bad habits, he sent me here to live with my aunt and get away from all the fame. This, the biggest change, was also brought about because my dad loved me, and didn't want to see me throwing my life away to the horrible decisions I was making. And now I'm here. I'm not always happy about it, and I miss my life in California. But because I love my dad, and my mom, and my sister, and everyone else who helped me become who I am, I want to show them that I can change, I can be better. I can be the mature and responsible person they want me to be and still pursue a life of acting and possibly more fame. But being here a week has taught me something else."

Here he looked up, surveying the classroom quickly. Then his eyes caught mine in a way that made it impossible for me to look away.

"So you see, I'm the same song as I was before, but I need a few beats replaced. And I've realized if I don't change, if I don't accept why my dad sent me here, if I'm not better, I just might lose out on a love story that could change my life forever."

A collective sigh washed over the room. The way Micah spoke had kept us all in a trance, mesmerized in his deep smooth voice and the way his energy filled the room. Everyone started clapping, and he broke our eye contact. I fell back in my chair, my heart racing as I tried to figure out what in the world had just happened.

Micah came back to his desk, giving me a little wink before he turned to sit down. I spent the rest of class fiddling with my pencil, lost in thought about what Micah may have just admitted to. Was I reading too much into this? Surely, he couldn't mean me. We'd only known each other for a little over a week. And even if he did have feelings for me, did I have feelings for him? Were the butterflies I felt because I was starting to fall for him, or because he was handsome and charming and famous? I had too many questions and not enough answers.

When the bell rang, I scooped up my bag, grateful for the students who swarmed around him to tell him how incredible his word essay was. I beelined it for the door before Micah could say anything. I'd only made it a few steps out of the class-room before Brock stopped me.

"Navy, hey," he said as he pulled me to the side of the hall and leaned on the lockers we stopped in front of.

"Hi," I smiled, suddenly aware of how out of breath I felt. How long had it been since I'd taken a full, deep breath?

"Are you feeling okay, you looked flushed," Brock put the back of his hand on my forehead, and then moved it to my cheek, checking my temperature.

"Oh yeah, I feel fine," I said, enjoying the warmth from Brock's hand, and reveling in the tingling feeling his touch left behind. "Maybe I just need some water."

"Yeah," Brock nodded, shifting his book bag on his shoulder. "So, we're trying to decide on a place to go to dinner before Homecoming, and we all just wanted to check with our dates. Is there a type of food you just absolutely cannot stand?"

I'm sure my wide smile looked ridiculous, but I couldn't help it. I was giddy to be Brock's date. "Hmm, I really don't like seafood, but other than that, I'm pretty easy to please."

"Great, I'll make sure wherever we go has a lot of options that aren't seafood for you."

"Perfect." My eyes inadvertently settled on Brock's mouth for a moment before I blinked and looked back up.

"Also, do you know what color tie I should get?"

"Not yet, sorry," I shook my head, "Becca and I are going dress shopping tonight though, so I'll let you know."

"That's great. I'm excited, Navy." He lowered his voice a bit, and put his hand on my arm. Even though he had told me we were going as friends, I couldn't help but wonder if this dance could be the beginning of something more.

"Me too," I said, trying to keep my voice steady despite the butterflies in my stomach.

"Talk to you soon," he said, turning to leave. "Oh, and remember to drink that water," he winked.

"Yeah, I will." I smiled as I watched him disappear into the crowd of students hurrying to class.

I walked to my next class gripping the straps of my book bag to keep my hands from shaking. As I slid into my seat, I tried to forget Micah, and remember that Brock was excited to go to Homecoming with me, and listen to what my teacher was saying, but after this morning, my mind was far too preoccupied to focus on school.

"AND THEN HE looked right at me and said something about a love story that will change his life forever," I said, stepping out of the dressing room and giving Becca a little twirl. "What about this one?" I paused in my story about Micah's word presentation that morning to get her opinion on the dress I was wearing.

This dress, the seventh one I had tried on, was a deep, Christmas green. It had a sequined bodice and a short tulle skirt. It wasn't the ugliest of the ones I'd tried, but I still wasn't feeling it. At this point, even though I'd only tried seven dresses, I'd felt like I'd been in every color of the rainbow, every fabric, skirt length, sleeve length, neckline, and silhouette, and nothing felt right. Nothing made me feel beautiful. I'd never had much trouble finding dresses for dances, but this dance wasn't just any old dance. This was my first date with Brock, and I wanted to look perfect.

Becca shook her head and scrunched up her nose. "No. I thought that color would complement your eyes, but it just washes you out. Try another one."

She was right. As I looked myself over in the mirror, I not only looked pale, but sickly. The knee-length skirt did nothing but accentuate my knobby knees.

I sighed and returned to the dressing room, pulling the heavy red velvet curtain behind me.

"Can you believe that?" I resumed our conversation about Micah as I unzipped the dress, hung it carefully back on the hanger and moved it to the *no-go* pile. "We're in high school. No love story he's going to find here is going to change his life forever. It's probably not even going to change his life past June."

"Who cares if the love story won't last past high school," Becca called back. "He was looking at you when he said it. He wants you. You're the love story that's going to change his life forever."

"Yeah, right." I rolled my eyes even though Becca couldn't see it.

"Why don't you go for it?"

"He's a celebrity."

"So what? He's here now. What makes him any different than any other guy at Park City High School?"

"He's a *celebrity*," I said again, dragging out every syllable of that last word because she obviously didn't hear me the first time. "And I like Brock."

"I thought you were getting over him."

I poked my head around the curtain. "I've known Brock for years, and Micah for a week. And I can't get over Brock overnight, especially when he asked me to Homecoming. How am I supposed to move on while daydreaming of finally slow dancing with him? Let me have this."

Becca rolled her eyes and smiled. "But it's *Micah Moore*. And he so *obviously* has a thing for you. What girl in her right mind would pass that up?"

"Yeah, Micah's great. Don't get me wrong. Maybe we'll just

be good friends." I lifted the last dress off the hanger and unzipped it.

This dress was my last hope before we'd have to go back and evaluate the dresses in my *possibly* pile or go back to the floor to find more to try on. It was floor-length and navy blue, with long sleeves, and a sequined peacock feather decal spreading from my right shoulder down across the bodice and spilling over the skirt. As I zipped it up and turned to face the mirror, my breath caught in my throat. Although I'd had my doubts about the dress on the hanger, I felt a new level of stunning now that I had it on. This was the one. I thought that the moment I found the dress, I'd think of Brock and slow dancing with him at Homecoming, but instead, I heard Micah's voice in my head, calling me Navy Blue. I was surprised that the memory made me smile. Pushing the thought away, I gripped the skirt in my fists before walking out to show Becca.

I pushed the curtain aside and walked out. I didn't even have to ask what she thought before her hand flew to her mouth. "Spin around," she said through her fingers.

I turned on the balls of my feet, letting my arms lift up a little bit.

"Navy, you look stunning," she said, breathless. "That's totally the one."

"I know," was all I could say. I wondered if this was what those girls on *Say Yes to the Dress* felt like when they fell in love with their wedding gowns. "I don't ever want to take it off."

"How it the world has Brock not fallen for you yet?"

"You're biased," I said, facing her again and putting my hands on my hips.

"Absolutely. But seriously, look at you." She put her arms

out in front of her like she was waiting for a hug. "Look at this dress. I hope he realizes how lucky he is."

I didn't know what to say to that, so I turned back to the mirror and admired how the sequins glittered in the light.

"Well, one thing is for sure." Becca moved to stand by me. "Micah's going to fall over when he sees it."

I blushed, "No, he's not."

Becca folded her arms, popped out her hip, and raised an eyebrow, "We'll see."

THE NEXT DAY, I cringed at the thought of AP Chemistry. I got there early, slid into the same seat in the very back and watched as everyone else trickled in, looking every bit as excited and awake as I was; that is to say, sleepy and dreading it.

The bell rang just as Micah opened the door and walked into the classroom. He ducked his head down and made his way to the back. I could tell he was trying to attract as little attention as possible as he came in late.

"Good morning, Navy," he said, taking a seat next to me.

"Morning." I nodded in reply.

Before we had time for more conversation, Mr. Thompson instructed us to take out a sheet of paper and started his lecture. He went on and on and on until there were only five minutes of class left.

I dropped my pen and massaged the massive cramp in my hand as Mr. Thompson taped a piece of paper on the board.

"This," he pointed to the paper, "is the list for lab partnerships. I have paired you up alphabetically, and before you ask, no you cannot change who your lab partner is. Labs will be after school for about two hours. You must come in six times a semester so that you will have the required twelve lab write-ups by the end of the year." Mr. Thompson clasped his arm behind his back, pacing in front of the board. "Get together and decide on afternoons that work for both you and your partner, and then sign up on the lab schedule in the back of the classroom. If you have any questions or conflicts, just come and work it out with me. You may pack up and check the list and you are excused when the bell rings."

Monroe and Moore were dangerously close when names were listed alphabetically. An unexpected excitement bubbled in my stomach at the thought of being lab partners and getting more opportunities to spend time with Micah, even if we were doing chemistry homework. I shook my head, trying to deny how increasingly hard it was to view Micah as the acquaintance he was while battling free-fall feeling in my stomach every time I was around him.

I flipped my notebook closed and packed up my book bag as quickly as I could, anxious to see who my lab partner would be.

Together, Micah and I walked to the front of the classroom. As we got the board, the crowd parted to let us through.

"Let's see here," Micah said, running his finger down the list until he found his name. "Navy Monroe and Micah Moore."

I smiled, feeling the glares of everyone in the classroom on my back. Micah and I shuffled towards the classroom door so the other students could check the list.

"I'm glad you're my partner," Micah said, lifting up his hand for a high-five. "Two-hour chem labs would be unbearable with anyone else."

"Yeah, you know," I slapped his hand before folding my

arms and leaning on the wall, "Maybe they won't be so bad after all."

On Friday, we were back in chemistry. I sat reviewing my notes when Micah brushed passed me as he slid into the seat behind me.

"Navy, I'm going to look at cars tonight, wanna come with me?"

"Sure, sounds fun." I turned around and rested my elbow on his desk. I felt a strange excitement in my stomach, and I was terrified, so I pushed it down and ignored it. I still didn't know where I was with my feelings for Brock, or my feelings for Micah, and until someone, Max or Becca or maybe even Micah himself, made me face it, I didn't want to think about it.

After school, I was sitting at my drafting table when Max rushed into my bedroom, out of breath.

"I asked Melanie on a date."

"What?" I spun around in my chair, gripping the back. "When?"

"Just barely."

"And when are you going?"

"In, like, an hour." Max checked his watch, pulling back the sleeve of the blue plaid button-up he was wearing.

"Do you have any idea what you're going to do?"

"I was thinking an EBF," Max smiled.

"Yes." I smacked my hands together. "Perfect."

EBF stood for Epic Backyard Forts, and, thanks to Pinterest inspiration, Max and I were pro at building them. We gathered all the old sheets, strings of white Christmas lights and almost every blanket and pillow we could find in the house. I texted Micah to find out Melanie's favorite movie and we raided the pantry for snacks.

"So what inspired you to ask Melanie on a date so spur the moment?" I asked as we walked outside.

"One day, she's going to be my girlfriend."

"You can't be serious." I looked sideways at him.

"I'm dead serious. I think she's the most beautiful girl I've ever seen. She's my age and now she's going to my school. What's stopping me?"

"Oh, I don't know," I rolled my eyes. "She's famous."

"So what? She's here now."

Becca had said the same thing about Micah earlier this week when we were dress shopping. Was I the only one who felt the Moore's fame was a legitimate reason a relationship between them and us couldn't work? I mean, surely we'd be setting ourselves up for heartbreak because at the end of the school year, they would leave, and we would stay here.

"She's going to our high school," Max continued. "As far as I'm concerned, she's just like any other girl at Park City High School, and I am going to date her."

"Micah and Melanie Moore are not like everyone else. They live a different life. Who's to say they will even be here long enough for you to make her your girlfriend?"

"Navy, you keep saying they are so different, that they live a different life." Max dropped the blankets and sheets he'd been carrying on the grass and started helping me untangle the Christmas lights. "But what if they're not? What if they're just like you and me? Their aunt teaches high school theater, for crying out loud. How much more ordinary can you get?"

"They are not their aunt. She may be an ordinary member of society, but that doesn't mean they are."

"Navy, how about you let go of your preconceived notions of

these people and get to know them for who they really are. You might be surprised."

"Alright, alright." I waved off his comment, wanting to move on because I knew I couldn't get him to change his mind. Who was I to stop him? If Melanie made him happy, and as long as she treated him well, I was happy for my brother. "We have to make this fort the most romantic thing she's ever seen."

"Yeah we do," Max answered enthusiastically as we dragged the chairs from the deck table into the middle of the grass. "Wouldn't it be funny if I actually did get to date Melanie, and you fell in love with Micah. Siblings dating siblings—it's straight out of a romance novel."

I laughed. Perhaps my brother had been hanging around Becca too much lately because it sounded like something she would have said. "Oh Max, I'm happy that you aspire to date a celebrity who's going to our school. I, however, will probably not fall in love with Micah Moore."

"Why not? He practically admitted in front of your whole English class that he's falling for you."

"First of all, we do not live in a romance novel. This is real life. And second of all, he probably doesn't even know what he's talking about. We've known each other for two weeks, and had only a handful of conversations that have lasted for longer than two seconds."

"Ah, but he's been to your treehouse, and that's something. I know you don't let just anybody up there," Max said as we situated the chairs across from each other, facing them out to form the skeleton of our fort.

"I didn't invite him into my treehouse," I said. "That was mom."

"And you're going out tonight."

"I'm not 'going out' with Micah. I'm helping him pick out a new car." When I said it out loud, I was struck by how odd it seemed. I didn't think teenagers went out buying their own cars very often, maybe more often than I thought, but still, it reminded me how different Micah and I were.

"Believe me, no boy needs help picking out a car that will be driven by him and only him. He already knows what he wants. He's using the whole thing as an excuse to spend more time with you."

As I strung the Christmas lights in random formations between the trees and chairs, I felt that strange feeling I'd felt when Micah had asked me to go with him that morning, that feeling like something was changing and it was out of my control. Again I suppressed it, choosing to ignore it.

"We are hanging out tonight as friends. You know better than anyone that I have feelings for Brock."

"And where has that gotten you?" Max asked as we threw a sheet over the lights and let it fall to the ground. The fort was coming together perfectly.

"Hey, we're going to a dance together. We're finally going on a date."

"Have you ever stopped to consider why you like Brock so much, why you've been so hooked on him?" Max asked, clipping the sheets in place with clothespins. "Maybe you've talked up Brock so much in your head these past seven years that you liked the idea of him more than you ever really liked him. Perhaps the fact that his affection constantly eluded you made you believe he meant more to you than he really did. Look, I've always wanted to be supportive of you, but now you have a chance to move on and fall for someone who's developing real feelings for you, and who's willing to act on those feelings, and I don't want you to miss it."

My mouth fell open and I dropped the clothespin I was holding. Something about what my brother had just said gave me a sinking feeling in my stomach, like I knew he was right, but I wasn't willing to admit it.

I shook my head, "No, I like Brock because he's kind, and—" I trailed off. Brock *was* kind, but beyond that, I really didn't know much about him. Yes, he made me feel like the center of the universe the few times we'd talked since eighth grade, but did I know anything below the surface? I knew little facts and snippets from watching out the window or stalking his Instagram page, but I'd never had a single deep conversation with him. He was my neighbor and my crush of seven years, and I barely knew anything about him. I'd put him on such a high pedestal that it was like admiring a celebrity. The irony was not lost on me. Even after two weeks, Micah felt more real to me than Brock had in a long time.

"And what?" Max asked as we finished pinning the sheets in place. The outside of the fort was complete.

I didn't know what to tell him, but I couldn't just go from liking Brock for seven years to suddenly being over him to feeling this way about someone else in a matter of a single conversation with my brother.

Or perhaps it wasn't this single conversation. Perhaps it was a culmination of moments, thoughts, glances, and denials that started the moment I met Micah in the music hall, or the moment I saw Brock kissing another girl with my own eyes, or the moment Micah called me "Navy Blue" for the first time. Perhaps love never begins or ends as abruptly as it seems to.

Perhaps none of this was love at all. Perhaps it was all delusion. Perhaps they were the same thing.

And scariest of all, perhaps I finally was moving on but refusing to admit it because I didn't know how to be Navy without being infatuated with Brock. I didn't know how to be a Navy who had feelings for anybody else.

"I don't know," I finally admitted as Max and I finished laying out blanket and pillows, and situating the laptop and the treats inside the fort. "I'm still having trouble sorting out how I feel about Micah."

"Word of advice, sis," Max checked his watch as we walked back inside. "Don't let him slip through your fingers. Who knows, maybe he could be the love story you've always wanted."

"We'll see," I laughed.

"Okay, it's time to go," he said, a small tremor in his deep voice. "How do I look?" He reached up to his neck, adjusting his collar.

"Like a million bucks," I smiled at him. "She's gonna love every second of it."

He gave me two thumbs up as he headed out the front door. I watched him walk up the street to Miss Moore's house and waited until I could see them walking back before I left.

I went to the garage and drove three houses down to pick up Micah. I stayed in the car and texted him to let him know I was here. He must have been watching out the front window for me because he almost immediately stepped out the front door, jogged down the driveway, pulled open the passenger side door, and ducked in.

"Hey, Navy Blue," he said, pulling his seatbelt across his body and clicking it into place.

"That's not my name," I smiled at the greeting that had

become our tradition. I was secretly starting to like my new nickname, but I'd be hard-pressed to admit it.

"Do you know what Max and Mel are doing on their date?"

"Yeah, we built the most amazing fort in our backyard, and I think they're ordering in and watching a movie in it."

"Do you have a picture of this fort? I love forts." Micah looked over at me, holding his hand out for my phone.

I laughed. "No, I didn't think to take a picture, but maybe we can go take a peek after we get you a car."

"Sounds like a plan."

"So where are we going?" I asked, realizing I was driving to the only car dealership I knew of around here, and that was a dinky used car lot just outside of Park City. Surely Micah didn't want that. He probably wanted to drive to Salt Lake where they sold luxury cars and search for something there.

"I hear there's a used car lot not far from here. Do you know where it is?"

"Yeah, actually."

"You sound so surprised," Micah laughed at me. "Do you not know where a lot of places around here are? Haven't you lived here your whole life?"

"No, I'm not surprised that I know where the dealership is, I'm surprised you want a used car. I assumed you would have wanted a Benz or a Ferrari."

"Oh, well, I already have a Lamborghini back in California, and I probably won't be here past next summer, so really all I need is a semi-nice car in working order that can get me to school and back." He shrugged his shoulders.

His logic gave me a defeated feeling that surprised me. I was reminded why I kept pushing those nagging feelings for him away. He was Micah Moore, a movie star who wasn't meant to be just an average person. Max believed Micah and Melanie were just like us, but they lived worlds away from us despite the fact we were living on the exact same street. Their lives would never let them stay here because I'm not even sure they wanted to be here in the first place. So things with Melanie may work out for Max, but even then, only for a little while, and that was exactly why I couldn't let my feelings for Micah progress past a fond friendship. I had already spent seven years of my short life waiting for a hopeless love story, and I didn't need to waste a minute more.

So I sat up a little taller in my seat, refusing to let myself feel defeated for long, and we drove the rest of the way to the dealership in comfortable silence. I found myself wishing I knew what Micah was thinking at that moment. I snuck a glance at him to see if his expression would give me any idea, but he was looking away from me out the passenger side window.

When we pulled in the parking lot and parked the car, Micah got out and walked over to a bold, cobalt blue Corolla whose shiny, sleek lines sparkled in the setting sun. It seemed Max was right. Micah knew exactly what car he wanted.

I joined him as he was hunched over, shielding his eyes from the sun as he peered in the windows at the interior. I had to admit that for a used car, this one actually looked pretty nice.

"I like the color," I said lamely as Micah stood upright again, apparently pleased with the interior of the car.

"Yeah," he said, looking around for a salesman. "I saw this car on their website earlier this week but wasn't sure it would still be here. Wanna take it for a test drive with me?"

"Sure," I smiled.

We sought out a salesman, and he told us to wait by the car while he got the keys. A few minutes later, he returned with a pamphlet about the Corolla, car keys, and a license plate. He put the license plate where it was visible through the back window, and turned to us, pointing out some of the features of this particular car. Micah seemed genuinely impressed, but I just stood there and nodded my head when Micah did.

"Enjoy the drive," the salesman told us as he walked away. "And let me know if you have any questions."

Micah opened the passenger door for me before walking around to climb into the driver's seat. He started the car and played around with the controls on the dashboard. There was a screen that popped up, allowing us to choose GPS, music, Bluetooth calling, and more. I had to admit it was pretty fancy. Micah plugged in his phone and shuffled the music he had on it. I was surprised when a familiar country song came on.

"You like country?" I raised my eyebrows.

"Yes, definitely my favorite."

I tilted my head and stared at him smiling.

"What?" He smiled back at me. "Why are you looking at me like that?"

"I just didn't think country would be your jam. I imagined punk rock, maybe alternative, but never country."

"There's a lot you don't know about me, Navy Blue," he said, putting his arm around the back of my seat and turning around to back out of the parking space.

Once we were out on the open road, Micah gripped the top of the steering wheel with his left hand and leaned his right elbow on the center console between us. His hand dangled relaxed over the cup holders. It was the first time I had ever really noticed what his hands looked like. He had long fingers, with nails that weren't long, but not extremely short either. His skin looked irresistibly soft, and I thought to myself how wonderful it must feel to hold them. I thought back to a thousand cliché quotes I'd pinned on Pinterest about how your fingers are made to fit perfectly in the spaces between someone else's. Would my hands fit perfectly in Micah's? Would I ever know?

*What the heck*, I almost said aloud, derailing my train of thought. I rubbed my own hands together, suddenly self-conscious about how rough the dry Utah weather had made them. I slipped them under my legs, feigning sudden deep interest in what was going on out the window to my right. I knew the thought had made me blush, so I flipped my hair behind my shoulder and adjusted the vents so they blew cool air on my face.

"How do you like it?" I asked.

"It's so smooth," he said, turning a corner. "I'm sold. I was the second I saw it."

"That was fast."

"When I see something I want, I get it, no beating around the bush, no going back and forth between options." He shot me a sideways smile.

"But what if there is another car that you might like better?"

"Navy Blue, there will always be something better. There will always be distractions, shiny objects that try to take away from the perfectly good things standing in front of you. If you want the most out of life, you have to find something, someone, somewhere that helps you feel genuinely happy, and run with it. Stop looking when you're content. You can spend your whole life asking 'what if' and looking for more, but the more you look, the more you compare, the less content you're going to be. Before you know it, a perfectly good life will have slipped through your fingers."

He continually surprised me. I had assumed that he was the kind of person that would always be looking for bigger and better things. Maybe he was more content here than I realized or that he let on, but could he be happy here forever? Would my reluctance to admit my feelings for him change if I knew he wasn't as fleeting as I'd thought?

"What are you thinking about?" he asked, breaking the silence. I hadn't realized that I hadn't replied to his personal philosophy on happiness.

"I don't know," I said, leaning my arm on the passenger side door, resting my head in my hand. "You're just surprising."

"You say that a lot."

"You surprise me a lot. The fact that I'm sitting here on a test drive in the same car as you is just something I never thought I'd be doing."

"Why not?"

"Because you're Micah Moore. You're this big-shot movie star and I'm just a girl living in a city most people don't even know exists. You and I are so opposite, we shouldn't even know each other."

"Are you mad that we do?"

"No, not mad. I'm glad I get to know you, *really* know you." I shifted and leaned my elbow on the center console, cradling my face in my hand. Micah made me want to be flirty. "You are an extremely pleasant surprise."

He stopped at a red light. The world around us seemed to slow down as he glanced over at me with a half-smile and a mischievous glint in his eye. I sucked in a breath and begged the light to stay red just a little longer so I could hang on to this moment when I finally admitted to myself that Micah Moore had left the friend zone.

7
_____

# MICAH

AFTER BUYING MY NEW CAR, Navy and I went out to dinner, and then back to her house so I could see the fort they'd built for Max and Melanie's date.

"Come here," Navy said, waving her hand to motion me over to the back window. She turned off the kitchen lights so we could see out into the dark night and pulled back the drapes, pointing. "There it is."

Outside was one of the most romantic scenes I'd ever seen. The twinkle lights strung between the trees made it look like the stars had come down especially for Max and Melanie. I saw my sister's bare feet and Max blue and white striped socks sticking out from the fort they'd made with white sheets.

"It's beautiful."

"Yeah," Navy smiled, leaning on the window frame. "We make some pretty amazing forts."

"You've done this before?" I asked, looking over and raising my eyebrows at her. Was Navy's romantic past more than just an unrequited crush on Brock? Had she had special nights in a fort like the one we were looking at? It wouldn't have surprised me, honestly. Navy was beautiful and smart and easy to talk to. I suddenly wanted to rush outside, push my sister and Max out of the fort, and take it for Navy and me.

"No, never for a date," Navy shook her head, looking sideways at me. "Sometimes Max and I build it because it's a beautiful night and we want to play games or watch a movie outside. Sometimes I build it for Becca when one of her two-week flings comes to an end. We've had lots of tearful conversations in a fort like that one."

"We could go out and join them, or go to your treehouse." I folded my arms and leaned against the window.

"No," Navy's voice softened, and she rested her forehead on the glass. "Let's not disturb them."

I looked over at Navy, watching as she looked dreamily, longingly, out into the back yard. I wanted to close the distance between us, grab her hand, pull her into my arms and dance in the kitchen. I wanted to create a moment for her that was more romantic than the fort. Normally I would have, but something held me back. Maybe it was because I knew she had feelings for someone else. Maybe it was because I wasn't supposed to get into a relationship here. Maybe it was because as much as I tried to view Navy through the lens of the Kissing Game, just a pointless conquest with no attachments to pass the time, I wanted more. I knew that if I ever kissed Navy, I'd never be able to quit her.

We stared out into the backyard in silence for a few moments more, before Navy flipped on the lights and we moved to the kitchen table. We played a game of scrabble that took far longer than a normal game would because we kept talking instead of playing. There were very few people easier to talk to than Navy. With her, something in me just clicked, and I felt the balance between normalcy and fame that I'd been looking for since I'd been launched into stardom. I didn't need to drink to dull my senses, I just need someone to treat me like I was just another boy at school even though she knew I was a celebrity.

After their movie, Max and Melanie came in, and Navy and I watched from the front window as Max walked her home. I didn't want to spoil the already awkward porch scene by walking home with Melanie, and of course, I wasn't ready to leave Navy for the night. I wanted to hang on to every moment I had with her.

When Max came back, I finally excused myself and walked up the streetlight lit sidewalk back to our house. Melanie and Aunt Juliet sat in the living room, talking about her date.

"Did you have fun?" I asked, slumping into the plush recliner next to them.

"So much fun." Melanie's eyes lit up as she turned her attention to me. "It was one of the most laid back and relaxing dates, but I still feel like he put a lot of effort into it. It was probably the best date I've ever been on."

"You haven't been on that many dates."

Melanie rolled her eyes at me, "Yeah, but I've been on enough to know the bad ones, and this one was exactly what I always thought a date should feel like."

"Was it easy for you to talk to him? Did you ever feel awkward at all?" Aunt Juliet asked.

"Not at all." Melanie shook her head. "I feel like I could have talked to him all night and we'd never run out of things to say."

That makes two Moores who want to talk to their Monroe counterparts all night.

"Did anything happen in that fort?" I raised my eyebrows teasingly.

"Yeah, we just ate dinner and watched a movie." Melanie looked down, obviously avoiding what I truly meant by my question. She was also very obviously blushing, giving herself away.

Now I was the one rolling my eyes. "You know that's not what I meant."

"If you must know, we held hands. And it felt wonderful." Her cheeks reddened even more.

"That is so precious," Aunt Juliet let out a girly squeal of excitement, clasping her hands together over her heart.

I sat up a little straighter, surprised at what I felt at the news that my sister and Max Monroe had held hands. I was excited for her, for sure, because I could tell she was starting to like this kid. But I felt something else, a sinking feeling, perhaps a little jealousy, but for what?

*You know for what,* a nagging little voice in my head said. Because even though I'd only known her for two weeks at this point, I wanted to hold Navy's hand too. There was no denying I was falling hard for Navy Blue.

I had thought that the opportunity might present itself while we were test-driving my new car, but she had spent the whole ride sitting on her hands. My heart sunk lower at the thought that perhaps she would never see me more than just a friend. It shouldn't have bothered me. After all, if I got that part in France, I'd be leaving in just a matter of months. Even if life in Utah was our normal, I couldn't ignore the fact that we were just in high school, and those relationships rarely lasted. But something about Navy was worth the risk, like some time with her was better than never having her at all.

I stood up, stretching my arms over my head. "Alright, I'm going to sleep," I announced, leaving my aunt and sister to finish talking about her perfect first date.

I walked up to my room, pushing open the door and standing in the doorway, looking over it. I'd still refused to put on the new bedding and had yet to fully unpack my suitcase. Everything I'd brought to Utah was a jumbled mess in front of my closet doors. As I looked at the mess, my heart was torn in two directions. I did still miss my life in California, and for Melanie's sake, I did want to get back sooner rather than later, but tonight was evidence that life here wasn't so bad. After all, Mel did just have one of the best, most romantic dates of her life, and to say I had enjoyed my night car shopping and playing scrabble with Navy was an immense understatement.

I walked across the room and dragged my suitcase away from the closet doors. I took out the new bed set and stripped my bed of the purple quilt and white sheets that had been there when I showed up. The new dark blue sheets and green and blue plaid down comforter were much more my style. Even though I was about to climb into bed, I made it up perfectly, tucking the sheets with the fancy nurse's corner my mom had taught me to do, and arranging the pillows at the head.

Next, I unpacked all my clothes, hanging them in the closet, or folding them neatly into the chest of drawers. It was the most organized I'd ever been. At the bottom of the suitcase, I found the picture of our family Melanie had insisted I pack, and put it on the nightstand. Finally, I unpacked my backpack, moving all of my school supplies onto the desk.

I stepped back, admiring how cozy and comfortable that

room was now that it looked like someone actually lived here instead of just staying for the weekend.

"You finally unpacked," Melanie said, coming into my room.

"Yeah," I said, turning to face her. "You know, life isn't so bad here."

"I would even go so far to say that life is good here," Melanie smiled.

WHILE I HAD ADOPTED my dad's habit of not looking at the tabloids since my drunk driving incident, Melanie had not. The next morning, she rushed into my room, pulling my covers off.

"What," I mumbled, stuffing my face in my pillows. "I want to sleep in."

"I think you're going to want to see this." Melanie sounded panicked as she threw her phone down on the bed next to my head.

I picked it up, lifting my head to see what she was so worried about. I saw a stream of pictures; Navy and I standing next to the Carolla as I looked in the window, me getting Navy's door for her as she slid into the passenger seat, Navy and I in the car, smiling at each other, Navy and I walking into the restaurant.

*Micah Moore spends a romantic date night with a new fling in Utah*, the headline read.

I sat up, running my fingers through my hair. "How did they get all this? I didn't even see anyone taking pictures."

I was usually on guard for people trying to sneak a quick picture of me, and was even more conscious of paparazzi and journalists, but either I'd been so wrapped up in Navy that I hadn't been paying attention, or the rule at school that no one could take pictures of me had made me soft. I rubbed my eyes with the heels of my hands. It was going to be alright, I was pretty used to this by now. However, it was still slightly annoying.

"Everyone is a paparazzi now." Melanie sat on my bed, taking my phone from me before I could read the accompanying article to hear what it said about me dating Navy.

My head snapped out of my hands. Had Navy already seen this? What would she think? What if she thought I'd planned this, trying to use her for a publicity stunt? What if she hated me forever after this?

I leaped out of my bed, pulling on a sweatshirt and bounding down the stairs two at a time, not even bothering to check the time, brush my teeth, or tell my aunt or sister where I was going.

I ran all the way to Navy's house, banging on the door when I got there. Max opened the door dressed in a white tee-shirt and plaid pajama pants.

"Is Navy here?" I asked before he could say anything.

"Yeah, she's still asleep," Max said, turning slightly and pointing his thumb over his shoulder.

I felt slight relief. If she was still asleep, she most likely hadn't seen the article yet, but she was bound to see it sometime, and I wanted to be the one to explain. "Can you wake her up?"

"Yeah," Max stepped aside, motioning me inside. "Is everything okay?"

I lifted my phone for him to see. "Some idiots snapped some pictures of us buying a car and going to dinner last night, and now they think we're dating."

Max looked back and forth between the phone and me. He opened and closed his mouth a few times, apparently not knowing what to say or how to react.

"We're not dating," I rushed on, "but I don't want her to think this is some sick way to boost publicity while I'm here, or that I set her up. If she has to see this, I want to be the one to show her."

Max nodded, "Good call. I'll go get her up. I think you'd better just wait here."

I stood in the entryway, rocking back on forth on my feet. When Navy finally came down, she was dressed in sweatpants and an oversized tee-shirt. Her long dark hair was piled on top of her head in a messy bun that was falling out, and thick green-rimmed glasses framed her mascara-smeared eyes. I didn't know she had glasses, and I was momentarily speechless at how effortlessly beautiful she looked for having just woken up. What's more, it didn't even look like she had tried to put herself together before coming down. Maybe Max had told her about the urgency of the situation, or maybe she just didn't care. It was refreshing.

Recovering myself and remembering why I'd practically banged down the door and dragged Navy out of bed in the first place, I handed her my phone.

"This was published this morning, but I want you to know I didn't plan this. I didn't know people were taking pictures of us, and I'm sorry you got caught up in this." I rushed it all out in one breath, panicked to think about how Navy would react and if this would be the downfall of our growing friendship.

Navy slid her finger up and down the screen, reading and looking at all the pictures of us. She looked up at me and then back to the phone with much the same expression Max had when I showed him.

"So what happens now? What do we do?" Navy looked at me.

I shrugged. "There's really nothing we can do. It's out there now."

"So now everyone thinks we're dating, and we're just supposed to sit here and take it?" She handed the phone back to me.

"Not everyone will believe it. We, and everyone important to us, know we're not dating. They know the truth."

"Yeah, but some people will believe it. Micah, you know how important Notre Dame is to me. Nowadays, they'll probably look at my social media and online presence as part of the admission process, and no offense, you don't exactly have the greatest reputation. What if they think I'm just an irresponsible partier too?" She put one hand on her hip, and the other went to her head, squeezing what hair was left in the bun as she paced in front of me.

"I know," I looked down, hurt that she thought being seen with me would ruin her chances at getting into her dream university, even though I understood. She was right, I wasn't exactly a boy scout. "I'm sorry. I don't know what to say."

I tried to remember the first time I'd showed up in the tabloids or when someone I didn't even know tagged me in a picture on social media, and how strange it felt to know that someone had been watching me and taking pictures without me knowing, how weird it was that someone thought they knew enough about me to write completely untrue things about my personal life as if they were fact. However, even then, I knew I'd signed up for that. It came with the job and lifestyle I wanted.

Navy had never chosen this. Now that she knew that this was part of spending time with me, I worried that she'd never be able to move past just being friends. If we started dating, she would have to open herself to this part of my life too.

"Tell me what I can do to make it better." I gripped her shoulders to stop her pacing.

"I don't know, Micah." Her arms dropped to her sides, defeated. "What if everything changes? What if I don't get accepted to Notre Dame because of this? And what about Brock?" She twisted the knife in my already panicked heart. I wanted to walk across the street and punch him in the face. "What if I never get a chance with him because he thinks I'm with you?"

"Navy, I know this has never happened to you before, so I know it's strange. But what these people write about me, what they write about us, doesn't make any of it true. It doesn't define the reality of our lives. We don't change based on what they write."

"But what will people think?"

"That was never in our control to begin with."

"Can't we say something to clear it up, tell everyone we're not an item?"

"No, don't say anything. Keep your head down. Go on with life. These people will take anything and everything we say and spin it to tell the story they want."

Navy let out a long sigh.

"I'm sorry I dragged you into this. I honestly never thought anyone was watching last night." I let go of her shoulders.

"I just need a minute to think, work through it all."

I nodded. "I totally understand. Can I do anything to help?"

"No," Navy shook her head, looking down. "I think I just

need some space. If they don't see us together, they can't specu-late, right?"

My heart sank, and I felt sick. I wanted to stay and work through her feelings together. I wanted to wrap her in my arms and let her know that we were going to be okay, that this really didn't mean anything, that life would go on, and that this wouldn't jeopardize her bright future. I wanted this to be a bonding experience, not one where she pulled away. But what could I do?

"Okay," I reached for the door behind me. "Can I call you later?"

"Yeah, okay." Navy still wouldn't look me in the eye. She stood by the door as I walked out and down the front steps. "Talk to you later."

I walked slowly back to our house and found Melanie in the front room when I got there.

"I'm assuming you went to talk to Navy?"

"Yeah," I nodded, running my fingers through my disheveled hair.

"And," Melanie made circular motions in front of her with her hand, prompting me to go on.

"She was shocked, doesn't quite know how to handle it."

"Understandable."

"Yeah, I'm just going to go back to sleep for a little bit." I started walking towards the stairs.

"Micah, it's going to be okay," Melanie called behind me. "This isn't going to change anything. After all, a month ago, you were in a drunken car accident. If that didn't ruin everything, this silly puff piece won't either."

I knew she was right, but this time I felt like I had so much to lose.

The two weeks that followed had both Navy and me walking on eggshells around each other. True to what she said when our tabloid story showed up, Navy kept her distance. We only managed to get little conversations in here and there between the two classes we had together every morning and play practice after school, but they only consisted of the usual pleasantries, and me asking questions about certain homework problems I already knew the answers to. I overanalyzed every interaction, trying to gauge how she was feeling about me. I watched her Instagram profile relentlessly and even set up notifications so I would know the second she posted something, but she was silent on there too. At play practice, I spent far too much time stealing glances at Navy in the pit when I should have been focusing on the scenes we were blocking. Perhaps I was boarding on obsessed stalker, but I craved more time with her.

On Friday afternoon, the bell rang, and all my classmates scrambled to get out. It was the weekend, and what's more, it was Homecoming weekend. The whole school was buzzing with excitement for the football game that night, and the dance the next day, but I couldn't think of that. I had our first chemistry lab to do with Navy. While I wasn't looking forward to the chemistry part, I was excited for the extended amount of alone time in the lab, where I knew we would be safe from prying eyes and unwanted pictures. I hoped it would finally give us a chance to talk everything through.

I shuffled to the classroom to find Navy already there, decked in green goggles and a white lab coat. She had pulled her curly hair up into a messy bun on the top of her head and was chewing on a pencil as she read over the lab.

"Hey," she said, looking up as I walked into the room.

"Hey," I smiled as I slipped my arms into my own lab coat. "Alright, what is this lab all about?"

Navy explained to me what she had been reading in the instructions our teacher had given us, telling me that we would be starting small fires to observe how each chemical changed when burned. I suddenly didn't think chemistry labs would be so bad. What boy didn't love playing with fire?

Navy and I made small talk as we weighed out 5,000 milligrams of ammonium nitrate powder and 5,000 milligrams of zinc powder in a glass petri dish and measured 40 milliliters of hydrochloric acid in a plastic dropper.

"When I say go," Navy said, "add the acid to the powder. I'm going to time the burn, and then we have to make observations about the mixture after it's burned."

I didn't think there would be much to observe besides ashes, but I just nodded, positioning the dropper over the powder on the petri dish. "Ready when you are."

Navy gripped the stopwatch. "Go."

I released the acid from the dropper, but instead of the little flame I expected, a huge fire erupted. Navy and I jumped back as the fire reached the ceiling, leaving what I was sure was going to be a gnarly burn on the white tiles.

"I thought you said a small fire," I yelled, panicking. I grabbed my water bottle and twisted off the top.

"Micah, don't!" Navy shouted, trying to stop me from pouring water over the flame.

But she was too late. I dumped the contents of my water bottle on the chemical fire and instantly knew I'd made a huge mistake. With a deafening pop, the fire grew even bigger. I felt the suffocating heat on my face and neck as Navy and I stumbled back, and the hairs on my arms were singed as I lifted them to cover my face.

Luckily, Navy kept her head on straight and remembered the emergency lab procedures we'd learned at the beginning of the semester. She threw the fire blanket over the flame, and once it was extinguished, we faced the mess that our lab station had become. I breathed heavily, putting a shaky hand over my racing heart, but Navy started laughing.

"What happened?" Mr. Thompson asked as he walked back into the classroom and saw our disastrous lab station. "Are you okay?"

"I don't know," I said, turning to him. "We added 5,000 milligrams of—"

"5,000!" Mr. Thompson rushed over and retrieved the lab instructions. "You were only supposed to use 500 milligrams of each powder, and 4 milliliters of the acid. You must have misread the instructions."

"Will all due respect, I don't think we did," Navy said, pointing to the typo on the lab instructions.

Mr. Thompson looked at the sheet, and then shook his head, "I am so sorry, I should have caught this. This could have turned into a huge catastrophe. I'm glad to see that you remembered the emergency lab procedures."

"Actually, Navy remembered the lab procedures," I said. "My mind went absolutely blank."

"Ah yes," Mr. Thompson let out a small laugh. "Mine did too the first time I had a mishap in the lab. I can't believe I made such a major oversight. You could have been seriously injured."

Mr. Thompson helped us clean up our lab station before

turning to us. "You can head home and do this lab another time. Have a great Homecoming weekend."

We took off our lab coats and goggles, and headed for the parking lot.

"Do you need a ride?" Navy asked me as she scanned the lot. "I don't see your car."

"Yeah, I drove with my aunt today. Would you mind?"

"Not at all, hop in." Navy threw her bag in the back seat and climbed into the driver's side.

When we got to my house, Navy put the car in park, her hand still resting on the gearshift. Before she could say good-bye, I put my fingers over hers and said, "Do you want to hang out tonight, maybe get some dinner? We could order in so we don't have to go out."

I held my breath as I waited for her reply. I'd been wanting to spend more time with her all week, but was worried she needed more of the space she'd asked for when our tabloid story broke.

Navy looked at our hands, and then up at me, her eyes flickering between mine.

"That would be fun," she said, smiling.

Butterflies fluttered in my stomach and I felt like reaching over and pulling Navy into a hug. But instead, I just said, "Sweet."

"Do you want to just come over now?" She looked down, and if I wasn't mistaken, a little pink blush crept into her cheeks.

"Yes," I answered eagerly. "Absolutely."

When we got to Navy's house, we dropped our bags by the door and went into the living room.

"Do you want a blanket?" Navy asked, lifting an oversized

fluffy blanket out of a basket near the wall and offering it to me. I only wanted a blanket if Navy was going to snuggle under it with me and make the sweatshirt I was wearing smell like vanilla, but I knew I needed to tread lightly until I could clear the air about what happened earlier with the tabloids, and gauge how Navy felt about me.

"No, I'm okay," I said, settling down on the couch.

Navy wrapped herself in the blanket before plopping down next to me.

"Can we talk about what happened a couple weeks ago?" I asked. "I don't feel like we've even had a real conversation since then."

"Can we not, actually?" Navy looked sideways at me. "Look, it was weird for me. I had to field all these questions about you at school, and got these random nasty comments from people I don't even know, and who don't know who I really am or that we're not actually dating. The internet really has a way of bringing out the worst in people." She rolled her eyes, and blew a stray piece of hair out of her face. "But you were right. It happened, and our reality shouldn't change because of it. Can't we just—"

She trailed off, not finishing her thought.

"Can we just?" I prodded after a few seconds ticked by in silence.

She leaned her head on the back of the couch, looking up at me through her lashes.

"I just want to go back to normal."

"We can definitely do that." I smiled.

"But you're not normal. You're Micah Moore."

"No, I'm just Micah."

"But what if every time we go out, I have to worry about

pictures invading what I think is a private moment, or dodging questions from nosy people at school and jealous fans online? I know you're probably used to it by now, but that's not how I want to live my life."

I understood where she was coming from. "Should I go home? Do you need more space? I realize that I signed up for massive invasions of privacy when I chose to pursue acting, but that doesn't mean you have to. I can leave, and we can just be classmates and wave as we pass each other in the hall."

I held my breath, waiting for her reply. I was asking all the questions I didn't want answers to. I didn't want to give Navy up, to be just mere acquaintances at school, but that wasn't my decision to make. This was her life.

"No, Micah," she shook her head quickly, "No, stay here."

"Okay." The tension in my shoulders released, and I let out a sigh, relieved.

"I may not want all my privacy invaded, but I also don't want to just give up and go without you." Navy fiddled with the corner of her blanket. "I'm just confused."

"What are you confused about? Talk to me, Navy Blue."

She smiled. "That's not my name."

"Then why do you get a little smile every time I say it?" I leaned towards her, lowering my voice.

Navy didn't say anything, her eyes darting between my eyes and my mouth. She reached out from the blanket cocoon she had wrapped herself in and swiped a finger across my cheek, leaving a trail of tingles behind.

"Look," she smiled, holding up her finger. "An eyelash. Make a wish."

I'd never been one who believed in making wishes on silly

things like stars and eyelashes, but I closed my eyes, imagined a life with Navy, and blew the eyelash off her finger.

"Don't change the subject," I smiled, sliding my fingers up and opening her closed hand so our palms were pressed together. My whole body warmed at her touch. "Tell me what's confusing you."

Navy's eyes stayed fixated on our hands, before she moved her arm back into the blanket, pulling it tighter around herself.

"Alright, fine." She let out a sigh. "But this goes in the vault with the fact that you know I sing."

"My lips are sealed." I pressed my thumb and forefinger together and dragged them across my mouth.

"Tomorrow, I'm going to Homecoming with a boy I've had a crush on since the fifth grade."

It felt like a ton of bricks had just been dropped on my heart, which then fell into my stomach and left a gaping, uncomfortable pit there. Was there a chance for Navy and I, or would she never fall for me because of her feelings for the boy who asked her to Homecoming? I didn't even want to say his name.

I swallowed, nodding. "Does he like you too?"

"He said he did, once, when we were younger." She kept her eyes down, and her fingers busy playing with the corner of her blanket.

"And has anything happened since?"

She shook her head. "Not until he asked me to Homecoming."

"So what are you confused about?"

Her eyes flicked up to mine and she chewed on the corner of her lip. "I'm not sure he's everything I thought he was. And just when I'm about to go on a date with him, I don't even know if I want it, him, anymore."

I wanted to ask if there was someone else, someone who made her question her near-decade-long crush, but I was afraid of her answer, afraid she would recede even further into her blanket cocoon, and afraid that needing to know if she wanted me right now would ruin any chance that she might want me in the future. I wanted to go deep with Navy, to know what she was thinking and to know every part of her mind. I wanted to be the one to help her clear her head, but I didn't want to spend tonight talking about someone else. I wanted to spend tonight helping her get over this other guy, and maybe help her fall for me instead.

"Do you want to dance?" I asked, standing up and facing her.

"What?" Navy looked up at me, her eyes wide.

"You know, to practice for tomorrow?" I reached toward her, my palm up.

Navy smiled, slipping her hand in mine. "Yes. I'd love to dance."

I pulled her into me, wrapping my arm around her waist. She slipped her free arm up over my shoulder, resting her hand on the back of my neck. Butterflies flitted down my spine to my stomach. I noticed for the first time that her eyes weren't just different shades of green, but there was some gold flecked in there too. They were intricate and beautiful and mesmerizing, just like Navy.

"We don't have any music," Navy whispered, as we rocked back and forth.

"It's okay." I shook my head. "We don't need it."

"Micah, we always talk about me. I want to talk about you."
She looked up at me, searching my eyes.

"What do you want to know?"

"Tell me about your parents."

I smiled. Had she asked me this earlier, I would have told
her I was angry with them, that I felt they were too strict, and
that they didn't understand, but I knew all of those things were
wrong. After all, it was thanks to my dad that I was standing
here, dancing in Navy's living room.

"They're amazing. My dad is so talented. Some of my
favorite memories are of sitting in his chair on set, and
watching him direct, watching him in his zone. And my mom,
she's always been so supportive of him." My parents were the
whole reason I believed amazing love stories could exist, even
in Hollywood. "When I was young, I didn't realize how incredible it was that she chose to forego her own career so she could
stay home with Mel and me, but I'm so glad she did."

"What's their story? How did they meet?"

"At college, they were both studying film. Before Mel and I
were born, they would direct together. Now, even if my mom
can't be on set every day, she helps my dad block out scenes, or
talk through his more difficult projects. We always traveled with
my dad if he had to shoot on location. They don't like to be
apart, they say they're better together."

Navy smiled. "That's so romantic. It strikes me love like your
parents doesn't happen very often in your line of work."

I shook my head. "Definitely not." I lowered my forehead to
Navy's, and her eyes fluttered shut, a small soft smile turning up
the corners of her mouth. "I want a love story like theirs one
day," I whispered.

"Me too."

I let my eyes close too, and breathed Navy in, intoxicated. If we were in a crowded bar, and if I was playing the Kissing Game, and if Navy was just like anybody else, I would lean in and win, but now all I wanted was for time to stand still. I wanted Navy to be my last first kiss, and I wanted to remember every little thing about this moment. I wanted to tell Navy exactly how I felt, tell her how hard and fast I was falling for her, lay everything out on the line, and hope she would take the leap with me.

"Navy Blue," I whispered.

"What?"

Before I could say anything we heard the front door open, and Max and Melanie laughing as they came in. Navy and I froze, looking at each other.

"Duck," she said.

We hid behind the couch, peeking out as Max and Melanie meandered into the kitchen holding hands. Max wrapped his hands around Mel's waist, lifting her up onto the counter. She draped her arms around his shoulders, running her fingers up the back of his neck and into his dark hair. Max laughed at something she said, and they brushed their noses together in an Eskimo kiss. I felt like I was intruding on a special little moment between them, but they were too cute, I couldn't look away.

"They're so precious," Navy said in barely a whisper next to me, gripping my arm.

I looked over at her, and secretly hoped Homecoming would absolutely suck, because I wanted her, needed her, to be mine. Navy was it. She was my end-all. I hadn't even kissed her yet, but I knew there was no quitting her now.

# 8

## NAVY

AFTER MICAH LEFT, I kissed my parents goodnight and went to my room. I laid on the bed and stared at the ceiling, letting out a long sigh.

Tomorrow, I was finally going on a date with Brock, something I had wanted for seven long years of my life, and I was excited, but all I could think about was how much *more* excited I felt when *Micah* asked me to dance, and how right it felt to be so close to him.

Brock was my dream. There were hopes and expectations and a thousand scenarios tied to him and my feelings for him. It was hard to let that go. As much as I tried to convince myself, and anyone who asked, that I was trying to move on, Brock had been my dream for so long I wasn't sure I could.

But then there was Micah. I should run, trip, fall at his feet. What was the point of holding on to Brock when Micah was right in front of me, ready and willing to give me the whirlwind romance I so desperately wanted despite what I told everyone else? Micah wasn't, to my knowledge, running around flirting with everyone. He wasn't the player I thought he would be. I was so happy when I was with him, and I wanted to make him happy too, so why couldn't I let go of Brock, a boy who hadn't made me feel like Micah did since eighth grade.

I realized that everything came down to what I wanted. Because if I wanted to stay hopelessly in love with Brock and watch him date everyone but me, I could. But if I wanted to fall hopefully in love with Micah, I could, because I was pretty darn sure he was falling for me too.

I turned on my side and faced my homecoming dress hanging on my closet door. I felt so beautiful in it and I couldn't wait for Brock to see it, but I was a little sad Micah wouldn't get to see it too.

And there it was, that little thought, that little twinge of sadness in my heart that helped me make up my mind. I laid on my back again, clenching my fists to my side. I took a deep breath, and on the count of three, I opened them, palms facing up, as I imagined letting go of Brock, and all the hopes, dreams, desires, ideas, and expectations tied to him. And then I closed my hands again, this time gently, wrapping them around all the hope Micah promised if only I'd let myself fall.

THE NEXT AFTERNOON, I sat on a stool in my bathroom. My mom stood behind me, curling my hair, and Max sat on the edge of the bathtub, scrolling through something on his phone. I stared at myself in the mirror, trying to decide how to do my makeup.

"Max, why aren't you going to Homecoming with Melanie?" I asked, picking up an eyeshadow pallet.

"I don't know," Max ran his fingers through his hair. "Our first date was just a couple weeks ago, and I wasn't sure if she wanted to go on another date with me so soon."

"Oh please." I would have rolled my eyes if I wasn't busy blending eyeshadow on them. "Micah and I saw you two in the kitchen last night. Clearly, she's into you."

Max's ears turned red, and his wide grin gave him away. I met my mom's eyes in the mirror and we laughed. It had been a long time since we'd seen him so excited over a girl.

"I just don't want to smother her, you know."

"Believe me, she won't feel smothered. Just ask her," my mom said, as she let the last piece of my hair out of the iron. "What's the worst she can say? No?"

Max bit his lip, looking between my mom and me. "Alright," he finally said, nodding.

He left the bathroom to call Melanie, and my mom finished styling my hair into a simple side braid. She pulled pieces of it loose, making the braid thick and elegant. The hair-do was perfect for me; not too fancy, still beautiful, natural, classy.

We went to my room and my mom helped me step into my dress and zip it up without ruining my hair or smudging my makeup.

"How do I look?" I asked, twirling around.

"Absolutely gorgeous." My mom smiled at me, handing me my earrings.

The doorbell rang, and a flood of butterflies filled my stomach.

"Here we go." My mom smiled, gripping my hands in hers. "Are you ready?"

"Yes," I said, feeling breathless.

I went to the door and pulled it open. I'm not sure if I

expected angels to start singing, or the world to blur around us when I saw Brock, but it all felt just normal. Sure, he was handsome as ever in a grey suit, and he looked so suave with one hand in his pocket and the other gripping the clear plastic corsage box, but I always imagined this moment would feel so much more spectacular than it did.

"Navy, you look beautiful," Brock smiled at me. "Did I choose a good tie?" he asked, lifting it up.

"You look great," I smiled, "Come in."

My mom brought me the boutonniere and I made awkward work pinning it to his lapel. I tried to stop my hand from shaking as he slipped a beautiful corsage with little white roses and blue ribbon on my wrist. Brock put his hand on my waist and pulled me close to him as my mom snapped a few pictures of us, and I finally felt the butterflies again.

We were just about to walk out the door when Max came running down the stairs. "Navy, she said she'll come. And Micah's coming too."

"That's great," I said breathlessly as Brock put a hand on the small of my back to guide me out the door. "I'll see you at the dance."

I tried to drink it all in, live up every moment from the second Brock knocked on the door, but more often than I cared to admit, my thoughts wandered to Micah. I wondered if he would think my dress was beautiful too. Thinking about him made everything else blurry.

We met the rest of our group at a restaurant for dinner, and Brock pulled out my chair before sitting down across from me. He leaned forward, all attention on me, making me feel like even though we were on a group date, he and I were the only ones at the table.

"So, Navy," he said, "what looks good to you?"

"Hmm," I said, scanning the menu. The butterflies that had taken up permanent residence in my stomach had robbed my appetite. I thought I might get a salad, but then I remembered what I looked like when I ate salad and thought I should probably find something neater for me to eat. "The chicken looks good."

"That does sound yummy," Brock agreed, looking up from his menu. "But I think I'll get the pork chops."

"Pork chops are good too," I nodded.

Now that we had decided what to eat for dinner, Brock set his menu down and leaned forward on the table again. "So what do you want to do after high school?"

I took a sip of my water. "I'll go to college, hopefully Notre Dame."

"That's cool. Do you know what you want to study? Music?"

"No, I think I'll study architecture. Music is a good hobby, but I'm not sure I could make a career out of it. I'm not sure I'd want to."

Brock nodded. "Oh yeah, you told me that at the gala in the summer. Sorry, I have a terrible memory."

"It's okay," I smiled. "What about you?"

This was definitely the longest conversation we'd had in years, but it felt so strained and awkward. I was starting to wonder myself why I'd crushed on him for so long.

"College, for sure. But I don't know where, and I don't know what I'll study." He straightened the menu in front of him and picked up his straw wrapper, twisting it around his fingers.

Of course, I knew this already. We'd had a strangely similar conversation during our dance at the City Council Fundraiser. I tried not to let it bother me that he didn't seem to remember anything I'd told him at the gala.

"That's okay, you've got time to figure it out. Where are you applying?"

"All the Utah schools, of course, but I'm not sure I want to stay here. Don't get me wrong, Utah is great, but I just kind of want to spread my wings, you know."

"I get what you mean. I mean, obviously, Notre Dame is in Indiana, but even if I don't get in there, I don't think I want to apply to schools in Utah," I said and sipped my water again before going on. "It's not like I want to leave forever. My family is here, and I love Utah, but I'm just restless."

Brock nodded again and changed the subject. "Do you ski?"

It wasn't bad that conversation with Brock was surface level, and I didn't necessarily mind that he changed the subject quickly, like a butterfly flitting from flower to flower, never staying too long in one place. But Micah would have asked me why I was restless, and without meaning to, his inquiries into the deepest parts of my mind would challenge what I thought, and make me defend it.

"No, I don't ski," I said as I rested my head in my hand and leaned on the table.

"What," Brock slammed his hands on the table in surprise. "Navy, we live in the middle of the greatest snow on Earth and you don't ski."

I laughed. His response was just like everyone else's when they heard that I didn't ski. "It's just not something that's ever interested me. Do you?"

"I snowboard. One of the only reasons I might stay in Utah for school would be for the snow."

The waiter interrupted before I could reply, and Brock

motioned to me to give him my order first. When the waiter left, we turned and continued our conversation with another couple in our group.

The rest of dinner was light and easy, and butterflies fluttered in my stomach as we drove to the dance. Would Micah already be there? Would he be jumping in the middle of the mosh pit, impossible for me to see? Or would he just be getting there and see me the second I walked in the doors?

When we walked into the dance, I was certain we'd been transported to a beautiful castle. Surely this wasn't our same old dingy gym. Long, flowing white fabric had been draped over the dance floor and strung with white twinkle lights, giving the appearance of a low ceiling in the gaping gym and making it feel intimate and classy. Tall Grecian pillars had been placed randomly throughout the dance floor, supporting the drapes and lights. The whole place was regal and oozed romance.

"Let's go!" Brock said excitedly, wasting no time in taking my hand and pulling me into the middle of the dance floor.

It took me a minute not to feel incredibly awkward, but eventually, I got into the rhythm of things. Brock even complimented my dancing, though I knew it was horrible. I was having such a fun time with Brock, but I kept surveying dance floor, looking for Micah.

A slow song came on and the crowd dissipated a little. Wasting no time, Brock took my hand and spun me into him, resting his hand on my lower back. Before I could look up into his eyes, I looked over his shoulder and I finally found Micah. For a second, the whole world seemed to stop. I should have looked away, focused on Brock and his arms wrapped around me, but I couldn't. Micah looked majestic, standing there in a dark suit, and my world blurred around him.

Max stood next to him, their heads leaned together in conversation. Neither one took their eyes off of me. Max took Melanie's hand and they walked away, and I had to stop myself from running to him as I watched Micah walk towards us.

"Would you mind if I stole your date, just for one dance?" Micah asked, placing his hand on Brock's shoulder.

Brock looked back and forth between Micah and me, but eventually nodded. "Sure. I needed some air anyway."

He let go of me as Micah slipped his hand into mine, pulling me towards him. A warm, comforting excitement spread throughout my whole body to have him close to me again. I took a deep breath, reveling in the woody scent that made me want to melt into him.

"Hi, Navy Blue," he smiled.

"Hey," I smiled back. "I'm glad you came."

"I hope you don't mind missing one dance with your date. I know you're, like, in love with him."

Although he said it teasingly, I sensed a little pain. It made me want to reach up, hold his face in my hands, and tell him he was wonderful too, tell him everything I'd been too nervous to say last night. I'd had the perfect opportunity too, right after he told me about wanting a love story like his parents. Now I was kicking myself for not saying it.

"Not at all."

"Navy, you look absolutely breathtaking."

"Every girl dreams of being told that." My cheeks were starting to get sore because I hadn't stopped smiling since I'd seen him. "And you look incredibly handsome yourself. It's no wonder every girl in the world falls at your feet."

"Oh not every girl, I'm sure. I haven't even noticed any, actually."

"You must be terribly blind then."

"Not blind, just focused on something else."

"Yeah?" I asked. "What's that?"

Something flickered in Micah's bright blue eyes for a fraction of a second, and then he said, "School."

"Oh, yeah, that is pretty important."

"Are you enjoying your night?" he asked, pulling me a little closer.

"I am. Brock has been a really fun date. But I have to admit, seeing you is really good." I watched Micah's face carefully, not wanting to miss his reaction. I shy little smile turned up the corners of his mouth, and my heart fluttered. I would do or say anything to see that reaction more often. "Are you enjoying yours?"

"I am now."

"Good." I smiled, giving his hand a quick squeeze.

We rocked back and forth in silence for a few seconds before Micah said, "I've stopped looking for a way out of here."

The thought made me happy. I liked having him here, and I liked spending time with him. Maybe if he was here, and if he liked it here, a relationship with him could be real and not so out of reach as I first thought.

"What made you stop?"

"You," he said with a look in his bold blue eyes so piercing I wanted to step back, and so magnetic I wanted to pull him closer.

"Me?" I asked, breathless. Was this a confession of his feelings for me, or just a confirmation of friendship?

"Like I said a couple weeks ago, when we were buying my

car, when you find someone that makes you happy, you run with it. There's a lot I still don't know, but I still want to run."

The soothing slow song turned into a bouncing beat again, and the crowd swarmed around us. Brock walked up just then, "I'll take my date back now, thanks."

I wanted to tell Brock no, that I need just a few more minutes. I couldn't just go the rest of the night knowing how Micah felt and not be able to talk about it, explain to him everything that was going on in my head.

"Let's talk more later," I said to Micah, giving his hand one last squeeze before I let go.

"Yeah, enjoy your night, Navy Blue." Micah gave me a wink and a dazzling smile before he turned and walked back to my brother.

Micah Moore had just laid his heart out on the line, and he was confident enough not to need an answer right away. I was grateful because I didn't quite know if I had one for him. But would it be so bad if he, too, were my answer? What if I stopped making excuses as to why he and I could never work out and starting running too?

"Can you excuse me for a minute," I turned to Brock.

"Yeah, I'll just be dancing over there." He motioned to where the rest of the group was jumping up and down on the dance floor and went to join them.

I turned, lifting up on my toes and looking for Becca. I desperately needed to talk to her. I weaved through the dancing crowd, almost getting knocked over once by an overzealous football player. I had to squint in the dim light, but as I emerged from the center of the crowded dance floor, I finally found her near the refreshment table.

"Becca," I said, grabbing her hand and dragging her away from the table. "We need to talk."

I didn't stop dragging her until we were in the bathroom, where I kicked in all the stalls to make sure we were alone. It was a miracle the bathroom was empty.

"What's going on?" Becca leaned on a sink, her brow creased.

"Micah just told me he has feelings for me."

Becca's hands went to her perfectly glossed lips with a little squeal. "I knew it!"

"What do I do?" I pinched the bridge of my nose pacing in front of the mirrors.

"What do you mean what do you do? You run back out there and tell him you have feelings for him too."

"But I'm here with Brock, and I thought it would be everything I'd ever wanted, and it's not. And then we're slow dancing, and Micah comes up and asks to steal me, and then he drops this bomb on me, and now all I want—"

I trailed off. What exactly did I want? I was on a date that I'd wanted for as long as I could remember. Wasn't I supposed to be on cloud nine? But when I silenced the voice that told me what I was *supposed* to do, when it all came down to it, I wanted to spend the night with Micah, because with him, I was finally confident in myself. He made me feel worth it.

"You want what?" Becca prodded, leaning forward.

I stopped in front of the middle sink, leaning down to grip the sides of the porcelain. I stared down, focusing on the drain, and then I looked up. I was surprised at the girl I saw staring back. She looked like me, but there was something new in her eyes. I stood up straight again, still looking in the mirror. What I really, truly wanted, what I'd been so afraid to admit, was on the tip of my tongue. I wasn't sure I was ready to open my mouth and say it, I liked the way the words felt sitting there.

Becca moved over so we were in the same mirror. She wrapped an arm around my shoulders and leaned her head against mine. "What do you want?" she asked me again.

I took a deep breath. "Micah."

"I knew it," she whispered with a giddy smile.

"Am I crazy?" I met her eyes in the mirror.

"Why would you be crazy? An amazing guy just admitted feelings or you. You'd be crazy not to run right into his arms."

And here's the thing; for once in my life, I didn't actually feel crazy. I felt supercharged, like I could do absolutely anything I wanted. I knew I needed to spend the rest of the night with Brock, because he was my date after all, but there was one more thing I wanted to do.

"Becca, thanks for your help, I've got to go do something." I bunched my skirt in my fists and ran out of the bathroom.

I surveyed the floor again, this time looking for Micah. When I couldn't find him on the outskirts of the dance floor, I braved the crowd. He was dancing with Max and Melanie near the middle of the floor.

"Hey, can I talk to you?"

"Sure," Micah smiled, following me outside.

We walked around the side of the building, I didn't want anyone to interrupt. We stood against the building, a single street light illuminating us.

"What's up?" Micah's eyes flicked between mine. If his heart was beating as hard and fast as mine was, he didn't let on.

I reached up, holding his face. Suddenly, everything I wanted to say to him felt inadequate. How could I tell him that I was falling for him, even if it was slow going? How could I tell him that when I looked at him, I no longer saw Micah Moore, the movie star? I saw Micah, my lab partner, my friend, and possibly the love story that could change my life forever.

So instead, I wrapped my arms around his neck, pulled his forehead to mine and whispered, "I'm running too."

9
_____

# MICAH

JEALOUS that I wasn't the one who got to enjoy Navy all night at Homecoming, I spent Sunday morning planning a fancy, romantic, over-the-top date to make up for it. That afternoon, I roped Melanie and Max into helping me find a dress for Navy, which was the first step in my perfect plan. I wanted this one to be even more beautiful and elegant, even more *Navy,* than her Homecoming dress had been because I wanted this date to surpass that one in every way. However, given how absolutely beautiful Navy had been at the dance, it was turning out to be quite difficult.

"What about this?" Melanie said, holding up a strapless black dress.

"Navy doesn't do strapless," Max said, shaking his head before I could answer.

Melanie hung the dress back on the rack and ran her hands through the others hanging behind it. We'd been shopping for nearly two hours.

"What do you think of this one?" I said, holding up a green number with a sequined bodice and a wide sash around the waist. "Don't you think the color would bring out her eyes?"

"Maybe, but I don't think that would look very good with her skin tone." Melanie shook her head.

"Hmm," I hung the dress back on the rack, wondering why women worried about how their clothes made their skin tones look. I guess it was just something I'd never noticed before.

Max, Melanie, and I took turns holding up dresses and asking each other for opinions. One of the dresses was lime green, floor-length and extremely poofy. I was almost suffocated as I tried to hang it back up, stuffing the oversized skirt back in line with the other dresses. Melanie found a deep purple one. It was form-fitting and knee-length, and although we liked the color, we all agreed it didn't look quite like Navy either. After the purple one, Max pulled a beautiful red dress off the rack. Like the green one I'd found earlier, it had sequins, and a satin sash, but Melanie held it up to her body and declared the tulle skirt was far too short to be elegant. Exasperated, and extremely tired of dress shopping, I pulled a floor-length deep grey dress out and held it up for Melanie.

"It's definitely classy," Melanie said, cocking her head as she scrutinized the dress.

Max nodded, "And the prettiest of all the dresses we've seen so far."

"I think we should go with this one," I said, checking to make sure it was the right size.

Melanie walked towards me, running her hand over the skirt. "Navy will love it."

"Sweet, let's do it."

As I moved around Melanie to go to the register, she

grabbed my arm, stopping me. "No, Micah," she seemed wonderstruck as she walked towards another dress hanging on a mannequin tucked in the back corner of the store. "I can't believe we didn't see this one before."

I turned to see the dress and instantly understood why she loved it. This dress was different than any of the other dresses we had seen in the store. It was pale pink with a high neckline and a flowy skirt. It was simple and understated, but just like her Homecoming dress, this one was stunning, gorgeous, breathtaking; the epitome of Navy.

"*Now,*" I said, searching for a store attendant to take the dress off the mannequin, "we have found the perfect dress."

I watched as the clerk folded the dress neatly in a box, covering it with tissue paper and sealing it with a store logo sticker. Placing the lid on the box, she handed it to me over the counter in exchange for my card.

Now that I had the dress, I couldn't wait to ask Navy on our date.

We walked into the Monroe's house to find Navy's parents lounging in the living room.

"Where's Navy?" Max asked. "Micah has a question for her."

"She's in her treehouse," Mrs. Monroe looked up from her paperback, smiling at me. "You're welcome to go on out."

"Thanks," I said, going to the back door.

I walked across the yard thinking about how I was going to ask her. The sun was setting over the mountains, casting a warm hazy light over the backyard.

"Hey, Navy Blue," I said, cupping my hands around my mouth. "Can I come up?"

"That's not my name," she said, sticking her head out of the door and smiling.

"Is that a yes?" I joked back, climbing up.

Once I was situated across from her, I pushed out my question in one big breath. "Do you want to go on a date with me?"

She smiled, her eyes lighting up. But it was only for a split second before her face fell. "Are you sure that's a good idea?"

I scrunched my forehead together. "Yes?"

Navy leaned towards me, putting a hand on my arm, "No, I definitely want to. I just mean are you sure we should be seen out together? Will there be more pictures stories about us dating if we go out in public?"

"Well," I tilted my head and gave her a flirty smile, "We kind of are, aren't we?"

She looked down at her lap for a second, and then looked at me through her lashes. "I guess you're right." She let out a little laugh and pushed a piece of hair behind her ear, "Let's go on a date then."

"Perfect. How's next Friday?"

"Sounds great. What should I wear?" she asked.

"It's a surprise." I gave her a wink and turned to leave. "Well, Navy Blue as much as I'd love to stay with you in this treehouse all night, I haven't even started that chem assignment we have due tomorrow, so I'd better leave."

"Wait, no," Navy wrapped her hand around my wrist and pulled it towards her. "You can't just walk away! Tell me what we're doing for our date."

Now that she was touching me, I was even more tempted to just stay with her, but I pulled my wrist free and lowered myself back to the ground. "I told you, it's a surprise."

"You can't just walk away!" She called out as I walked back to the house.

"Oh, but I just did," I said, over my shoulder

"Micah." I stopped and turned around. She was leaning out of the treehouse, smiling. "I will get it out of you."

"We'll see," I grinned.

Try as I might, I couldn't wipe the smile off my face for the rest of the night. This had been the best weekend of my life. Each day seemed to drag on while I waited for Friday. Navy tried hard all week to get any information out of me, but I wouldn't budge. I couldn't wait to see her face when she found out what I had planned for us.

As Friday drew closer, my attention span went from that of a 17-year-old boy, to that of a three-year-old, to that of a squirrel.

After school, Aunt Juliet, Melanie, and I all drove home together. I went up to my room and pulled a sticky note off of the pad on my desk.

"Put on this dress," I wrote, "and be ready by 6. Don't eat. See you soon."

I signed it "love, Micah," and pulled the box with the dress inside off the top shelf in my closet, pressed the sticky note to the top of it, and walked to Navy's house. Max had told me earlier that week that if I came right after school, Navy would either not be home yet, or in her treehouse doing homework, as was her after school routine when we didn't have play practice. I was hoping it was the latter. I didn't want her coming home before I could plant the surprise dress and leave.

Max let me in and led me up to her room. I'd never been up here before. The whole room smelled like vanilla and roses. There was a drafting table set against one wall, with a cup of pencils, a few books, and some blueprints scattered across it. Her bed was on the opposite wall and was neatly made with a pink floral quilt. Polaroid pictures with Becca, Max, and her parents were pinned to a corkboard above the bed. On her nightstand, there was a pink lamp, a glass with a few sips of water left, and a tube of chapstick. I knew I should hurry, but it was exciting to be in Navy's space and I wanted to remember everything. Finally, I laid the box gently on her bed, took one more look around the room and followed Max back downstairs.

"We should go on a double date sometime," Max said as we walked back up to my house.

"Absolutely. Looks like things are going great with you and Mel."

"They are." He nodded. "I'm just hoping we can work something out long-distance once you guys have to go back to California."

I'd been so wrapped up in Navy lately that I hadn't thought much about going home, and I hadn't heard back yet about my audition tape. Part of me didn't even want the part anymore if it meant I could stay here longer. But the other part of me was practical and knew that even if I didn't get this part, there would be another one to audition for and I couldn't stay here forever. It felt like I was on borrowed time, and Max's comment made me question if things could work out long term with Navy. Would she want a long-distance relationship? In any other relationship, I doubted I would be thinking so much about the future, but with Navy, it was different. I knew one day, probably sooner rather than later, I'd have to figure out what would happen once I left Utah, but I didn't want to worry about it right now. I had a whole night with Navy to look forward to.

With three hours to kill before picking up Navy for our date, I tried to be productive and get some homework done, but ended up snoozing in front of the TV while Melanie and Max cuddled on the couch and watched the Food Network.

When it was finally time to get ready, I showered and put on the same pinstriped suit I wore to homecoming. I tied the pale pink tie I'd bought to match Navy's dress, and slipped my wallet and some gum into my pocket.

"Well you look spiffy." My aunt smiled, handing me my keys as I walked towards the garage. "Have fun tonight."

"And remember everything. I want every detail when you come home," Melanie said as I pulled open the door.

"Will do," I smiled at them.

I had never felt anything quite like I did as I drove three houses down to pick up Navy. No girl had ever given me the feeling that my stomach was in free fall while simultaneously being carried away by butterflies. I tried repeatedly to calm myself down, as I wanted to be a cool, calculated gentleman when I saw Navy, but none of the breathing exercises I'd learned from my acting coaches were working on me tonight.

I pulled into her driveway, pulling the keys from the ignition. Shoving my hand in my pocket, I walked up to the door and knocked. This was it. The moment I'd been waiting for.

Navy pulled open the door, absolutely flooring me.

"Micah," Navy's face was glowing. Her dress was too, although in a much different way, the porch light glinting off of sparkles on her bodice. "This dress is absolutely the sweetest thing anyone has ever done for me."

"You look absolutely beautiful in it."

"Thank you. For the compliment, for the dress, for this date."

"Should we go?"

"Yes! I've been waiting all week."

I smiled, glad she was excited. I opened her door and helped her inside the car.

"So are you finally going to tell me where we're going?" she asked as I pulled out of the driveway.

"Ah, that is still a surprise."

We drove for 20 minutes, making small talk about our week at school, and our excitement over the holidays coming up. Finally, I pulled up to the restaurant.

"We are right on time. Our reservation is at 6:30," I said, checking my watch.

"Micah, this is amazing. I can guarantee I have never eaten food this fancy," she said staring up at The Blue Spoon.

It was the fanciest restaurant I could find without having to drive for hours. I had called ahead and had a table waiting for us in the ballroom, complete with sparkling cider in champagne flutes, and chocolate-covered strawberries for dessert. I knew it was cheesy, and cliché, but I wanted this to be a fairy-tale-level date straight out of a chick flick.

Navy rested her hand in the curve of my elbow as we walked inside. Although we walked on white marble floors and were surrounded by white marble pillars, the black drapery, and the dim lighting made the restaurant dark, mysterious, romantic.

"Good evening, sir," the hostess said from behind the podium.

"I have a reservation for Monroe," I told her.

Navy looked at me, surprised I had used her last name. I leaned in, whispering, "I don't want anyone knowing I'm here. I don't want anything to ruin our night."

"Smart," Navy winked.

"Yes, Mr. Monroe, right this way."

The hostess led us out into the main dining area. The ballroom was circular, with black carpet and a large white marble circle in the center of it. A black baby grand was in the middle of the marble sending up soft, classical notes as women in long dresses and men in tuxedos swirled around it. The dining tables were on the carpet surrounding the dance floor. The hostess led us to one on the far edge of the room.

"I feel so fancy," Navy said, sitting up straight in her chair, carefully sipping her drink. "I'm not sure I know quite how to act."

"You fake it 'til you make it," I smiled back at her.

"Duly noted."

A black-vested waiter took our orders, and we nibbled on bread while we waited for our food.

"So," Navy said, leaning forward. "You've been in Utah for almost two months. What do you think?"

"You know, at first I hated everything, and I was dying to get out. I even auditioned for a part in France to try and get out early. But now, I'm not so mad. I actually really like it here. And my dad and I have talked. We're back on good terms, and I don't really resent him anymore."

"Well, I'm glad you're not mad anymore. Utah's not that bad. It's actually quite beautiful. Especially where we live."

"Oh, Utah is gorgeous," I said, staring right into those captivating green eyes of hers. She may have been referring to the mountains, but what I was looking at was far more beautiful than they were.

And for the first time, I thought about what might happen if I stayed in Utah. I'd been so sure leaving was inevitable, but did I actually have a choice? Sure, I would probably have to travel to film, but what if I could always come home to Navy. Was she worth shaking up my whole life for, and changing all my plans? Looking at her now, sitting across from me sipping our fizzy apple cider, I thought yes, absolutely she was worth it. It wasn't often I found a girl who made me feel like this.

"What's your favorite part?" she asked, leaning forward.

"Of Utah?"

"Yes."

"Quite honestly, you."

"Micah," Navy blushed. "I've never met anyone quite like you."

"Is that a good thing or a bad thing?"

"Oh, most definitely a good thing. When I ran into you that first day of school and everyone was moving out of the way for you, I thought you would be a haughty, self-serving jerk who thought he deserved the whole world to fall down at his feet."

"You're the only person who's interested enough in the real me."

"Really?"

"To be fair, you're really the only person I've let get this close."

"I love being close to you," Navy whispered, leaning in across the table. It was the most vulnerable thing she had ever said to me.

I pushed my chair away from the table and took Navy's hand, leading her into the middle of the ballroom floor. I pulled her towards me, putting my hand on the small of her back. "I love being close to you too," I whispered in her ear.

We danced like this until I lost track of how many songs had started and ended. When we got back to our table, our food had arrived. After we finished our meal and paid the bill, Navy looped her arm through mine as we walked out of the restaurant. I expected the calm of a starry night, still on a high from dancing so close to Navy, but in the matter of moments men and women with big black cameras stormed out of their cars. My heart sank as I realized that my romantic night with Navy had been ruined by the paparazzi. Soon we were overtaken with camera flashes and voices.

Navy gripped my arm. "Micah, what do we do?" she yelled over the sounds of all the shouts and camera shutters.

"Smile and run!" I yelled back, taking her hand and pulling her toward the car.

I hurried to help her into the car and raced around to the driver's side. I started the ignition and pulled out of the parking lot, hoping I was quick enough to lose the photographers, but they had already seen my car, and they were quick too. Soon, I was leading a caravan down the road.

"What was that?" Navy asked, gripping the car door, her eyes wide.

"Shhh. Let's just find somewhere to hide, please." I don't know why I was quieting her. It wasn't like anyone could hear us. But I felt so surprised, caught off guard and invaded that I felt like we needed to whisper.

"We can go to my treehouse," Navy suggested. "No one will find us there."

"I'll take it," I said. "Just give me a minute to lose these lunatics."

The problem with the rural county we lived in was that there were very few buildings to shield us from the view of the paparazzi. When we got closer to our neighborhood, I took unnecessary turns to lose the caravan behind us and drove in circles for five more minutes to make sure we truly lost them. There was no way I was going to lead them right to our houses.

Once I was certain we had lost the paparazzi, we parked a block away from our street.

"Let's run," I said, pulling the keys out of the ignition. "Fast."

Navy kicked off her high heels and bunched her skirt in her fists, leading the way to her house. She unlatched the gate to the backyard and we hurried through it, running to the tree-house. By the time I made it there, Navy was already in. She helped me up, and we both sat trying to catch our breath.

"What was that?" she asked.

"I cannot believe that just happened." I pushed my fists into my eyes.

"Did you honestly think we could go out like that and not get noticed?" she said in disbelief.

"Yes," I said, still squeezing my eyes shut. "I'm supposed to be normal here."

"Micah, I hate to break it to you, but you'll never be totally normal. Everybody knows you."

"I'm so sick of people thinking they know me. Nobody knows me. I hate it. For once I want someone to let me offer a complete introduction. I want someone to take the time to get to know me, from me. Not from those stupid tabloids." My chest heaved up and down as I struggled to catch my breath and calm down.

"Maybe it's because you don't let them. You said so at the restaurant."

"Well, I'd like to see someone at least try."

Navy and I weren't exactly fighting, but I was shaken up by our recent high-speed chase, and I could tell Navy didn't know how to react, to the paparazzi or to me.

"What about me?"

"You're not like everyone else."

"Good or bad?" She asked, lightening her tone and leaning in. She was regaining her calm a lot quicker than I was.

"Definitely good." A small smile spread across my mouth.

"Then tell me all the things I don't know about you." She lowered her voice, and reached out, cupping my face in her hands. I took a deep breath and closed my eyes, her gentle touch finally calming me down.

My eyes fluttered open again and I started talking. "Well, my name is Micah Andrew Moore. I was born on July 16. I grew up in Malibu. My first role was as an extra in an action film. All I had to do was yell, 'run,' but even from just that, I knew I would always crave to be on set. I love the rain. I would love to kiss someone with real emotion behind it, not because the script calls for it or a girl is pushing herself on me. I love staying up late and sleeping in. I'm finding out that school is a lot harder than it looks in the movies. I love lazy days and watching movies, but not the ones I'm in. I think it's weird to watch myself. I love hamburgers and French fries, McDonald's is my guilty pleasure, and I have a huge sweet tooth. Plain vanilla ice cream is my favorite. Uno is my favorite card game, but I'm not a huge fan of games otherwise. I love stargazing, and I'm just like anyone else."

Navy smiled as she listened to my stream of consciousness. "My name is Navy Elizabeth Monroe. I was born on April 25, and I grew up here in Park City. I love playing the piano. I like rain, but I love snow better; the kind that falls softly in big fat flakes that stick to your nose and eyelashes. I'd rather go to sleep early and wake up early. I love school, depending on the day. I agree that lazy days and watching movies are some of the best pass-times ever. Hamburgers and French-fries are yummy, yes, but I really love anything Italian. Sweets are also my weakness. I love making wishes. And it is very nice to meet you." She stuck out her hand.

"It is very nice to meet you too," I smiled at the cheesy introductions we'd given each other even though we'd known each other for almost two months now.

"Can I show you a secret?"

"Please do."

She propped herself on her knees and pushed up on the roof of the treehouse. The ceiling swung open like double doors, revealing the beautiful starry night above us.

"My dad built this contraption for me when I was a little girl. It's why I love this treehouse so much," she said, lying down on her back, her long dark hair splayed out around her.

I lowered myself next to her, our arms touching. "It's beautiful."

We laid there, staring up the stars without talking. I liked that Navy didn't feel the need to fill the silence. My heart pounded in my chest knowing how close my hand was to Navy's. All I had to do was move it ever so slightly.

Taking a deep breath, I moved my hand over Navy's, praying she'd take it. I hoped I wasn't pushing boundaries Navy didn't want to cross. I smiled as she laced her fingers through mine, squeezing gently before relaxing her hand. It was amazing how perfectly our hands seem to fit together. I had done a lot of handholding; for movies, on the red carpet, randomly because the opportunity was just there, but I don't think I had ever held some one's hand because I had genuine feelings for them. Never before had it ever felt so right, so comfortable, like Navy's hand was created to fit into mine.

We stayed up in the treehouse for a few more hours, with silence and sound, and never letting go of each other. Just before our curfew, we climbed out of the treehouse and walked out front.

"I'll walk you to your car if you'd like," Navy said as she unlatched the gate.

"Actually, if it's alright, can I walk you to the door? It wouldn't be a date without that good-old porch scene."

"Of course," she smiled.

We walked up to the front door and Navy turned to face me. "Thank you so very much for tonight."

"No, thank you. I'm sorry the paparazzi ruined it."

"That is an apology I thought I would never have to accept," she laughed. "But seriously, don't you worry about it. This was the best date I have ever been on."

She wrapped her arms around my neck, pulling me close to her. After our hug, she loosed her arms, but didn't let go.

"Goodnight, Navy Blue."

Wrapped up in the romance of the moment, I wanted so badly to lean in and know what it was like to feel Navy's lips on mine. But I had already expended my twenty-seconds of insane courage tonight, so I left a kiss on Navy's forehead instead.

"Goodnight, Micah," she smiled before going inside.

I couldn't stop smiling as I walked back to my house. This had been the best night of my life thus far, and if this was what falling in love felt like, I suddenly knew why everyone was so drunk on it.

THERE WAS a nasty cold going around the school, and even being on Cloud Nine couldn't stop me from catching it. On Monday morning, I woke up excited to see Navy at school, but my body had a different idea. I ached all over and got dizzy when I stood up. My aunt sent me bed rest for the day, and I listened as she and Melanie left for school.

I laid there in silence, disappointed I wouldn't get to see Navy at school. However, I was not one bit heartbroken over missing AP Chemistry.

But maybe this was a good thing, I thought. Although Navy and I had spent all of Saturday and Sunday sending each other flirty texts, we had not discussed our date, or the romance that transpired during it. I worried I had crossed the line. Did Navy enjoy holding my hand as much as I enjoyed holding hers? Did the fact that she didn't readily let go of our hug on the doorstep mean that she'd wanted me to kiss her, even on the first date? I guess I could have asked her, but I was too afraid of the answer, too afraid that maybe I'd missed my chance.

I knew that if I didn't find something to take my mind off of Navy, the questions would keep coming, I would dive deeper into overanalyzing every moment of our amazing date, and I would drive myself insane.

As I looked around my room for something I could do without standing up, my phone vibrated. It was Navy.

*Where are you?* Her message illuminated the screen.

I smiled. Her text made my aching body feel a little bit better. I replied that I was sick, and I spent the rest of the day clutching my phone waiting for her replies as we sent messages back and forth.

After a long and unproductive day, I was ready for company and was happy to hear my aunt and Melanie come home from school. I heard someone on the stairs and was happily surprised by who it was.

"Hey," Navy said, poking her head into my room.

"Hey, Navy Blue." I sat up quickly but instantly regretted it as a sharp pain shot through my head, sending it spinning.

"How are you feeling?" she asked, sitting on the edge of my bed.

"I've been better." I tried to smile as I lowered myself to the pillow again.

"I'm sorry." She frowned. "I brought you presents."

"Oh, you really didn't need to bring me anything."

"First, I have this." She tossed a packet of paper on to my stomach. "Courtesy of Mr. Thompson. I can help you with it if you'd like."

"Oh, you *really* didn't need to bring me this," I said, sarcastically, picking it up and flipping through it. "But I would love some help on it when my head feels better."

"Sure thing. I also brought you these," she said, handing me a grocery bag.

Curious, I sat up slowly, waiting for my head to stop spinning. I opened the bag and smiled as I saw what was inside.

I pulled out a McDonald's bag and peeked inside.

"A hamburger and French fries," Navy said. "I'm not sure if you have an appetite or not, but I figured I'd bring you your favorite, and if you weren't hungry, I'd only be out a couple of bucks."

"Oh, I'm always hungry for McDonald's," I winked at her as I set the bag aside and went back to the rest of the contents in the grocery bag. I pulled out a can of cream soda, Uno cards and a tub of vanilla ice cream.

"Navy, you remembered all my favorites?"

"Of course I remembered."

"Thank you." I couldn't stop smiling. "This is the nicest thing anyone has ever done for me."

"Anything for you," Navy smiled back at me. "Being sick is awful. Hopefully, this helps."

"More than you know. Will you stay while I eat? And maybe even help me out with this ice cream?" I asked.

"Of course," Navy said, sitting cross-legged on my bed. "Dig in."

After I had finished my hamburger and fries, Navy pulled two spoons out of her backpack.

"Here," she said, handing me one of them. "I was hoping you'd want to share the ice cream."

We opened the tub and sat facing each other with the ice cream in between us. "How was your day?" I asked her.

"It was good, I guess," Navy said, licking a drop of ice cream off of her finger. "Chem was hard as usual, not actually sure how much of a help I will be when we look at that packet. We did nothing in Business Marketing, so nothing to complain about there. Play practice was good too. We worked a lot on the opening scene."

"Did Rachel slaughter it?" I asked. It was no secret to Navy that I had not agreed with who my aunt had chosen to play Belle. Perhaps I was biased.

Navy laughed. "No. Micah, she is a really good actress, she has an amazing voice, and she looks like a Belle."

"You sang better."

"You only heard me that one day on the stage. You probably remember it better than it actually was. How was your day?" Navy blushed and looked down.

"As good as sick days can be," I shrugged as I ate a spoonful of ice cream. "I found a new show on Netflix. I'm already two seasons into it. I'm on a roll."

"Sounds like you have been so productive," Navy laughed at me.

"*So* productive," I agreed. "Do you have lots of homework?"

"Nothing that's due tomorrow," Navy said, digging her spoon into the ice cream.

"So you don't mind staying here? For a little longer at least?" I was afraid there was a little too much hope in my tone, but I figured I had already given myself away. Navy knew how I felt.

"Of course not. I'd rather be with you anyway."

I smiled.

We finished off the entire tub of vanilla ice cream before playing a few rounds of Uno. By round four, my head was starting to hurt again, but I didn't want Navy to go. I powered through round five, but by the time Navy was dealing round six, I knew she could see past my act.

"You look tired. Why don't I let you get back to resting," she said, scooping up the cards and pushing them into a neat deck in her hand.

"No, it's okay," I said, trying to keep the eager tone out of my voice. I'd rather be spending time with her than resting, but I couldn't deny the pounding pain in my head.

"Get some sleep, and if I don't see you at school tomorrow, I promise to come visit again."

"Okay," I smiled, settling back into my pillows. "As long as you promise."

"I pinky swear," she said, lifting her hand, little finger extended, in front of me.

"Goodnight, Navy Blue," I said, wrapping my pinky around hers. "See you tomorrow."

"See you tomorrow," Navy said. "Rest well."

I definitely could now.

# 10

## NAVY

ALTHOUGH I HAD EXPECTED Micah to be sick the next morning, my heart sank a little when Creative Writing started and the seat he usually occupied in front of me was vacant.

*Playing hooky again, I see,* I texted him five minutes after class started.

*You know me, love breakin' the rules,* he replied quickly with a winking emoji.

*Will you be up for visitors tonight?*

*Absolutely!*

I smiled as I slipped my phone back in my bag and focused on the tasks at hand: getting through school and play practice so I could go spend time with Micah. It surprised me how anxious I was to be near him, and how comfortable I felt when I was. He was unexpected in every way, and I wanted to know more. Our date the past weekend had solidified any question I had that I was falling for Micah. It was nerve-wracking and amazing all at the same time. I was scared, but feared letting go far more than holding on.

After play practice, I rushed home for dinner and then walked to Micah's house. Miss Moore answered the door and let me upstairs to his room.

"Hey, you still up for a visitor? I can let you rest, if you'd rather," I said, poking my head through the door.

"No, come in," he said, pushing himself up slowly. "I've been waiting all day."

I blushed. "I've been pretty excited to come see you too. How was your day?"

"It's been okay. I tried to take a crack at that chemistry assignment, but I gave up."

"It's okay. Once your head feels better we can look at it together. It's not due until next week anyway."

"That's a relief. How was your day?" he asked, situating the pillows behind him so he could sit up.

"It was good. Nothing too exciting to report."

"I've been watching more of that show I started yesterday. Want to watch a couple episodes with me?"

"Of course," I smiled, excited at the thought of relaxing with him all night.

I moved from sitting on the end of the bed to reclining next to him. Micah hit play and propped the laptop up on his knees so we could both see the screen.

Max had told me that next time Micah and I were together, I should make the first move. He said it would give Micah reassurance and confidence that this is what I wanted too. And seeing how well Max and Melanie's budding romance was going, I knew he knew what he was talking about. As we leaned close together, focusing on the small screen, I noticed Micah rest his hand at his side. It was the perfect opportunity to offer the reassurance Max told me Micah needed, but all I could do was rest my hand next to his. I didn't pay much attention to the show as I was battling fear and want in my mind, anxious to feel the warmth of Micah's hand around mine, but scared to move my hand ever so slightly.

Before I knew it, the episode was over.

"Should we watch another one?" Micah asked as the credits played.

"Yes," I answered quickly, maybe a little too eagerly. I wasn't going to miss this chance.

Micah started another episode, and finally, I closed my eyes, held my breath, and moved my hand into his, giving it a little squeeze. I smiled as I felt the familiar warm feeling spread up my arm and eventually over my whole body.

I laid my head on his shoulder, snuggling a little closer to him. He moved his arm around me, and I settled into him, laying my arm across his chest. We watched two more episodes like this and I even started to doze off a little bit, before Micah moved, waking me up.

"I better get home," I whispered, looking up at him. "We have school in the morning, or at least, I do."

"Can I walk you out?"

"Only if you feel well enough too."

He slipped on some shoes and pulled on a sweatshirt before we walked downstairs.

"Do you think you'll be at school tomorrow?" I asked, turning to face him when we were on the porch.

"I hope so. I'm going a little stir crazy after two days in bed."

"Well, sleep good, and feel better," I wrapped my arms around his neck.

"I'll do my best," Micah said, hugging me back.

As I let go, running my hands down his arm and slipping them into his, it started snowing, the big fat flakes kind that I loved.

"I love when it snows," I beamed, looking up. "It is so beautiful."

He wrapped his arms around me again. "I can see why this kind of snow is your favorite. It's perfect."

"Isn't it, though." I pulled away just enough to look up at Micah.

"Navy, will we still be close after high school is over and you go to Notre Dame, and I go back to California?"

I nodded, "I hope so."

The thought of having to be a whole continent away from Micah, made me want to stand here with him forever, just so I could be close to him. Silence fell between as I looked up, watching the snow fall on me and thinking about what would happen once we graduated high school.

I looked back at Micah and found him watching me intently. I knew that he was sick, but here we were, in each other's arms, surrounded by my favorite, most romantic kind of snowfall. We were so close I would hardly have to move at all. I wondered if our lips would fit as perfect together as our hands did.

"Micah," I whispered, moving ever so slightly closer to him. "I'm scared."

"Of what?" Concern creased his forehead.

"That everything is going to change," I was still whispering.

He moved closer and I was sure he was going to kiss me in the snow, but instead, he leaned close to my ear and whispered, "Don't worry, Navy Blue, not all changes are bad."

I tightened my grip before letting go and smiling up at him. "Get some rest. I'll see you tomorrow."

I walked home with a lot on my mind. Although plans for college and my life after high school had always been at the forefront of my mind, I had never given thought to what that might mean for my relationship with Micah. Granted nothing was serious right this moment, but I wanted it to be, more than I had ever wanted anything.

As I pulled off my sweater to change into my pajamas, I could still smell Micah on it. I smiled at the memories of tonight, our date the past weekend, and the friendship that had been forming the past months, and decided to put the future out of my mind. It was a long way off. I could cross that bridge when I came to it.

# 11

## MICAH

THE NEXT MORNING woke up finally feeling better and it was sweet relief. I got out of bed without my alarm going off, and was ready for school before Aunt Juliet and Melanie even came down for breakfast.

"I see you're feeling better," Aunt Juliet said, starting the coffee maker.

"So much better," I replied, through a mouthful of cereal.

"Glad to hear it. It will be good to have you at play practice again."

"Micah, you're out of bed," Melanie said, walking into the kitchen. "How was your night with Navy?"

"Incredible," I smiled at the memory.

"What did you do?" Aunt Juliet asked.

"Oh, we just watched Netflix."

"Smooth," she replied sarcastically.

"Hey, I was sick."

"I could see you guys having a pretty incredible moment on

the porch," Melanie winked at me as she poured milk into her oatmeal.

"You were spying on us?"

"Why didn't you kiss her?" Melanie asked, dodging my question and sliding into a chair next to me. She picked up a banana from the fruit bowl in the middle of the table and started peeling it.

"I was sick," I said again.

"That's never stopped you before," Melanie laughed, taking a bite.

"Yeah, well, Navy's different."

That afternoon at play practice, we were running the "Be Our Guest" scene. I wasn't in it, but it was one of my favorites because the choreography was intricate and the costumes were bright and colorful. It was fun to watch. I jumped down in the pit and slid onto the piano bench next to Navy.

"Can I turn your pages?" I asked.

"Sure," she winked at me.

Navy started playing, and I wasn't paying any attention to what was going on up on stage when we heard a collective gasp from the cast. Rachel had stepped a little too far and fallen into the pit. Even over the piano, we heard a sickening crack.

Navy and I hurried over to see if she was hurt, and we saw her leg turned at an unnatural angle.

"Are you okay?" Navy asked, kneeling down next to her.

Rachel propped herself up on her elbows and tried to move her twisted leg. She winced, "No, I can't move it."

Aunt Juliet joined us in the pit, but we all sat helplessly around Rachel, unsure of what to do. None of us wanted to move her, afraid we would hurt her leg even more. We ended up calling an ambulance and her parents, and Aunt Juliet told the rest of the cast that they could go home.

Rachel's parents showed up at the same time the EMTs did, and Aunt Juliet, Navy, and I watched as they stabilized Rachel's leg, lifted her onto a gurney and wheeled her out of the auditorium.

Aunt Juliet sighed as we watched the ambulance drive away, rubbing her eyes.

"You okay?" I asked.

"Just worried about Rachel. That leg looked painful."

"What are you going to do about the musical?"

"We'll wait to hear for sure how badly her leg is injured, but for now, let's just go home."

On our way home, I turned to my aunt, "If Rachel's leg won't be healed in time for opening night can Navy be Belle?"

"Navy doesn't sing. She's our pianist."

"Actually, Navy does sing. On the first day of school, I walked in on her singing and she made me promise not to tell anyone that she could."

"But then we'd be out a pianist, and I can't just go around filling holes in the production to leave new ones behind them." Aunt Juliet rolled her eyes, and maybe I should have stopped pressing her about this, but I really, *really* wanted Navy to be the new Belle.

"But did you know Luke, the third cellist, can play the piano too, and you really only need two cellos."

"How do you know that? Did you walk in on him playing the piano, too?"

"No, Navy told me."

"Ah, I see," Aunt Juliet smiled. "Let's wait to hear about

Rachel's leg before we make any decisions. It may not be as bad as we think."

"But you would seriously consider letting Navy have the part?"

"Let's cross that bridge when we get to it." She reached over and patted my leg.

The next morning, Aunt Juliet got a call. Rachel had not only broken her leg, but torn her ACL, and she would need surgery. Even then, her doctors weren't sure she would be healed and mobile enough to be dancing around by opening night in March.

"Please, please, please, please," I begged my aunt when we heard the news. "Please, can Navy be Belle."

"Navy is an amazing pianist, but she has no acting experience, and I'm not even sure how well she can sing. I'm not sure I can give her the leading role with only three months until opening night."

"I know, I know, but trust me. Navy's voice is amazing, and I'd work with her every single day to make sure she would do a good job. I'll help her learn her lines, and teach her all the dances. Give me a week or two to fill her in and she will be the best Belle you have ever seen."

Aunt Juliet filled her cheeks with air as she thought. "Okay," she said finally, letting out her breath. "Talk to Navy today, and ask her if that is something she'd be interested in doing. If she's up for it, I'll give her an audition, and then make my decision."

"Sweet!" I said, rushing out of her classroom. "See you at practice."

When I got to Creative Writing, Navy was already in her seat, her nose in a book.

"Navy, I have the most amazing news," I slid into my desk behind her.

"Yeah?" She looked up, smiling.

"Rachel needs surgery and she won't be healed enough by opening night."

Navy laughed, "That's not exactly amazing news."

"I haven't even gotten to the best part yet. We need a new Belle, and my aunt said she would consider you for the part if you sang for her."

"Oh Micah, not this again." Navy rolled her eyes at me.

"I know that you've never done anything like this before, but I could help you. We could spend these next few weeks getting you all up to speed. Besides, you've watched this all in the pit, you know how it all goes. I *know* you can do this."

"You *believe* I can do this. And I think you're a little biased."

"I am absolutely biased and I don't care one bit," I had one final argument I hoped could sway Navy. "And just think about how great this would look on your college resume."

Navy pressed her lips into a thin line as she considered what I'd said. The bell rang and Miss Ackekian started class, cutting our conversation short.

"I'll think about it," Navy said as she turned around to face the front of the classroom.

I asked Navy about filling the part again at lunch, but still didn't get a definitive answer. After school, I hurried onto the stage, anxious to persuade Navy one last time.

"Navy!" I yelled, unable to see if she was in the pit.

"I'm in the pit," she called back.

"Navy, please, you have to sing for my aunt, and at least put yourself in the running to be the new Belle."

"Micah, we've been over this already." She shuffled through

her sheet music. "Sure, hypothetically, I would love to be Belle. I would love to dance and sing and be the princess I've loved since I was a little girl. But that is not who I am. I belong in the pit, I belong at the piano."

"Navy, to heck with where you belong. Embrace the change."

Navy stared back at me, tilting her head to one side in that quizzical look she often gave me. "I will never hear the end of this until I at least try, will I?"

"Probably not."

"Fine," Navy threw her head back and let out a breath. "Go get Miss Moore."

"Thank you!" I was so excited I threw my hands around her waist, lifting her off the ground and spinning her around. "You will not regret this," I said, holding her face.

I went to Aunt Juliet's classroom, sticking my head in, "Hey, Navy agreed to try out for the part."

"Really? Okay, I'll come listen to her sing, just one second."

I walked back to the stage to find Navy playing the piano, singing the same song she was singing on that first day. "Is this the only song you know?" I joked.

"No," Navy smiled. "It's just my favorite."

"Can we sing it together while we are waiting for my aunt?" I asked, sliding onto the bench next to her.

"Sure," Navy said, playing the intro.

I let Navy sing the first verse alone, and then I started singing with her in the chorus. When we finished the song, I looked at Navy, and she looked eagerly back at me. It was like the romance of the lyrics and the vulnerability of our voices was pulling us together. We were so close. My gaze lingered on her mouth. Her lips were only inches from mine.

"Navy, that was amazing," Aunt Juliet beamed, walking over to the pit. "I had no idea you could sing like that."

"Oh, Miss Moore," Navy said as we scooted away from each other on the piano bench, trying to recover from the moment we had been caught in. "I didn't know you were here."

"I overheard you as I was walking on the stage, and decided to let you keep going. Your voices sound so beautiful together."

"Does that mean she gets the part?" I asked, standing up.

"I still have a couple of options to go over, but I'll let you know soon," my aunt said as the cast started to file onto the stage.

I tried to focus on the scenes we were practicing that day, but all I could think about was singing with Navy, that almost kiss, and the possibility of getting to spend even more time with her if she was cast as the new Belle.

I pestered my aunt as we drove home from school, while we ate dinner, before we went to bed, and even the next morning on the way to school.

"Micah," she finally said, exasperated, "asking me more often won't help me make the decision any faster. I'm still going over some things. But I promise you I will have the answer by this afternoon at practice."

"Alright, fine," I sighed. "I'll stop asking. It'll be a long day, you know."

"Sorry love," Aunt Juliet winked at me. "You'll just have to focus on something else."

I walked to class and slid into my seat behind Navy.

"Any word yet?" she asked, turning around to face me.

"So you do want the part. I knew it."

"Well now that you've gotten my hopes up, yes, I really do want it."

"No final decision yet, but I feel confident you'll get it."

"Really?"

"Really. You were absolutely amazing. And my aunt said our voices blended really well together. Besides," I said, leaning close to her, "our on-stage chemistry would steal the show."

"I suppose you're right." Navy smiled, leaning her elbow on my desk and resting her face in her hands. "And who doesn't love a good on-stage romance?"

It was not the on-stage romance I was gunning for, but the bell rang and class started before I could reply to Navy.

At lunch, Navy and I visited my aunt to gauge if she had figured out who she would cast as Belle, but we swore we weren't going to ask any questions.

"Hi," Navy said as we walked into the classroom. "How are you?"

"Oh hey guys," Aunt Juliet said, erasing the whiteboard. "I'm good. How are your days going?"

"Pretty good," I replied. "AP Chemistry was difficult as always, but at least I have the smartest lab partner."

We continued the aimless small talk for a good five minutes. Navy sat on a desk in the front row, swinging her legs. I paced around the edge of the classroom, stopping to thumb through the collection of playbills my aunt had in a bin at the back of her classroom to keep my hands from fidgeting.

Finally, Aunt Juliet let out a laugh. "Alright, alright, I was going to wait until play practice to tell you this, but I guess I'll put you out of your misery. Navy is the new Belle, and we'll have Luke take over on the piano."

"Really," I said excitedly, running back to the front of the classroom.

"Yes, but Navy, you're going to have to work hard to get up to speed with everything. Micah said he'd help you."

"Oh thank you, Miss Moore. I promise I'll be the best Belle you've ever seen," Navy clasped her hands in front of her heart.

"Let's get started right now," I said, giving Aunt Juliet a hug, and pulling Navy out of the classroom. "We'll be on the stage."

Once we were on the stage, we dropped our bags and threw our arms around each other.

"Micah," Navy buried her face into my neck, "I am so excited."

"Me too, Navy Blue," I sighed, running my fingers through her hair and feeling completely content with her in my arms.

My mind raced with all the possibilities ahead of us now that she was the new Belle. We would have late nights on the stage, and lots of dances, and spend so much time together that Navy would know me better than anyone else. Even though we were only in high school, and everything ahead of this year was so uncertain, this moment gave me hope that we could make it through whatever we had to because I wanted Navy Blue to be the last girl I ever fell in love with.

## 12

---

# NAVY

THE WEEKS after I was cast as the new Belle were some of the best weeks of my life. Between AP Chemistry labs and getting me up to speed for the musical, Micah and I spent almost every waking moment together. I saw sides of him I didn't know existed, like the silly little dance he'd do when he was excited, or how he tripped over his words when it was late and he was tired. Even the little things he did that annoyed me, like chewing on his pencil erasers, or always running late for our chemistry labs and play practice, made me love him even more. I was never tired of spending time with him.

Having heard Rachel recite the lines and sing the songs when she was Belle, I was able to memorize those things with ease. Even the acting came quickly. But we all have our weaknesses, and mine was dancing.

We spent hours—on the stage and off of it—trying to master every step. My favorite dance was the last one, the grand finale where Belle and the Prince finally lived happily ever after. This dance was a beautiful waltz—well, in theory, it should have been beautiful. However, Micah and I spent most of it tripping over each other.

"I'm so sorry," I sighed, exasperated after messing up for what felt like the hundredth time. "I don't understand why I can't get this."

"Don't worry," he said, smiling at me. "You're doing fine. Just follow my feet."

He put his hand on my back, pulling me just a bit closer. "Just relax. I know you can do this."

I bit my lip and looked down at our feet.

Micah started counting and we started waltzing again. We went along slowly, doing surprisingly well. I was finally starting to get it, and I was feeling more confident as we continued to dance.

"Look at me," Micah said.

"What?" I asked, looking up.

"We have to look at each other in the play."

"Oh, of course."

"Do you trust me?"

"Yes."

"Close your eyes."

"Close my eyes?" I arched an eyebrow, looking at him quizzically. I could barely dance with my eyes open, surely I would never be able to do it with my eyes closed.

"Yes, let me lead you."

I hesitated, but eventually let my eyelids fall.

As Micah tried to lead me along, I tripped over my feet, and over his, making the dance anything but graceful.

"You're not trusting me," he said quietly.

"I can't see anything."

"So feel it instead." He pulled me closer. "Let me be in charge."

Micah began again, gently pushing and pulling me where I needed to go. As I relaxed, the dance became more fluid, and we waltzed around the stage as if we were figurines in a music box.

The moment I had been waiting for—the big dip—finally came. Without skipping a beat, Micah leaned me back.

"Micah," I gasped, caught off guard by the feeling of falling backward even though I knew it was coming.

"I got you," he laughed. "Trust me."

I loosened my grip, opening my eyes. "Did we do it?"

"We did it," he smiled.

And here I was, in Micah's arms, inches from his face. It seemed all I could do was stare at his mouth and will it to come closer.

"So," I said, finally breaking the silence. "Should we take a small break? I have peppermint M&M's in my book-bag."

"Oh, of course." Micah helped me to my feet again as I tried to pull my thoughts together.

I let go of him and walked over to my bag. With the M&M's in hand, I motioned him over to the edge of the stage.

"Tell me a secret," he said as we sat with our feet dangling into the pit.

I laughed, popping an M&M into my mouth. "That's a hard question."

"Hard because you don't want to tell me, or hard because you don't have any secrets."

I nodded, chewing the M&M in my mouth slowly.

"I have never been kissed," I finally said.

"What?" Micah said in complete surprise. "You have never been kissed?"

"Don't make me say it again," I joked. "And I am terrified for two reasons. I'm scared that my first kiss will be staged. Kisses aren't supposed to be prefaced. They are supposed to be spontaneous, in the moment. They are supposed to happen when you just can't wait any longer. I don't want to know my first kiss is coming."

"You could always get your first kiss before we run the stage kiss?" He winked at me.

I giggled, pushing his arm as if to say *Then kiss me already,* but instead I said, "Again, not something I can really plan."

"What's the second reason?"

"I don't know how to kiss. What if I mess it up? After all these years of dreaming, what if it is nothing like I thought it would be because I don't know how to do it." My heart raced and my hands started shaking as I admitted this to Micah. He'd probably kissed so many girls he'd lost count. I was afraid he would think my lack of experience was silly. Or what if he tried to kiss me, and I was such a horrible kisser that he wouldn't like me anymore.

"I could teach you," he said. "I mean, I won't really kiss you here, this stage is unromantic. I'll just show you how to set it all up, and then all you'll have to worry about is getting kissed before we run the stage kiss." He winked at me.

I started laughing. It seemed to be the only thing I could do to cover up how much I wanted him to kiss me.

"Come on," Micah said, standing up, "kisses are always much more romantic standing up."

"Okay," I said taking his hand to help me up. "What do I do?"

As I stood there looking up, I had half a hope he'd just kiss me right then and there. I didn't think the stage was so unromantic as he said it was, and kisses were supposed to be spontaneous, right?

"Here," he said, resting each of my hands on his hips. "Put your hands there."

He reached up, lacing his fingers through my hair, holding my head. My whole body seemed to buzz, especially where his hands touched my bare skin.

"Relax," he laughed. "This isn't supposed to be tense."

I let out a little nervous laugh, not realizing I was tense at all. "I'm trying."

"Try harder," he rubbed his thumbs along my jawline and I slowly felt the tension leave my neck.

"Close your eyes," he whispered, moving his thumb under my bottom lip, pressing down slightly to part them.

Now that I couldn't see, my other senses kicked into high power, becoming all the more vibrant. I could feel the heat of Micah's body all up my arms and in my chest. Close to his face, his skin smelled warm and musky, not quite as strong as cologne. My face tingled where Micah was holding it, just a heartbeat away from his. Every part of me craved to be close to him, to kiss him, and to never let go.

"You see, Navy," he whispered the words almost right into my mouth. "Kisses are not so much how you set them up, as they are about how you are feeling in the moment."

We stood like this for what felt like ages, and for every second of it, I was praying he would kiss me right there. All we had to do was move ever so slightly.

My heart sank as Micah let go and stepped away, and I opened my eyes.

"So yeah," he said, shoving his hands into his pockets. "That's pretty much it."

"Thanks," I said, twisting the ends of my hair around my fingers. I looked at him, tilting my head slightly. Something about Micah seemed so small, so ordinary, so vulnerable in this moment. I'd been so used to the confident guy making all the moves to make sure I had no doubt about his feelings for me, but now he seemed nervous. Did he honestly think that if he tried to kiss me, I would turn him down? Or perhaps, no matter how much experience you did or didn't have, first kisses were always nerve-wracking in an exciting kind of way.

"What?" he asked, looking down.

"I've just never seen you quite like this before."

"Good or bad?" He looked back up at me, a nervous little smile turning up the corners of his mouth.

"Good. Most definitely good."

"Are you done for today, or do you want to keep practicing?"

"No, I think we're good for today."

"Alright, well, I guess I'll see you tomorrow."

"Yeah," I said, standing there.

I didn't make any move to leave, and neither did Micah. It was probably awkward, but the idea of kissing him was all I was thinking about. My whole body was still tingling from being so close to him.

"Well," I turned to walk off stage. "Goodnight, Micah."

"Navy, wait," he said, taking a step towards me.

He reached for my hand and spun me back into him. He laced his fingers through my hair again and this time, he didn't stop.

*Finally.* His lips slipped between mine more perfectly than I had even imagined.

Warmth exploded, radiating from my lips and filling my whole body. I suddenly knew why people called it *falling* in love because my stomach felt like it was in zero-gravity free fall. We were way past butterflies.

Micah tasted like mint and cream soda, and I was keenly aware of every place his body touched mine. I sighed as his woodsy scent filled me, enveloping me in a warmth I knew I'd never forget. I leaned into him, kissing him back. He sighed softly like he had waited just as long for this. He broke our kiss, still holding my face close to his.

"Micah," I whispered, looking up into his eyes and wrapping my arms tighter around his waist. I never wanted this to end. I stayed silent for a moment, but couldn't stop smiling.

"Micah, are you ready to go?" Miss Moore walked on the stage.

I tried not to let a disappointed sigh escape as Micah and I stepped quickly away from each other.

"Yeah," Micah nodded, breaking eye contact with me and looking at his aunt.

"How is the dance coming along?" Miss Moore asked, looking at me for the answer.

"It's going great," I smiled. "Micah is a great teacher."

"Glad to hear it. See you tomorrow."

"Yeah, see you tomorrow," I said over my shoulder as I walked off the stage.

"Goodnight, Navy Blue," I heard Micah say behind me.

I walked to my car, unable to stop smiling. Once I was safely in the driver's seat where no one could hear me, I let out a squeal. I couldn't wait to call Becca and tell her all about it, and to dance around in excitement with my mom when I got home, but for right now, I wanted to revel in the memory all by myself. I traced my lips, trying to hold on to every little detail of our first kiss to tide me over until Micah kissed me again.

# 13

## MICAH

I WAS FALLING in love with Navy. That kiss on the stage had solidified it.

It was a funny feeling—feeling confident that I could say I loved her instead of just liked her. But it wasn't just that I wanted to kiss her, or that I thought she was beautiful. I was falling in love with her mind, the way she saw the world, her intelligence. I wanted to know how she felt about everything, and I wanted to do everything in my power to fix anything she felt was wrong.

I had never felt like this before. In Hollywood, every girl I had ever been romantically linked to had been for the press, or to rebel against my parents. Not once had any of those relationships been backed up with a genuine interest in who they were as a person and that was why I knew I loved Navy, at least to the extent that I knew how.

The next day, after play practice, Navy and I sat in the middle of the stage, sprawled out on our stomachs, working on homework. The impending Christmas break made it hard to focus An open box of peppermint M&M's and a bottle of cream soda sat between us. We weren't talking, but it was comforting to feel Navy next to me.

My phone started ringing, pulling us out of focus.

It was my mom. "I better take this."

Navy smiled up at me, "Okay."

I walked off the stage, pacing the hall between my aunt's classroom and the stage doors, "Hey."

"Micah, I have the most amazing news," my mom said excitedly.

"Yeah? What's up?"

"You got the part."

"That's great news," I said, smiling. "When do we start filming?"

"Right after Christmas. Dad and I thought we could fly out and celebrate Christmas in Paris before you start. I know it will cut your stay with Juliet short."

"That's okay, I've been dying to get out of here," came my knee-jerk response, but as soon as I said it, my heart sank. I knew it wasn't true. Yes, perhaps I had wanted to leave when I first got here, but now I genuinely loved this place, and I wasn't ready for it to be over.

"Perfect, we'll send the jet to pick up you and Mel tonight."

"Wait," I said without thinking. Tonight was too soon.

I leaned against the wall, a lump in my throat. Did I have to take the part? Did I really have to go? I paused for a moment, truly considering turning down the part, but I knew I wouldn't do it. This could open up so many doors for my career. But my heart was torn in two. I'd just kissed Navy, I loved her, and now I had to leave. Wasn't there any way I could have both an amazing girl and the incredible career opportunity? Maybe there was enough time to explain everything to Navy before we left. Maybe she would wait for me.

"What is it?" my mom said, pulling me out of my thoughts.

"Nothing," I said, shaking my head and swallowing the lump. "It's nothing. I'll see you soon. Love you."

"Love you." The line went dead.

I hurried back on the stage, working out everything I was going to say to Navy, but the auditorium was empty. She was gone. My laptop and our treats sat alone in the middle of the stage.

My heart was beating out of my chest. I knew there was so much I needed to do before I left, but all I could think about was getting to Navy. I couldn't give her up. I shoved everything in my backpack and ran to my aunt's classroom. She met me halfway down the hall.

"You're dad just called," she said, wrapping me in a hug. "Congratulations! I'm so excited you got the part."

I pulled away and saw her eyes were glossy with tears. I wanted to cry too. "I'm sorry," I said. "I'm sorry we're leaving, and I can't be the Beast anymore."

"No, don't be," she shook her head and let out a little laugh. "We found a new Belle, we'll find a new Beast too. This is incredible for you."

I didn't say anything. I knew she was right, but I'd never felt so conflicted before. For so long, acting had been my main focus, the only option, and a mere four months earlier, the decision to take the part and leave would have been a foregone conclusion. Now I felt like there was so much more.

"Come on, let's get you home," Aunt Juliet ushered me

towards the back door. "We've got a lot to do before your parents get here."

"Where's Melanie?" I asked as we walked through the parking lot.

"Max took her home. I'm sure your mom called her."

I dialed my sister's number, but it went straight to voicemail.

We raced home to find Melanie had already packed and was waiting in the kitchen. She had her arms folded across her chest, her head cocked and her forehead furrowed.

I took the stairs two at a time to my bedroom. "Dying to get out of here?" Melanie said, following me upstairs. "Micah, why would you say that?"

I pulled the suitcase out from under my bed and flipped it open, throwing clothes and toiletries in it without thought or order. "You talked to mom, huh."

"Yeah, I did."

"I'm sorry, okay," I straightened up and turned to get more clothes out of the closet. "Aren't you happy I got the part?"

"Do you realize that in the past four months, my life has been uprooted twice, and both times because of you?"

"Mel, not all changes are bad," I said, falling back on what was beginning to feel like an excuse instead of a mantra to get me through hard times.

"But not all changes are necessary either."

"Look, I did not ask to be sent here, and I did not ask for you to come with me. That was on dad. And you know what, yes, I do love it here. But face it, Mel. It was never going to last. We are actors; we go where there are parts for us. Life like this, here, is not meant for us."

She was silent for a moment, and she chewed on her lip.

"Yeah, well, I wish it was," she finally said before leaving my room.

After tossing everything I'd brought to Utah back into my suitcase, I zipped it up and dragged it down the stairs. I checked my phone, relieved to see no message from my parents yet. I still had time.

I sprinted up the street and banged on Navy's door. Max pulled it open.

"Is Navy here?" I panted, out of breath.

"No," Max shook his head. "I don't know where she is. She hasn't come home from school yet."

I pulled out my phone, scrolled to Navy's name, and pressed it up to my ear. "Please pick up," I whispered as I listened to each hollow ring. "Please."

It went to voicemail.

I heard a car pull up behind me, and soon Melanie was by my side. "Micah, mom and dad are here. It's time to go."

Max stepped out onto the porch with us, and pulled Melanie into a hug, cradling her head and running his fingers through her hair.

"Let me know when you land safe, okay," he said into her neck.

That was it, this was where I broke. Tears filled my eyes watching Max and Melanie together.

"It's not goodbye," she said softly, holding Max's face and giving him a kiss. "I'll see you soon, okay?"

"Max, will you tell Navy to call me? Please?"

"Yeah, man," Max slapped my shoulder. "I'll tell her."

The ride to the small municipal airport was long and quiet. When we pulled up to the jet, my parents walked out, giving us hugs and kisses.

We turned to our aunt, who was teary-eyed but smiling. "I'll miss having you two here with me. The house will be so quiet without you."

"Thank you for everything," I said, giving her a hug. I felt like I wanted to say more, but the lump in my throat stopped me.

Aunt Juliet, Mel, and my parents said their goodbyes, and we walked single file up the stairs to the jet. Before I ducked in, I turned around, taking in one last look at Kimball Junction. I felt the cold winter wind on my cheeks, and my mind reeled back to the warm August afternoon I'd stepped off the jet for the first time. I hated the mountains, hated the tan Camry, hated my aunt's cheery attitude, and I was bitter at having to be here. Now, as my eyes fell from my aunt, to her Camry, to the mountains surrounding us, I couldn't imagine hating any of it.

I turned and ducked into the jet, taking my seat opposite of Mel, and buckling my seat belt. I leaned my forehead on the window, sighing as the plane took off and I said goodbye to Kimball Junction.

A LITTLE OVER ten hours later, we stepped off the plane, tired and jet-lagged. My clothes were rumpled, my hair was a mess, and I wanted nothing more than to sleep.

A car was already waiting for us, and we all climbed inside while our driver loaded our bags into the trunk. My dad made conversation with him in impeccable French as we drove to the hotel.

We pulled up to a five-star hotel and security guards surrounded us as we walked in. I'm not sure that was necessary considering no one seemed to know us here, but I didn't question it.

My room was spacious, but I didn't have much time to admire it. All I saw was the bed, and that's all I wanted. I vaguely remember my mom tucking me in and telling me that when I woke up again we would explore Paris. With that, I drifted to sleep.

When I opened my eyes again, I was still groggy and confused. I didn't exactly remember where I was. The curtains by my bed were drawn back and I could see clearly the gorgeous view of the Eiffel Tower and the Paris skyline, lit up against the dark night. Then I realized where I was: far away from Navy.

Before I had time to think much more, my mom walked in, carrying a black tuxedo and dress shoes.

"Do you feel more rested, my dear?" she asked, hanging the tux in the bathroom and setting the dress shoes out next to my bed.

"I think so," I said, stretching.

"I'm so glad, because tonight, we are going to a Christmas party." She smiled as she ripped the covers away. "So get all showered up and put on that tux. The limo will be here in an hour."

I sat up, rubbing my eyes.

"I am so excited," she said as she left my room.

I pushed myself off the bed and got a good look at everything. Our suite consisted of a sitting room, three bedrooms, each with their own bathrooms, a balcony and a gorgeous view. All the wallpaper was a warm cream with faint floral designs, and the rooms were filled with rich blue furniture and gold accents. It was homey and majestic all at the same time.

I turned on my music and went about getting ready for this party my parents were so excited for. I quickly realized that there were a lot of things about this place that would remind me of Navy, and the music didn't help. I resorted to getting ready in silence. The motions of getting ready for the party kept my thoughts occupied.

I walked out onto the balcony as I tied my bowtie, drinking in one of the most stunning views I had ever seen. My thoughts wandered to Navy, and I let them. I thought about how much she would love Paris. I thought about how the city lights would reflect in her green eyes. I thought about how I didn't even get to say goodbye. How was it possible to miss Navy so much after only knowing her for such a short time? I wondered if Navy was missing me too and why she hadn't called yet. I rubbed a spot below my bowtie, trying to knead out the pain in my chest. I knew now that heartbreak was far more than metaphorical.

"Micah, the limo is here," my dad called, pulling me out of my thoughts.

I walked inside, telling myself with every step that I was going to be a good actor and that I was going to be happy and have fun.

Mel and I walked behind my parents as security escorted us to the limo.

"Are you still mad at me?" I asked, hoping sleep had put my sister and me on good terms again.

"I can't decide," she said, checking her lipstick in the window of the limo before ducking inside.

I felt like my whole world was falling apart and it was taking every ounce of will power I had to sit up straight and smile.

I stared out the window as we drove to the outskirts of Paris and pulled up to a mansion that resembled a medieval castle.

My parents stepped out of the limo first, and we followed close behind them. Melanie looped her arm through mine as we walked inside. I was grateful to feel her next to me, even if she was still a little angry.

The first stop we made on our way into the party was the bar. My parents both ordered wine, and my dad watched me closely as I stepped up to order a drink. I knew he expected me to ask for alcohol too, but I honestly didn't want it.

I stepped up to the bar, and a young man who looked just a little older than me asked me what I would like.

"Do you have cream soda?" I asked, leaning in, so he could hear me over the music and the hum of the party.

"Coming right up," he said in a thick French accent. "Enjoy yourself, *monsieur*."

"*Merci*." I nodded, using one of the few French words I knew.

I took a sip of the sweet soda hoping it would help the pain I felt in my chest. Mel and I followed my parents around most of the night, listening to them make conversation in a language we didn't understand. I tried making conversation with some of the party-goers who spoke English, but over the buzz of everyone's conversation and their thick French accents, it didn't go very well.

About halfway through the night, I refilled my cream soda and went exploring, trying to find a place to myself, where I could think, where I wouldn't have to force smiles and laughs.

I slipped up the spiraling stairs and down a hall, trying the first door I came to. It was unlocked and I stepped inside quietly. There were no lights on, but the luminescent full moon cast a silver glow through the floor-to-ceiling windows on the far side of the room. I was in a library full of French books I couldn't read the titles of. I heard the buzz from the party downstairs, but it was distant and quiet up here.

I walked over to the window, leaning against it. The view from this window overlooked a garden. In the middle of it, a couple sat on a stone bench despite the cold winter weather. They were turned towards each other, invested in their conversation. They looked beautiful together, and I couldn't help but wonder if Navy and I looked like that. Watching them made my heart hurt, but for some reason, I couldn't turn away.

I heard the door open and someone slip in. I turned to see who it was.

"I thought I'd find you hiding away up here." It was Melanie.

"Hey," I said, going back to watching the couple on the bench.

"Sick of the party?" Melanie moved to the opposite side of the window, looking up at the full moon.

"Yeah," I took a long swig of my cream soda, finishing it off.

"Me too."

We stood like this, looking out the window in silence, for a few minutes before Melanie spoke again. "I'm sorry."

"For what?"

"For being angry at you. I know you didn't mean to upset me."

"It's okay. I'm sorry I'm brainless sometimes and keep getting us uprooted. Even if I don't mean to."

"We all have our brainless moments."

"Me more than most, it seems."

Melanie let out a small laugh, "No, you're a lot better than you give yourself credit for."

"Thanks, Mel."

I went back to staring out the window.

"What are you thinking so hard about over there?"

"I don't know," I lied.

"Navy," my sister nodded, "of course."

I smiled, "You know me well."

"You want to talk about it?"

"I'm in this vicious cycle, beating myself up for leaving, for making you leave, regretting not getting to say goodbye and explain everything to her, then feeling stupid for feeling so heartbroken over a girl I only knew for four months and only kissed for the first time 72 hours ago."

"You kissed her?" Melanie exclaimed in surprise. "Why didn't you tell me?"

"Sorry," I said, rubbing my eyes. "I meant to, but everything got chaotic."

"Micah, it's okay to feel heartbroken. It's okay to miss her. Some people have that effect on us, no matter the amount of time we've known them."

"But what I'm feeling feels so much more earth-shattering than I think it should. I mean, we are in high school. The chances of our romance lasting longer than the school year were slim to nothing. We are two extremely opposite people planning on living two extremely opposite lives. And even if we were any semblance of normal, high school sweethearts don't last. We were driving down a dead-end road. It was all inevitable."

"But that doesn't mean it wasn't real. I've watched you build more of a relationship with Navy than I've seen you build with anyone. What you had with her was backed with real feelings, and the inevitability of the end doesn't make that any less special. Micah, you got the whirlwind romance we all hope for in high school, regardless of who you are, regardless of who Navy is. You don't have to give up just because your story took a turn you didn't expect."

"But what if I never see her again?"

"You are Micah Moore, for goodness sake. Don't give up so easily. Remember at the beginning of the school year when you felt like Navy wasn't giving you the time of day? Did you give up on her then?"

"No. But—"

"No buts. You said yourself that you worked hard for everything you had with her. So don't let go."

"How are Navy and I ever going to work out now? We are in France, and who knows when we will be done filming and back in the United States."

"Oh for Heaven's sake, Micah, use your head. We have phones, and laptops, and Skype for a reason. If you don't want your relationship with Navy to be over, don't let it be. Call her. To heck with time differences and long distances."

I let out a sigh. Melanie was right. My relationship with Navy didn't have to be over. I wanted what I had with Navy to last long past high school. And if I wanted us to last, I would have to get used to loving her long distance. After all, she had one more year of high school left and then had plans to go to college in the Midwest. I didn't even know what would happen when filming wrapped in two months, if I would go back to Utah and finish school, or if I'd go back to California with my parents.

As we left the party, I checked the time-zone converter app on my cell phone. It was 9pm in Utah, and I was sure Navy would be home studying. When we got back to the hotel, I was struggling to keep my eyes open but wanted to hear Navy's voice before I fell asleep.

I found her contact information and held the phone up to my ear. What would it mean if she didn't pick up? I rubbed my forehead, a sinking feeling in my stomach as I paced around my room. She hadn't called me or even sent a text, and I could only imagine she was furious at me. It rang for far too long before going to voicemail. I didn't want to just leave a message though, I wanted to talk to her, maybe even Skype so I could see her face when I explained myself. I hung up the phone and stared at the blank screen. I was determined this wouldn't be the end of us. I wouldn't give up on her so easily.

# 14

## NAVY

I TRIED NOT to eavesdrop on Micah's conversation, but his voice carried. I smiled as I heard him make small talk with whoever was on the other line, but then he dropped a bomb that made my heart stop: "I'm dying to get out of here."

It felt like falling off of the monkey bars, landing on my back, and having all the air knocked out of me. I slammed my laptop shut, gathered my things in my arms, and ran. It was the only thing I could think of to do. When I got to the car, I jerked the door open and threw myself in. Once I was home, I ran to my bedroom and slammed the door shut. I leaned against it, sinking to my knees.

I didn't want to cry, but I couldn't deny the anger and the aching heartbreak I felt. The tears came out and there was nothing I could do to stop them.

Everything I thought Micah and I had—dancing at homecoming, our incredible first date, and that stunning dress, holding hands in the treehouse, our kiss on the stage yesterday —was all a lie. I should have known. He never wanted to be here, and I just so happen to be a pawn in a little game he was playing to wait out his time. I was so stupid to think that someone like Micah Moore could really ever be in love with me.

I dropped my bag and stumbled over to my bed. Kicking off my shoes and pulling back the covers, I climbed into the security and safety of the blankets, willing them to take me away. I drifted off to restless sleep, hoping I would wake up and realize it was all a bad dream.

I woke up to someone shaking my shoulder gently.

"Navy," Becca said softly. "Navy, it's me."

My eyes fluttered open, and I could feel my face was sticky with tears and leftover makeup. I sat up and buried my face in Becca's shoulder. I didn't say anything, I just started crying again.

"Oh Navy, I'm so sorry," Becca wrapped her arms around me and started smoothing down my hair. "Max told me they left." Becca's voice cracked, and it sounded like she was about to cry too.

"Tell me what I can do to help." She put her hands on my shoulders, holding me at arm's length.

"I don't know," I sniffled, wiping my dripping nose.

"I can't believe he finally kissed you and then had to leave."

I nodded, "I know. But do you know what he said before he left?" I stopped, a new wave of tears flooding out. "He said," I hiccuped, "that he was dying to get out of here."

"What?" Becca's eyes flicked between mine. "No, I'm sure that's not what he meant."

"It was all a lie, Becca," I said, burying my face in my hands. "Everything was a lie."

Becca pulled me to her again and held me in silence for a minute.

"Take a shower," Becca said finally. "You'll feel better if you clean yourself up a little bit, and then we'll watch a movie. I think both you and Max could use the distraction."

"Oh my gosh, Max," I said, kicking the sheets off of me and stumbling across the hall to Max's room. He was spread out on his bed scrolling through something on his phone. "Did Melanie leave too?" I asked, going to sit next to him.

"Yeah," he sighed, sitting up. He wasn't crying, but his voice sounded so defeated my heart broke all over again.

"Did you get to say goodbye?"

"Yeah, I got to see her before they went to the airport." He nodded and let the phone drop into his lap. I saw that he'd been looking at Melanie's Instagram profile.

"Was she dying to get out of here too?" The words stung.

"No, she said she didn't want to leave. Wait, is that what Micah said?"

"Not directly to me, but I heard him say it to someone he was talking to."

"So you didn't get to say goodbye?"

"I left before he got off the phone," I said, shaking my head.

"Navy, I'm sure that's not what he meant. He came over before they left, wanted me to tell you to call him. Maybe you should give him a chance to explain himself."

"No, I don't want to hear any more of his lies." I couldn't take it. "But you and Mel are still together, right?" I gripped his shoulders. Micah may have been lying about everything, but I'd seen my brother and Melanie together, and there was no way she was faking her feelings.

"Yeah, we're going to try giving long distance a chance."

"Oh good," I sighed. Even if I was heartbroken, knowing Max's love story was still intact helped me feel better. "Thanks for calling Becca."

Max nodded, "I thought she might be able to help you feel a little better."

"Yeah, I'm going to clean myself up a bit," I said, standing up, "and then we're going to watch a movie. She thinks it will be a good distraction."

Becca was still in my room and had laid out a fresh pair of pajamas for me. She handed me a tissue and ushered me into the bathroom. "What movie do you want to watch?" she asked.

"I don't know," my eyes filled with tears again. Why couldn't I pull myself together long enough to say one thing without crying again? "Something funny."

"Got it," Becca said, closing the door.

I turned to face myself in the mirror. I looked awful. My hair was frizzy and giving in to the cowlicks, making me look like a mad scientist. Mascara had run down my cheeks with the tears and my clothes were wrinkled. I started the shower and peeled off the dirty clothes.

By the time I had changed into fresh PJs and combed out my wet hair, I'd gone a full ten minutes without crying and managed to make it through the movie with Becca.

"Text me in the morning, let me know how you're doing," Becca said, giving me a hug before leaving.

"I will. Thanks for coming over tonight. I'm sorry I'm such a mess."

"Don't you dare apologize. This is what best friends are for."

I locked the door behind Becca and went upstairs, but I didn't want to be alone.

"Can I sleep in here tonight?" I asked, cracking the door to Max's room open.

"Of course," Max said, scooting over so I could crawl under the covers.

We laid side-by-side, staring up at the ceiling,

"It will be better in the morning, right?" he whispered.

"I don't see how," I said, disheartened.

A flood of tears came back again, and for the first time in my life, I knew what it meant to cry myself to sleep.

THE NEXT MORNING, I opened my eyes, still moist from last night. I heard crackling and sweet sounds coming from the kitchen. But not even the thought of that delicious breakfast was enough to lure me out of bed.

"Sounds like Mom is making breakfast," Max said sleepily, rolling over to face me. "We should probably go eat."

"Probably," I agreed as we stumbled out of bed and downstairs. Mom was dividing scrambled eggs onto four plates, and Dad was seated at the table, sipping coffee and reading the newspaper.

"Good morning," Mom smiled, looking up as we walked into the kitchen.

"Morning," we said together as we took our seats at the table.

"Navy, your eyes are red. Are you okay?" she asked, setting plates of steaming breakfast food in front of us.

"Micah and Melanie left last night," Max said, noticing I was on the edge of tears again.

"Left for Christmas?"

That's right, I had forgotten that today was Christmas Eve.

"Nope. They left, like, forever."

"Why?"

It dawned on me then that because I hadn't stuck around school long enough to say goodbye to Micah, I didn't actually know why they were leaving. I stayed quiet and let Max finish the conversation.

"Apparently there was a part for Micah in a French movie, and I guess it would be really good for his career."

"Wait," I said, speaking up for the first time. "If the part was just for Micah, why did Melanie leave with him?"

Max shrugged, "I know they're going to celebrate Christmas over there, and they're a pretty tight-knit family, if one goes, they all go. At least that's what Mel told me."

A new wave of anger hit me. It was one thing to break my heart, but quite another to take Melanie away unnecessarily and leave my brother heartbroken too.

"Oh Navy," my mom said, coming around and hugging me from behind, kissing the crown of my head. "It will be alright." Then she sighed, "But I know saying that doesn't make it okay right now."

"That's okay," I said, reaching up an gripping my mom's arm. I wasn't sure there was anything anyone could say that would make me feel better.

"I'm sure with a little more time, it will hurt less," my mom said, letting go and sitting down across from us. "Grandma and Grandpa are coming in from Seattle today, and hopefully Christmas will help you keep your mind off of things."

I nodded, but wasn't so sure.

We finished eating and cleaned up breakfast while Christmas music floated through the house. While it did lighten my mood a bit, it did little to help the heavy feeling in my chest.

My parents left to pick up my grandparents from the airport, and Max and I went upstairs to get ready. As I applied my makeup, I mentally painted a face: I was a happy junior in high school and definitely not heartbroken over the boy who left last night.

When I was almost done curling my hair, my phone buzzed on the counter and I looked down. My heart sped up when I saw it was Micah. If I answered it, would he give me answers to put me out of my misery, or would he make me cry more? I wanted to hit the green button and hear his voice again, but nothing short of him telling me he was coming back here was going to lessen this heartache. Even if our whole relationship hadn't been a lie, I knew that Micah and I couldn't work long term. I'd been denying it all this time, but this was our reality. Even if it hurt, I needed to move on, and that was going to be easier if I could just hate him.

Once my parents got home with my grandparents, Christmas was in full swing and I didn't have much time to think about Micah's call or whether I should have answered it. We exchanged family Christmas presents and then I helped my grandma and mom make food for the family Christmas Eve party while the boys watched football. Excitement filled my house that night as my aunts, uncles, and cousins arrived with steaming comfort food and presents. The fun of being surrounded by my family would have almost helped me forget about Micah, but everyone kept asking me the same two questions: how was school going, and was I dating anyone? The wound, which hadn't had that much time to heal in the first place, was ripped open over and over again.

When everyone left, my mom gave us our Christmas pj's, as was tradition, and we left out cookies for Santa even though we had stopped believing in him a long time ago. It was comforting to do these little traditions, a reminder that not everything had to change.

The next morning we woke up early, and the excitement of new Christmas presents kept my mind busy and my heart happy as I was surrounded by my family and Christmas music. We stayed in our pajamas all day and ate leftover food from the Christmas party. I spent the majority of the afternoon putting away all of my new presents and organizing my room while my mom and Max sat on my bed talking. I tried to focus on their conversation, but all I could think about was Micah. I wondered what he was doing, and if he ever thought of me too. My mind lingered too long on our kiss on the stage, and unconsciously, my hand went to my mouth. The thought of never getting to kiss him again made me want to double over and cry. I would have thought I'd run out of tears by now.

The majority of the holiday break was spent lounging around the house, rarely getting ready, watching a lot of Christmas movies, and getting a lot of homework done. My dad took work off, and my grandparents stayed the whole break. It was refreshing to spend so much time with my family, but before I knew it, the break was over and it was time to go back to school.

I laid in bed that night thinking about what this week would bring. Would school help keep my mind busy, or would all the little memories I'd made with Micah there make it unbearable?

I was dreading going back to the stage. It was, after all, where Micah had both kissed me and broken my heart just hours apart. The thought of Micah and the things he said before he left brought back tears quicker than Christmas presents got me out of bed. I turned over and stuffed my face into the pillow, hoping that it would stop them. It didn't, and I cried myself to sleep for the second, and not the last, time that week.

## 15

# MICAH

PARIS MORNINGS WERE JUST as stunning as Paris nights were. It was almost easy getting out of bed despite having only a few hours of good sleep knowing that this was what I was waking up to.

I had almost forgotten that today was Christmas Eve. We took our time getting out of bed, but room service for breakfast and the beautiful sunshine coming through the windows encouraged us to get up and go exploring.

We walked to Le Champs Élysées to finish our Christmas shopping. The hum of the crowds around us and the Christmas decorations adorning each store put me in a hopeful mood. I walked around looking up, in awe of the elegant, archaic architecture reaching toward the sky around us, but when snowflakes started falling softly around us, my heart ached for Navy.

For lunch, we stopped at a cafe with a bright, red-painted

front and big windows, displaying all the delicious treats inside. I would have loved to sit outside the cafe, and drink in the sounds of Parisians chattering in French as they hurried by with packages tucked under their arms and bags dangling from their wrists, but it was far too cold to enjoy lunch on the patio. The aroma of rich coffee and fresh pastries wafted around us as we stepped inside. We ordered steamy drinks and warm sandwiches and tucked ourselves into a booth in the back of the cafe.

I was half-expecting my parents to tell us to suit up for another party when we returned to the hotel, but I was relieved to find out we would be enjoying a traditional Christmas Eve dinner just the four of us. We sat around the table for hours after we'd finished our food, sipping sparkling cider and telling our parents all about our four months in Kimball Junction. I did mention Navy, but only so far as to tell my parents she was the new Belle in the musical and that we were good friends. Melanie shot me a sideways glance, and I thought she would spill the whole story to my parents, but she kept her mouth shut as we told the story of why we needed a new Belle in the first place. I smiled at the memories we'd made in Utah, but tried to keep my mind busy with conversation and the excitement of Christmas.

As we talked together, sharing memories, I felt once again that my dad was proud of me, and that our disagreements back in the summer were water under the bridge. The irony of the situation was not lost on me as I thought back to those first weeks in Utah. I was so determined to be the good kid he wanted me to be so that we could leave. I'd hoped that we'd be gone by Christmas, and here we were, all together again half a world away. I had gotten what I wanted, or what I had thought I'd wanted, but it didn't feel as good as I thought it would. Of course, I was excited to start filming a new project, and for the thrill of being back on a movie set, but I missed Kimball Junction. Life was adventurous when I was shooting on location and living my dreams of becoming a great actor, but my simple life there had been good too.

It was late when we finally went to bed. As was tradition when we were little kids, Melanie snuck into my room after our parents had gone to sleep. When we were young, we would pull the covers over our heads and talk about what we hoped Santa brought us, too excited to fall asleep. Even now that we were older and it was easier to fall asleep, we couldn't let go of the tradition.

Once we were alone, Melanie let out a long sigh.

"What's wrong?" I asked,

"I miss Max."

"Not Utah?"

"No," she let out a small giggle, "just Max."

I nodded, guilt pooling at the bottom of my stomach because I knew I was the reason she was forced to miss Max in the first place. "I miss Navy too."

"I've never felt like this," Melanie admitted, twisting the corner of the sheets between her fingers. "I mean, I'm in Paris —" she motioned out the bedroom window where the Eiffel Tower was lit up, "—and all I want is to go back to the relatively unremarkable Kimball Junction."

"No," I shook my head. "Kimball Junction is not unremarkable."

"I never thought I'd hear you say that."

"I never thought I'd love it." I reached up, tucking my arm under my head.

We stayed quiet for a moment before I spoke again. "You could go back, you know."

"What?" Melanie turned her head on the pillow, looking at me with surprise. "No, I couldn't leave you. I want to be here to support you while you film your first international film. This is big for you."

"If you choose to leave, it wouldn't mean you don't support me. I feel like my whole life you've acted like the big sister, even though we're the same age. My whole life, you've stepped up and sacrificed for me. It was my fault you were dragged into going to live with Aunt Juliet in the first place, and it was my fault you had to leave right in the middle of your relationship with Max. It's time for you to do something for you."

I had to swallow a big lump in my throat before I went on because what I was about to tell my sister to do was exactly what I wanted to do. "Go back to Utah."

Melanie shook her head, snuggling close to me and resting her head on my shoulder. "I'm not going to leave."

"Think about it, though."

"Hypothetically, if I went back to Utah, would you come back too, when you were done filming?"

I shrugged the shoulder Melanie wasn't resting her head on. "I don't know. I'm not sure how long filming will take."

"I'll consider going if you come back."

"Melanie, you can't live your whole life based on what I'm doing."

"I know." She sounded slightly defensive, but then her voice softened. "But we're growing up, and life is about to change. I'm sure we'll always be close, but what happens when you move out, decide to get your own place. And what happens when we eventually get married and maybe move away from each other. How many more Christmases can we hide under the sheets and talk about what Santa is going to bring us?"

"I'll always be your big brother," I yawned. I didn't want to fall asleep yet, but I was having trouble keeping my eyes open.

"You're only six minutes older than me," Melanie laughed.

"I know, but we'll always be close, no matter what. I promise."

"I love you, Micah," Mel whispered, stifling a yawn of her own.

"Love you too, Mel."

Christmas morning in Paris was beautiful. It had snowed all night, and the sky was still grey and overcast. The city looked like it was snuggled up under a fluffy white blanket. Having only arrived in Paris two days before, we didn't have a Christmas tree or any other decorations, but the beautifully wrapped presents waiting for us on the coffee table made the room feel festive. We spent the day relaxing, watching movies, and ordering room service. We Skyped Aunt Juliet, who had gone back to California to be with our grandparents, and I even tried calling Navy again, but she still didn't answer. I tried to stay optimistic, but was anxious that she refused to take my calls. I typed out text messages to try to explain myself, but always ended up erasing them. Maybe she wouldn't be so angry if I had tried harder to find her before I left, but I just ran out of time. Surely she would understand if I could just explain.

With the time change and jet lag, I'd lost track of the days since our kiss on the stage, but I found myself playing the moment over and over again in my head. It took me on an emotional rollercoaster, filled with butterflies at the memory, and heartbreak at not knowing when, or if, I'd ever be able to kiss her again.

Luckily, the next morning, it was time to begin production on the new movie. I hoped it would keep my mind busy enough to keep my thoughts far from Navy.

When I showed up on set for the initial read-through, I didn't recognize anybody. In the commotion of finding out about the part, moving to Utah, making the audition tape, finding out I actually got the part, and then flying to Paris, I'd never bothered to look up what the director or producers looked like, nor to research who else would be in the cast. I felt entirely unprepared for filming, and it was excruciatingly uncomfortable.

"Micah, good to finally meet you," a tall man with salt and pepper hair and wide-set eyes approached me, shaking my hand vigorously. "Bennett Pardo."

So this was my director. He was wearing a bright red button-up shirt, toned down with a tweed sports coat. His crisp khaki slacks and freshly shined dress shoes made me feel like I should have dressed up for the read-through, even though it was 4:30 in the morning, and I'd be changing into new clothes for shooting anyway. I had thought, too, that he would have a thicker accent.

"Of course," I tried not to look surprised and act as if I knew who he was all along. "So good to meet you as well."

"I was so impressed by your audition tapes and so glad you agreed to take the part. I look forward to working with you."

"Thank you for the offer," I ran a hand nervously through my hair, messing it up even more than it already was, and doing nothing to look more professional in front of Bennett. "I hope I live up to your expectations."

"I have no doubt," Bennett said before moving on to greet more of the cast members trickling in.

I found an empty seat at the large round table and flipped through my script, my eyes skimming over my speaking parts. It was a modern interpretation of *Romeo and Juliet*, minus the iconic and tragic death scene. If I'm being honest, I wasn't much interested in portraying another love story when my own was so undecided and memories of Navy were still fresh. However, this movie was a big move for my career, so I would have to find a way to soldier through it.

"I'm Drake," the blonde boy next to me extended his hand. "Drake Andrews."

He had a subtle British accent and his name sounded familiar, but I wasn't sure I'd seen him in anything before.

"Micah Moore," I said, smiling and shaking his hand.

"Good to meet you. Bennett goes on and on about your talent. You're going to be the perfect Remy."

I continued smiling at him like an idiot. I had no idea what to say in reply. How did he know what part I was, and more importantly, what part was he playing?

"Thank you," I finally said. I looked around awkwardly and then leaned closer, whispering. "I'm sorry, but what part are you playing?"

He let out a loud laugh, defeating the purpose of my whisper, "I play Beckham, Remy's best friend."

"Ah good," I nodded, genuinely pleased with the prospect of working more closely with Drake. "And who plays—" I paused, consulting my script for the love interest's name. "Jacqueline?"

"Over there," Drake motioned to the far side of the room with his head to a girl with long, naturally curly blonde hair. "Fiona Fletcher."

She cradled a coffee cup in her hands, obviously engaged in a lively conversation with an older woman whom I wasn't sure belonged to cast or crew. Watching her facial expressions in just a simple conversation let me know she was a great actress. I was feeling more and more inadequate and less and less prepared the more I sat here. I felt like everyone else knew what was going on, and I'd been left completely in the dark. Wasn't Winston supposed to make sure I was prepared for this type of thing?

I pulled out my phone and checked my email. Turns out Winston did fill me in, sending me a full cast list, the contract, and the script, I'd just been too preoccupied to check.

We started the read-through, and I read my lines with as much enthusiasm as I could muster even though it was so early.

Next, it was off to hair and makeup to get ready for my first scene. I walked into the trailer, met by a wall of lights and mirrors facing me. A stylist with purple hair and a thick accent motioned me over to her station at the far end of the trailer, and I held my breath as I walked through clouds of hairspray and makeup powder to get there.

I settled in the chair in front of her and she ran her fingers through my dark, wavy hair, beginning to work a pomade that smelled like coconuts into it. After she'd worked my hair into place, she used stage makeup to cover up some of the zits that had popped up on my forehead and even out the rest of my skin tone. Compared to other movies I'd been in, I was in and out of the makeup trailer relatively quick.

I was led by a French-speaking producer from the hair and makeup trailer to another small trailer. He introduced himself to me as Nicolas before consulting a clipboard and chattering into his headset in French. I obviously couldn't understand what he was saying, but he sounded stressed out.

"This is your trailer. You'll find your clothes for today's scenes in here," he motioned over his shoulder to the trailer door behind him. "Change quickly, and come to Sound Stage 3, please."

"Will do," I stepped up to the door of the trailer as Nicolas hurried away to show other actors emerging from the hair and makeup trailer to their respective trailers to get dressed.

Inside my trailer, I found clothes laid out on a chair. The dark grey sweater and faded jeans resembled what I would have chosen to wear on a normal day. Putting on the clothes helped me step into the character, and I felt more confident I could do a good job with this part.

When I was finished getting dressed, I walked to Sound Stage 3, where expert carpenters had designed a set that looked like a beautiful Versailles chateau. Bennett promised that we'd be able to shoot some scenes on-site at Versailles, but for these interior shots, we'd have to deal with the fake one.

After a morning full of running scenes where I had to turn on the charm and convince the cameras Fiona and I had flaming hot chemistry, I was mentally, emotionally, and physically exhausted. I almost cried with relief when Bennett approached us after our last cut and told me my scenes were done for the day and I could go home.

After changing back into my own clothes and leaving my costume with Nicolas, I took a cab back to our hotel. Mom and Dad were out, but Melanie was reading on the plush couch in the living room.

"Back so soon," she looked up as I walked in.

"Yeah, I only had to shoot a few scenes today." I collapsed on the couch across from her.

"Want to go to lunch?" She closed her book, placing it beside her on the couch.

"Sure," I nodded, "as long as you help me prep for tomorrow when we get back. I was so behind today, it was embarrassing."

"Deal," Melanie said, standing up and pulling on her coat.

We walked to the little red-front cafe we'd eaten at on Christmas Eve, this time opting to sit by the window so we could look out at the street.

After we'd ordered, Melanie gripped her water cup, tracing the rim of it with her index finger. She didn't look at me, but focused intensely on the circles she was tracing around the rim of her glass. "Micah, I think I'm going to go back to Utah. I talked to mom and dad about wanting to finish school there. After all, the part here is just for you."

The lump that had formed in my throat when we'd had this conversation the first time on Christmas Eve came back. I tried to swallow it away, but that only seemed to make it bigger. "Okay," I nodded.

"But you have to promise me, that if you can, you'll come back too when you're done filming here."

I nodded. "I promise."

Melanie finally looked up at me. "Are you going to say anything else?"

I clasped my hands in front of me, not sure how to reply. I was glad Melanie was going back and giving her and Max a real chance. I was jealous because I wanted the same thing for me and Navy. This morning, shooting romantic scenes in a beautiful rendition of a French chateau had brought the memories of Navy and our little moments together right to the forefront of my mind, and made it hard to remember why I'd taken this part in the first place, why I'd willingly left Kimball Junction when I could have stayed. Was there a way I could stay here and shoot the movie and still have a chance to make things work with Navy?

"Micah," Melanie prodded again, bringing me out of my thoughts.

"I'm glad you're going," I leaned forward. "I really am. And I'll miss you while we're apart. I'm jealous too." I gave her a small smile.

"Don't be jealous. You're going to come back too."

"I wish I could have both, this movie and Navy."

"Who says you can't? Finish filming the movie, and then come back and pick up where you left off with Navy."

I let out a long sigh, debating whether or not to tell my sister one of my biggest worries, especially since Navy and I hadn't had any contact since I'd left.

"We haven't talked since I left. What if what we had was nothing to her. What if she's moved on, hooked back on Brock, or some other guy by now. What if I blew it because I chose this."

"Navy wouldn't ask you to alter your dreams for her," Melanie sat back in her seat, crossing her arms. "Surely she understands that this is your career and that this was a great opportunity for you."

"Maybe she would have, but I didn't get a chance to say goodbye and explain. We didn't get any closure or reassurance that we could pick this back up when or if I ever go back to Utah." It finally dawned on me how hopeless I felt and I couldn't cover it up no matter how good of an actor I was.

"When I get back, I'll talk to her, have her call you so you can tell her everything."

I gave my sister a half-smile. "Thanks."

And even though it should have felt like a resolution, like I might find a way to make both Navy and the film work, I still couldn't shake the sinking feeling in my heart.

## 16

# NAVY

I WALKED into Chemistry on Monday morning and took my normal seat. I made it through the class okay, grateful for Mr. Thompson's complicated lecture to keep my focus on something other than Micah and the huge void I felt being at school without him.

The bell rang as I was gathering up my things.

"Miss Monroe, would you come talk to me for a second?" Mr. Thompson asked as everyone filed out of the classroom.

I zipped up my book bag and walked over to where he stood, erasing the whiteboard.

"I know that Micah was your lab partner. Now that he is gone, would you like to join another group?" he asked, placing the eraser on the tray at the bottom of the board.

"No, it's okay." I bit my lip. "I can do them alone."

I knew it was silly, and I also knew it would be hard to finish the labs by myself, but this felt like one part of Micah I could hold on to.

"That is perfectly fine. If you need help with anything, just let me know," he smiled, dismissing me.

"Thank you," I tried to smile back as I turned to leave.

Even after everything my heart had been through in the week since Micah left, I was in no way prepared for the heartbreak play practice would bring. I walked on the stage, trying to prepare myself to find out who would play the Beast now.

"Navy, I'm so glad you're here. First off, I've cast James as the new beast," Miss Moore said, looking down at her clipboard.

I knew of him, of course, but had only had a handful of small conversations with him. We definitely weren't close. Not like Micah and I had been. I wanted to cry all over again. Knowing who the new Beast was put the final nail in the coffin. It removed all hope I had that Micah would come back.

"Also, after play practice tonight, I need you to do some costume fittings. Is that alright?"

"Sure," I nodded, trying to make my smile look real. I was an actress now, after all.

Just then, James walked on stage.

"Perfect timing," Miss Moore said, turning to face him.

I blinked the tears from my eyes as James and Miss Moore started discussing some blocking for the scene we'd be running today. Now was not the time to cry.

James and I made small talk until the rest of the cast filed on the stage and we began play practice. It was tiresome at best. We ran the dance scene, which I struggled with on a good day, and James wasn't much better at it. It was awkward and sweaty being this close to him under the hot stage lights, and my hand didn't fit in his like it fit it Micah's.

As we danced, I thought of the hours Micah and I spent on

the stage, even after play practice was over, learning the dance scene. I messed up so many times, but Micah was always patient. He would just laugh, and help me again. If I messed up with James, he'd roll his eyes and I would feel even worse about my mediocre dancing skills. I started to wonder if I could be a good Belle at all.

It was maddening to me that all I could think about were the good memories with Micah. I reminded myself over and over again that he never wanted to be here, and that nothing that had happened between us was even real. Yet, I held on to a slim chance, a foolish hope that it was.

Micah had called every day since he left, but I'd never answered. Max said I was being stubborn, I said I was being practical. Whether Micah was calling to apologize or not, I needed to get over him, and it was going to be easier to do that if I could just stay angry at him.

After play practice, Miss Moore and I walked back to her classroom together where a tall lady with jet-black hair and piercing blue eyes was waiting for us. Had she not been smiling, she would have looked frightening, but her high-pitched voice and bubbly personality immediately put me at ease.

"Navy, this is Jenna, our costume designer," Miss Moore told me.

"I have heard all sorts of wonderful things about you." Jenna smiled and offered her hand.

"Oh thank you," I said, blushing.

Miss Moore watched as Jenna showed me all the costumes she had made for me. There were beautiful dresses in all different colors, but my favorite was Belle's classic yellow ball gown. It had a sweetheart neckline and a bodice covered with little jewels that sparkled every time I moved. The wide skirt had pickups, and I had to resist the urge to spin as Jenna zipped it up and went about making her alterations.

I finally felt like a princess, like I was capable of playing this part despite my worries and reservations about it. Micah wasn't the Beast anymore, but standing in front of the mirror wearing that dress helped me realize something I'd struggled to see before: I was more than just a plaything to pass the time. I was worth a real love story, and it was time I started acting like it.

After the rest of my dresses were fitted, I changed and told Miss Moore goodnight, walking to my car. When I got home, Max was sitting on the couch. A book lay open on his lap, but he was flipping through something on his phone. I'm not sure I had actually ever seen him study.

"How was musical practice?" he asked without looking up as I collapsed on the couch next to him.

"I don't want to talk about." I curled into the fetal position, hiding my face.

"That bad, huh."

"I don't like the new Beast."

"Why not?"

"Because he's not Micah." Even though I felt like crying as I admitted it, I managed to reply with all the angst I had.

I was supposed to be mad, angry that Micah left and turned out to be exactly who I thought he was: a stuck up, lying movie star with better places to be and better people to see. I wasn't supposed to remember all the nights we laid in the treehouse holding hands or all the times we spent on the stage rehearsing and getting me ready to be Belle. I wasn't supposed to miss the way his arms felt around me, or the ways his lips felt when he spun me back into him for that Earth-shattering kiss.

Before Max could reply, someone knocked on the door. I lifted my head, checking the clock above the TV. It was 10:30, and my parents were already in bed. Who was coming over this late?

"Are you expecting anyone?" Max asked me, moving the book off his lap.

"No." I shook my head, uncurling myself from my dejected position on the couch and standing to follow him to the front door.

When we opened the door, Melanie stood on the landing, the porch light illuminating one side of her face. Snow, the big fat-flake romantic kind that I loved so much, fell around her, dusting the top of her head and the shoulders of her grey peacoat in sparkling ice.

As if I weren't standing next to him, Max rushed out onto the step the moment he saw her, wrapped his arms around her, lifted her off the ground and gave her the most passionate kiss before she could even say hello. It was so romantic I got butterflies for them.

He put her back down, letting go of her long enough to move his hands to her face, cradling it as he said, "You came back."

She nodded, the biggest smile I'd ever seen spread across her face. "I came back."

My heartbeat quickened. If Melanie was back, maybe Micah was too. Maybe if I ran to his porch, he'd give me the same welcome Max had just given his sister.

I didn't want to interrupt the idyllic moment they were having, but I had to know. Stepping forward eagerly, I asked, "Is Micah here too?"

Max turned, looking as if he'd forgotten I was there.

Melanie turned too, except her smile fell, and I already knew the answer.

"No." She shook her head, her eyes dropping to the ground around my feet. "He stayed to finish filming the movie."

I stepped back as if the fact had physically pushed me. My heart thudded to the bottom of my stomach again, and I placed a hand over the place in my chest where it used to rest. "Oh," was all I could say.

"But—" Melanie started to say something, but I put up a hand to stop her.

"No, it's okay," I said, blinking back tears, my voice tight. "Max, I'm going to bed."

"Navy," Max made a move to come in and comfort me, but I stopped him too.

"No, be with Melanie as long as you want." I tried my best to give him a smile. After all, I *was* happy that she had come back for him, or perhaps not for him specifically, but I was glad she was back and that they could be together again. "I'll see you in the morning."

I walked up to my room, changed out of my clothes from the day, didn't even bother to brush my teeth, and crawled into my bed. I laid on my back, pulling the covers up to my chin. I couldn't get the image of Max kissing Melanie out of my head, how clearly elated they were to see each other. It was so obvious that Melanie was so in love with my brother, and tears stung my eyes again as I thought about how much I wished Micah was in love with me too. I knew we were only in high school, and it would be silly to think he would give up a big opportunity like this, but I wanted him to come back too. I wanted to imagine him running through the airport like in the movies, not wanting to waste a second getting back to me. I wanted to believe that I meant the world to him. The truth was Micah may have been *my* life-changing love story, but I was simply someone to pass time with while he was here. I meant nothing to him. After all, he hadn't even bothered to say good-bye.

# 17

## MICAH

WE HAD BEEN in Paris for almost two months (53 days to be exact, but no one was counting.) I was sure that once I got back into acting and being busy with this movie, I would think of Navy less. But as the days went on, more and more things in Paris reminded me of Navy, and the longer I spent away from her, the more my heart hurt.

I'd gotten really good at counting back 8 hours to figure out what time it was in Utah, and I tried to call Navy every day, but she hadn't picked up a single time. After a month of this, I was losing hope, but I couldn't bring myself to give up.

My days in Paris were spent on set. I would often come for hair and make-up before the sun was even up, and leave set when it had gone down again, so I didn't get to see much more of the iconic city besides the set and our filming locations.

I tried to enjoy every moment in France. After all, how many 17-year-olds got to be the lead in a French film and work in such a beautiful place? But I struggled to really get into the part. Perhaps having just had my own amazing romance and lacking any resolution with Navy was a distraction. It wasn't that Fiona Fletcher wasn't beautiful, or talented, but even though our romance was totally fictional, I had trouble compartmentalizing work and my real feelings in my head. Every time I focused on an aspect of the character Fiona was playing, I was reminded of a part of Navy, and it threw me off.

On the last day of filming, I sighed with relief when the director yelled, "Cut!" on our final take. After tying up a few loose ends on set, and making sure I had everything out of my trailer, I opted to walk home instead of taking a car.

At this time tomorrow, I'd be on a plane back to Kimball Junction, and I couldn't wait. As I walked, I watched the tan cobblestones ahead of me and I weighed love and work in my mind. For so long, my drive and determination had always been focused on acting, on getting the next part and making the right moves to advance my career. When last summer hit, and I was suddenly a huge success, I didn't think there was anything more I could want. But now I knew there was more to life than fame, and I wasn't sure I wanted this life if I had to sacrifice love to have it. Based on how eager I was to get off the set and get on a plane out of here, I worried I would never enjoy acting as much as I used to. My parents' relationship had always given me hope that I could have both a successful film career and a love story, but the difference between my mom and dad, and Navy and me was that they both choose a life in the limelight, and Navy hadn't. Would she consider it though, if it meant we could be together? And if she didn't, would I be willing to alter my whole life plan so I could be with her? Could we compromise?

When I got back to the hotel, my parents were lounging on the couch.

"Micah," my dad looked up from his phone as I walked in. "You're sure you want to go back to Utah with Juliet and not just come back to California with us?"

I nodded quickly, "Yeah, I definitely want to go back to Utah. You know, just to finish the school year out. You always say it's important to finish what we start."

My dad looked at me like he was sure there was more to my desire to be in Utah a few more months before coming home. I hadn't told either of my parents about my feelings for Navy, or how desperate I felt to get back to her. I worried they might think I was silly or that I needed to get my priorities straight. My dad didn't press me, though, he just stood up and said, "Okay, sounds good. We'd better get ready for the cast party."

In the states, all the cast parties I went to were casual, or business attire at most, but tonight, our party was at Mont Saint Michel, an extraordinary French chateau, and casual just wasn't going to cut it.

I showered and dressed in the same navy blue suit I'd worn to Homecoming. Once I was dressed, I wandered out into the living room to lounge on the couch while I waited for my parents to get ready.

I scrolled through Instagram on high alert for anything Navy may have posted, but I knew I wouldn't find anything. She never posted on her social media profiles, and Max had only posted a few pictures of him and Melanie, which was cute and all, but I wanted to know what Navy was up to. I wondered what her life looked like now. Was she happy? Did she miss me too? Had she moved on? Was she dating somebody else?

After perusing social media a bit longer, I walked over to the window, leaning my head against it and staring out at the overcast grey sky. Little raindrops hit the window sporadically, like the clouds were trying to rain, but couldn't quite let it out.

Once my parents were dressed and ready, we took our car to the chateau. I'd seen a lot of beautiful things during my time in France, but this was by far the most mind-blowing. My mouth gaped as we drove closer to the secluded French monument. Lit up against the inky night sky, it looked more like a small town than a single chateau.

A valet took the keys from my dad as we stepped out of the car and walked into the ballroom reserved for our party. The domed ceiling towered above us, and pillars the size of hundred-year-old tree trunks outlined the room. Everything was embellished in gold, sparkling in the light from a dozen intricate crystal chandeliers hanging above us. The marble floor was so shiny I could see our reflection in it as we walked in.

Men and women dressed smartly in crisp white shirts and black slacks walked around, balancing champagne and hors d'oeuvres on silver trays.

I tried to enjoy the party, drinking in my last night in Paris, and being present and engaging with the cast and their family members, but my thoughts were elsewhere and I was restless. If it had been up to me, I'd be on a plane back to Utah by now.

"Hey," Fiona walked up to me by the bar. "Want to dance?"

I did not want to dance, not at all. Everyone had their phones out, snapping pictures and recording videos, and I didn't want a picture of me and Fiona dancing to end up on a gossip site. If Navy's aversion to social media was any indication of her online activity, there was a good chance she would never see it, but still, I didn't want to risk it.

I smiled apologetically, trying to have some tact, "Um, I'm not really up for dancing tonight."

"What are you planning to do next?" Fiona moved closer to me, resting her hand on my arm.

"Well, I'm going to stay with my aunt in Utah for a little bit, and then I'll go back home to California." I took a sip of my drink.

"You could stay here, you know." She tilted her head and looked up at me through her lashes, tracing circles up my bicep. "We could spend some more time together."

I'd been afraid of this. In the past month, Fiona had made a few moves that implied I was more to her than just her on-screen love interest. I'd tried to let her down easy and make it clear I didn't feel the same, but apparently, she was making one last-ditch effort tonight.

"Look, Fiona, you're great, and it was fun working with you. But you should know, my heart's tied up with someone else right now." I fidgeted with the button on my suit coat.

"Well," she leaned forward, resting her elbow on the bar and twisting a piece of her long curly hair around her finger. "I can't say I'm not disappointed. She's a lucky girl, I hope she knows it."

I nodded, "Me too."

When we got home, I said goodnight and packed everything so we could leave first thing in the morning. Even though it was late, I couldn't sleep. I laid awake, more excited than I had been on Christmas.

Butterflies filled my stomach as we drove to the airport the next morning. I watched Paris sink below us as the jet took off, and I settled back in my seat. I tried to catch up on the sleep I'd missed the night before, but my mind was racing, making it impossible to rest. I was nervous to see how Navy would react to me once I was back, given the fact that we hadn't talked at all while I'd been away, but I was determined to work it out with her. This was just a little bump in our road, and I was going to do everything to fight for her. After all, it wasn't every day you found a girl like Navy Blue.

## 18

# NAVY

MICAH HAD BEEN GONE for almost two months. I had convinced myself that night during my first costume fitting that I wasn't going to be hurt over him anymore, but it was so much easier said than done. I had good days where I felt like I was finally moving on, and bad days, where I spent the day on an emotional rollercoaster, willing myself to get over it. I just wanted to be done. I needed to get back to focusing on school and dedicating myself to my work and my future.

With a little less than a month until opening night, play practice was a nightmare. No matter how much time we spent on the stage, it felt like we would never be ready to perform the musical in front of people. I felt inadequate and was unsure that I could do any of it. I dreaded rehearsals with every part of me because it was something that reminded me of Micah, as he was the reason I was doing this in the first place. It was like rubbing salt in a wound.

Everyone had gone home and I was finally alone on the stage.

I bunched up the skirt of my beautiful yellow dress and jumped into the pit, walking over to the big black baby grand. I hadn't played in what seemed like forever. I sat down on the bench and ran my fingers over the black and white keys.

I started playing a song and all of a sudden I couldn't stop, even when I realized what song I was playing.

It was the song I was singing on the first day of school when Micah walked on the stage and discovered my secret. It was the song we had sung together when we were trying to convince Miss Moore to let me be the new Belle. I started to cry, letting out of the tears that had been on threatening edge for two months.

When I sang that song before, it was because I loved the lyrical genius of it, not because I related to it, but Micah had given every word a bittersweet meaning.

I finished the song and I was left all alone in silence. I missed Micah more than ever. I stood up quickly, knocking the piano bench down behind me. I felt trapped and had to get out. After hurrying backstage, and hastily hanging my yellow dress back with the rest of my costumes, I ran to my car.

When I finally got home, I found Max sitting at the kitchen table doing his homework.

"Hey, what's up?" I tried to sound lighthearted as I went about making myself a late dinner.

"Nothing much," he said, but didn't look up. "Hey, have you heard from Micah lately?"

"Nope," I lied.

Micah called every day, and I ignored him. He'd even left a message, but I had deleted it before I listened to it. All I could think of every time I wanted to pick up was what he had said on the phone the night he left and that he never wanted to be here. Every time he called, half of me hoped it would be to explain that he was all wrong, but I knew that would be a lie too.

"You ought to call him. Mel says he's been trying to get a hold of you since he left."

"Max, you know what he said before he left," I said, squeezing my eyes shut and rubbing them hard. I was sick of constantly feeling on the edge of tears.

"Yeah, but maybe it was just a misunderstanding." Max set his phone down and looked at me.

"Look," I said, finally breaking down. "I'm happy Melanie came back, and I'm happy you guys get to be together, but that's not how it happened with Micah, and I need to move on."

"Navy, I'm sorry. I didn't mean—"

But I didn't wait for him to finish his response. I ran out of the kitchen.

"Wait, Navy, your food," Max said as the microwave beeped.

"I'm not hungry," I yelled back as I ran up the stairs two at a time.

I was too restless to go to bed, so I walked into my mom's room and collapsed on her bed instead.

"Navy, what's wrong?"

"I can't take it anymore." I sobbed, letting all the tears out. "When will I be happy again? I'm so sick of feeling so hopeless all the time. I'm so sick of pretending to be all right. I'm not all right, mom. I'm absolutely heartbroken."

"Oh Navy," my mom sighed sadly, pulling me into her arms. "You will be happy again, I promise. I know it looks bleak right now, but one day you'll forget your heart was ever broken. It's going to be okay."

"But that doesn't make it okay now."

"I know, honey," my mom ran her fingers through my hair. "I know."

"Why did I have to fall in love with that kid? I'm so stupid."

"Navy, you are not stupid," my mom spoke softly, but firmly. "Our heads are logical. They immediately jump to worst-case scenarios and let doubts overtake our dreams. But our hearts, they are believers. They are the reason we love. Our head will wait all day to be able to say 'I told you so', to mock us for dreaming, but you've got to show your head whose boss. You've got to keep hoping for good things to come."

Frankly, I was tired of hoping. For seven years, I'd built up Brock in my head with all these ideas of what a perfect couple we could have been. Then Micah came along and brought all of my ideas about love to life, but it had all been a facade. Were all boys either players or liars or both? Were good men simply fiction, stories hopeless women made up to help themselves sleep better at night?

My mom tucked me into bed that night for the first time since I was little and told me it would look better in the morning.

It didn't.

I woke up feeling the worst I had felt since Micah left. I stumbled through my morning routine, putting absolutely no effort into looking nice that day.

Max was quieter than usual as we drove to school.

"I'm sorry I snapped at you last night," I said, on the verge of tears as I pulled into the parking lot.

"Don't worry. I haven't given it a second thought." Max slung his book bag over his shoulder and opened his door, not even looking at me. Something was definitely wrong with my brother.

"Max, are you okay? What's up?" I jogged to keep up with him as we walked into school.

"No, Navy, to be quite honest, I am not okay. I'll see you after school."

"Wait." I stopped and pulled him to face me. "What's wrong?"

"I broke up with Melanie last night."

"No," I said, feeling panicked. I looked deep into my brother's eyes, trying to find that playful glint they always had, but all I saw was rock-hard seriousness. "Why?"

"It dawned on me last night that Micah fooled you. He came here, and he made you believe he was falling in love with you, and he played your heart. I thought it was just Micah, I wanted to believe Melanie was different. But you're right, Navy, they live such different lives. Melanie may have come back, but they're going to leave again."

"Max, Melanie *is* different. Please, you have to go get her back."

"Micah hurt you more than I've ever seen you hurt. It scares me to see you like this. Is it only a matter of time until Melanie hurts me like that too? Is she going to walk all over me like Micah walked all over you? We are not their red carpets, Navy." I had never seen Max like this before. His firmness and anger set me back, almost scared me.

"Melanie is different," I repeated again. "She's not like Micah. Please, you have to believe me. She would never hurt you, she would never lie to you."

"How do you know?" Max almost yelled at me.

To be honest, I didn't. I didn't know if Melanie felt the same way about being here as Micah did, but she came back, and that was a good sign. Still, I didn't know if she was playing games with my brother like Micah did with me.

Last night, my mom told me I had to keep believing, and if I couldn't believe in Micah, I wanted to believe in Melanie. I wanted to believe that she was better, and wanted to believe she really loved my brother, I wanted to believe that some love stories worked out.

"I don't," I finally admitted.

"That's what I thought," Max said, pulling open the door and walking inside. "See you after school."

I stayed where I was, my hand on the door, leaning on it for support. I thought I had felt pretty hopeless last night, but it didn't compare to the hopelessness I felt right now. I felt the weight of not only my own heartbreak, but my brother's now too, crushing me. I didn't know if I could take much more.

The prospect of AP Chemistry didn't help me feel any better. Although I tried to understand what Mr. Thompson was teaching us, I couldn't concentrate. The rest of the day went by pretty much the same way.

I walked onto the stage that afternoon in a crabby mood. We started the show from the top, stopping now and then to rerun something that wasn't quite right or change some tiny detail to make the show better. Finally, three very long hours later, we made it to the final dance scene. I cringed as I anticipated the dip.

Thankfully, Miss Moore told us that we didn't actually have to kiss until the rehearsal right before opening night, but I hated relying on James to hold me up during the dip. I didn't feel as secure in his arms as I had in Micah's.

We made it through the simple four-step waltz part of the

dance, and I managed to stay in rhythm when the dance got a little more complicated towards the end. Finally, I spun out, focusing on my arm gracefully extended in front of me. I caught a glimpse of backstage, all the complicated ropes and pulleys that lifted the sets in place, and then closed my eyes and braced myself for the dip. As I started to spin in, I felt James's hand slip, but only for a second before he gripped mine again. I knew I must have been imagining things when a familiar warmth spread up my arm and our hands finally clicked into place, finally fitting together. But the arms I spun into were definitely not James's. These arms were strong, ones I knew wouldn't drop me even if given the chance. Before I even had time to think about what was going on, someone's lips were on mine, but this wasn't a kiss that made me cringe. This kiss took my breath away. I knew these lips, I knew these arms, and I knew that warm, musky smell that suddenly surrounded me.

They were Micah's.

I kissed him back, sighing as I melting into him before I came to my senses and my eyes flew open.

"Micah?" I broke our kiss. "What are you doing here?"

Was I dreaming? No, I had woken up this morning. Or at least I was pretty sure.

"We're done filming, which means I get to finish school here. Isn't it great?" He smiled down at me, still holding me in our dipped position.

"No," I said bluntly, struggling to pull myself upright again. "That is not great. You fooled me once, but I can assure you, I will not be falling for it again." I turned to Miss Moore. "Will you please excuse me?"

She nodded as I turned on my heels and stormed off the stage, scooping up my bag as I left. I was painfully aware that every eye in the auditorium was on me. Never before had I ever felt so humiliated. I couldn't believe the nerve of that stupid boy, coming back here and kissing me like that. If he thought we could go back to the way it was before he'd left, that he could pick up his little lies again and that I'd be naive enough to believe them, he had another thing coming. If he was only here because his dad sent him, and he was looking for a game to play until he could go back to his old life again, he would have to find someone else to fool with his pretty words because Max was right. I was not Micah Moore's red carpet.

# 19

## MICAH

NOT EXACTLY THE response I was going for.

I walked over to my aunt. "Did I do something wrong?"

"I'm not sure." Aunt Juliet bit the end of her pen and gripped her clipboard close to her chest. "Navy has been very on edge lately."

"I'm going to go find her." I ran out the backstage door, looking left and right up the hall, wondering where she had gone. I checked my aunt's classroom before I walked out to the parking lot, and saw her across it, halfway to her car.

"Navy," I called out, jogging towards her. "Wait."

She didn't stop, and I sped up. I had to get to her before she got to her car. It was close, but I slammed into the driver's side, stopping her just as she was about to open it and climb inside.

"What," she said harshly, finally turning to me.

"What's wrong? I thought you'd be happy I came back."

Navy laughed, but it wasn't her usual bubbly one. This one came out harsh and short and it felt like a knife in my heart.

"What's wrong? What's wrong is that you played me. You made me believe you were happy to be here, happy to be with me. You made me think you had real feelings for me." She stepped closer to me, jabbing her finger into my chest. "And perhaps worst of all, you made me fall for you too."

"What are you talking about? I do have real feelings for you. I came back because I want to be with you."

"You may have fooled me once, Micah Moore, but I'm not falling for it again."

"I didn't fool you," I gripped her shoulders and craned my head so I was eye-level with her. "I don't know what you're talking about. I'm sorry I left, it was just a really good opportunity for my career."

"Good, I'm glad." She folded her arms in front of her and most definitely did not look glad. "And good luck with the rest of your life, but if you'll excuse me, I need to get home."

She yanked the door open with surprising strength, forcing me to step away and let her get in. As I watched her drive away, I thought of a thousand things I wanted to ask her, a thousand things I wanted to say. I wanted to ask her why she never answered my calls, and I wanted her to tell me exactly why she thought I'd been lying. I wanted to tell her that being away from her had made me so certain of my feelings for her. I needed her to tell me that she still wanted me too. I wanted to tell her that I was going to do everything I could to make sure I never had to be without her again, even if we had to date long distance. I wanted to tell her I was in it for the long haul, and that she was my endgame.

By then, Aunt Juliet and Melanie were in the parking lot, ready to leave. My heart was already heavy as we drove home in silence, but it broke even more when Melanie spoke up for the first time, "Max broke up with me."

"What?" Aunt Juliet and I said together, looking at Melanie.

"He didn't think we were going to work out long-term."

I didn't know what to say. I wasn't one to cry, but I definitely felt like it right now. This wasn't what coming back was supposed to feel like.

As soon as we pulled in the driveway, I got out and went up to my room, not even bothering to say goodnight. I got ready for bed and climbed under the covers, but I couldn't sleep. I tried blaming it on the fact that my body was still used to Paris time, seeing that it was 5:30 in the morning over there, but I knew the real reason I couldn't rest.

Question after question ran through my mind. I had never seen a side of Navy quite like I had today. I couldn't think of anything I could do to make this better, especially because I still didn't know why she thought I'd fooled her. I suppose she could have been angry that I hadn't said goodbye, but I'd tried to fix that, and she was the one who wouldn't answer any of my calls. Who knew if she had listened to any of my messages, in which I had apologized and tried to explain myself. Something bigger had to be going on here. Melanie's newly broken heart weighed heavily on my mind, too.

The next morning, I tried calling Navy again. Still, she didn't pick up. I sent her a text, trying to apologize, pleading with her to call me back. I even went to her house, but she wasn't home, and Max seemed especially cold too.

Needless to say, that weekend was the longest weekend of my life. I tried countless more times to get ahold of Navy, but my efforts were fruitless.

On Monday morning, I got to Creative Writing early. Butterflies filled my stomach as I waited for Navy to arrive. As the time ticked closer and closer to 7:30, more and more students filed it. Navy was among the last of them.

"Good morning." I smiled, trying to sound lighthearted.

"Hi," Navy replied as she slid into her seat in front of me. Her voice flat.

I tried to focus on the lesson, and even tried to make a few jokes, but Navy blew me off, ignoring me completely.

After class, I jogged up to her, falling into step with her as she walked to her next class.

"I still don't understand why you think I've played you, or fooled you, or whatever you said on Friday in the parking lot. Can you please tell me what's going on?" I asked.

"Don't act like you don't know," she said, ducking into the classroom.

"But I don't," I sighed hopelessly, watching the door swing shut behind her.

Play practice was horrible. Given the fact that there were only two weeks until opening night, my aunt had made the executive decision to keep the new Beast. I was forced to sit through rehearsal and watch Navy with James, and I about lost it when they ended the run-through with a kiss. I tried talking to Navy again once practice was over, but she left without saying a word to me.

The next morning, I walked into AP Chemistry to find Navy already in her desk. I walked up to her, ready to try to explain and apologize, although I was still unsure of what I was apologizing for. It could have been the fact that I left without saying goodbye. Maybe she was upset that I had to leave so soon after kissing her, and when things were going so well. Had she heard what I said on the phone with my mom, when I lied and said I was dying to leave? My mind went back to that day, and I was certain the stage door had closed behind me. Unless she had followed me into the hall, there was no way she could have heard me, right? Or perhaps she was angry because now she had to do all the chemistry labs alone and it was a lot of work. Did she feel like she needed more help getting ready for the musical and I left even when I promised to help her? I would apologize for it all a thousand times over if it meant Navy wouldn't be mad at me anymore. I felt like she was slipping through my fingers and I was dying to hold on to her.

"Navy, I—"

"Don't bother." She stopped me, handing me a thick stack of papers. "Here, these are the chem labs I did while you were gone."

"Thanks," I said quickly, tossing the papers on my desk. "But if you would just—"

"I'm doing another lab tomorrow night if you want to help. If not, I can do it by myself."

The bell rang before I could reply and Mr. Thompson lost no time in starting his lecture, making any further conversation impossible.

The next night, I dragged myself to the chem lab after rehearsals to try and help Navy with the lab. Talking to Navy obviously wasn't working because every time I tried to start a conversation, she shut me down, and if I asked her a question that didn't pertain to the lab we were doing, she just wouldn't answer. She was stubborn, and my patience was wearing thin.

At the end of the night, Navy turned to me. "I'll email you the lab write up when I finish it."

"No, let me do it," I said, taking the lab instructions and our data from her. "You did them alone while I was away. I promise to have it done soon." I thought perhaps doing the lab write up, something I knew for a fact Navy hated, would get me in her good graces long enough to get a few answers out of her, or at least apologize for everything I thought I did wrong.

"Fine," she replied before walking out of the lab, leaving me alone, frustrated, and heartbroken all over again.

I drove home and went straight up to my bedroom. Pulling my laptop out of the desk drawer, I worked tirelessly for the next two hours, crafting the best lab write-up I possibly could. After making sure it was absolutely perfect, I opened my email and tried to compose yet another one of my pathetic explanations. I finally gave up and decided to send off the document with a short message saying I hoped everything looked good on the lab report.

The next morning, I walked into class with no intention of trying to force conversation with Navy. It hadn't worked thus far, and I was sick of feeling the rejection. I knew I needed to make a grand gesture, something to show her how much I cared for her, but at the moment, I didn't know what that was going to be.

"Thank you for sending me the lab write-up," Navy said. She looked me in the eye, but her words were forced and her eyes were empty.

"Yeah, no problem," I replied, searching her green eyes desperately. How was I ever going to get her back?

"Navy, would you please just listen to me." I pleaded.

"No. I have no desire to be part of your lie again." Her tone hurt and made me angry, my patience finally snapping. Why wouldn't she just listen to me? I was not lying to her, and I was done trying to get her to understand.

After school, I sped home, too angry to care I was going 20

over the speed limit. I pulled into my driveway, jammed the car into park, and yanked the keys out of the ignition. Navy was stubborn, but so was I, and if she wasn't going to talk to me, I was done talking to her.

Her unwillingness to talk to me confirmed my worries that I'd meant nothing to her. I was done fighting for someone who clearly didn't want me.

TWO WEEKS LATER, Navy and I had managed not to say a single word to each other. She'd taken to showing up extra early to chemistry and sitting in the front, instead of in the back with me. At musical practice, she wouldn't even glance at me. It was like I wasn't even there. My angry resolve to give up on her had morphed back into heartbreak and bitter nostalgia, and I didn't want to move on.

After school, I went up to Melanie's room and collapsed on her bed with an overly dramatic sigh.

"What's wrong?" she asked, looking up from her computer. "Is Navy still mad at you?

"Yes! We haven't talked in two weeks and all because she thinks I'm lying to her. She is so difficult!"

"Max said something like that too, that we were lying," Melanie huffed, pushing a strand of dark hair out of her face.

"I don't understand?" I asked, propping myself up on my elbows.

"We used to talk about a future, what we would do once the school year was over, but when he broke up with me, he said it was because we were lying to ourselves to think we could make it work. He said we were too different. He said it was better to cut our losses now and save ourselves from more heartbreak in the future. I wanted to convince him that we could work long term and long distance if he was willing, but he didn't seem to want to listen."

"But don't you want to fight for him?"

"The problem with love is that it takes two people to fall into it, and only one person to fall out of it." She moved onto her stomach and laid her head on her arms, facing me. "I don't want to dig deeper. It will only hurt more if I fight to hold on when he's so willing to let go."

I fell onto my back again. "I know it might hurt, but I just have to know why Navy thinks I'm lying. I can't just move on."

"If you're so desperate for closure, maybe you just have to talk even if she won't listen. Don't stop when she tells you to."

"I've tried, but every time I do we get interrupted or she walks away."

"So go to a place where she can't leave."

"Do you really think Navy will go anywhere with me right now?"

"So go to her," Melanie said matter-of-factly.

Melanie was right. I had to explain my side of the story and get Navy to tell me exactly what I had done to make her so upset.

"Come on," I said, getting off the bed. "We're making them listen."

The walk to Navy's house was silent. Anger drowned out the nervousness as I went over in my head exactly what I was going to say. Before I knew it, we were on the front porch, ringing the doorbell.

Max answered the door.

"Micah?" he said, his expression stern. "Melanie?" His

expression softened when he saw my sister and I knew there was hope for them.

"Is Navy here?"

"Yes," he said, "but she's not up for visitors right now."

"She's in the treehouse, isn't she?"

"I don't know."

"Fine. Navy may not want to talk to me, but can you at least clue me in to why she thinks I was lying to her?"

Max crossed his arms and leaned on the doorframe, his lips pressed together in a straight line. He didn't talk for a moment, and I thought for sure I would have to get on my knees and beg for an explanation. He looked at me, and then he looked at Melanie, and finally, he said, "Navy said that the night you guys left, she heard you tell someone that you were, I think she said, 'dying to get out of here.' Navy was falling hard for you, and hearing you say that made her think that you were playing some game with her heart for fun while you waited out your time here."

Finally, all the pieces fell together and it all made sense.

"None of it was a game. I'm falling in love, at least to the extent I know how, with your sister. When my mom told me I got the part, I panicked a little." I ran my fingers through my hair as I spoke. "I mean, I was excited about the new part and reverted back to who I was when we first got here. I said something I didn't mean at all. It's true, when I first got here I wanted nothing more than to leave. But as I got to know Navy, I didn't want to go anymore. None of it was a lie. And I'll find the right time to tell her all that myself, but for right now, I think you two need to have a long conversation."

I pushed Melanie into the house. "I swear if you two don't get back together, you'll both be making the biggest mistake."

"Micah." Melanie looked at me with wide eyes, her cheeks flushing red.

"What? It's true." I shrugged.

And as I turned to leave, I swear I saw them exchange a little glance that told me Max and my sister were going to be just fine.

As for Navy and me, she may not want to talk to me right now, but tomorrow we had a chemistry lab to do, and I would make her listen to me before she could run away from that too.

## 20

## NAVY

WHILE I'D BEEN good at pulling away since Micah's return, I knew that being alone with him that afternoon while we did another one of our chemistry labs would really test my resolve. I would have liked to tell everyone who asked that I hated Micah Moore with every ounce of my being and I would never fall for him again, but in reality, I was a wreck. Having him close again reminded me why I'd fallen for him in the first place, and it was getting harder and harder to remember all the reasons I'd come up with to hate him when he left.

Adding to the war in my heart was the fact that tonight was opening night, and to say I was nervous was an immense understatement. By now, I was confident in my ability to sing, act and dance, but this was the first time I'd be doing it in front of a full audience. Had Micah and I been on good terms, I'm sure he would have understood what I was feeling, and he would know exactly what to say to help me feel better. He'd pull me into his arms, maybe even give me one of his heart-melting kisses, and I wouldn't be so afraid anymore.

But no, I was forced to bear this alone.

I walked into the lab, picking up the instructions from Mr. Thompson. I read over them, keeping my mind busy as I slipped into my lab coat and fitted the green goggles over my eyes.

Micah rushed into the science lab soon after I'd gotten there. I watched out of the corner of my eye as he dropped his bag next to the door and pulled on his lab coat, but I didn't look up.

"Sorry I'm late," he said, breathing heavily as he pulled the green goggles over his eyes. "What have we got today?"

I didn't lift my eyes from filling out the lab report. "Testing chemical versus physical reactions. My call time is in an hour and a half, so we have to do this fast."

"Okay."

I walked over to the lab closet, searching for the right equipment.

Micah followed me over, holding the lab instructions. "I'll get all the chemicals, you get all the equipment, yeah?"

"Sure," I nodded, picking up four glass beakers, droppers, and Petri dishes.

I walked back to our station, arranging the glass lab equipment in front of me, mostly just so my mind had something to do.

"This should be everything," Micah stood next to me, laying out the liquids and powders in front of us.

I inadvertently looked up. He was staring back at me, those piercing blue eyes caught me off guard even through the thick green plastic of our lab goggles.

Micah smiled carefully at me, moving ever so slightly closer.

"Navy—" He started to say something, but I cut him off.

"We don't have time. We've got to get this done." I stepped away, turning my attention back to our lab. I picked up one of the bottles, twisted it open, and dipped the dropper inside. I narrated my every movement in my head, trying to keep it occupied while my heart beat so fast I'm sure it would burst at any moment.

Since he'd gotten back two weeks ago, I'd barely allowed myself to look him in the eyes, and I sure as heck never let my eyes wander to his mouth. But now that we were forced to be in the same lab, so close to each other, I felt like I was going to spontaneously combust. My ears buzzed with the energy between us, like our hearts were magnets that knew they needed to be together. The harder I tried to pull away, the stronger I was pulled to him.

I felt Micah's hand on the small of my back as I pulled the dropper out of the bottle. I stepped away from him, startled, letting go of the dropper. It hit the ground and shattered before I could catch it. I crouched to clean it up, but Micah caught me, pulling me up to face him.

My breath caught in my throat.

"Navy." He put his hands on either side of me, trapping me between him and the counter. "I know you're mad, and I know now why you're mad. And I don't care if you listen to me, but I'm going to explain."

"Micah," I fought to keep my voice steady and light, but it came out raspy, betraying just how riled up I felt. "Please, not right now."

"Why not? Why won't you just hear me out?"

I wanted to hear him out, wanted him to tell me he missed me every day, that he loved me and was willing to do anything and everything he could to make sure he never lost me, but I knew that even if what he said was true at this moment, too much would change in the very near future, and despite all of our good intentions, he would have to leave again. And when he did, I would be crushed all over again. As much as I hurt right now, it would be easier to move on if I didn't have any more good memories to hold on to, to dream about and wish for, to miss and to mourn.

"I know that you think I was playing some kind of sick joke on you, waiting out my time here, but you should know that every single part of us was real. I know you heard what I said on the phone that day I left. It was stupid and I didn't mean it. I was just excited about getting this really awesome part, and I guess I just fell back into the person I was when I first got here. And I'm sorry I don't always know what I'm doing, I'm still trying to figure everything out, but the one thing I know for sure is that I'm falling hard for you. Paris had its moments, but every day I wanted to come back. Every day I wanted you. Please believe me."

After his confession of love, the one I'd desperately wanted, half of my heart was rejoicing while the other half broke beyond repair. There was no way I could go on like this, living without him, denying myself this amazing boy because I was scared. Terrified. And yet, I'd have to, because he would go back to California, and eventually I would go off to college, and I would have to find someone else, someone more reasonable, to make me feel the way Micah made me feel standing in some-place so unromantic as our AP Chemistry lab.

*That will never happen, no one would ever make me feel like this,* my heart whispered. I knew it was true. But I'd find something close enough. I'd have to.

"Please." Micah's eyes flicked between mine. "I've been dying to be close to you and you're running from me."

He moved his hands from the counter to my back, pulling me into him. "Come back to me," he whispered, his eyes still glued to mine.

I put my hands on his chest, longing with every bit of me to give in, collapse in his arms and let myself love him. But I couldn't. I pushed him away. "We won't work."

"Why?" The hurt in his eyes as he let go of me broke my heart. I could feel tears brimming in my eyes, but I couldn't cry. Not here. Not in front of him. I bit my lip. I couldn't answer him.

"Navy." He stood in front of me, looking vulnerable and hopeless. "You know how I feel about you. Nothing has changed." He slipped off his goggles and leaned on the counter next to me.

"It has to, Micah."

"Why?" he asked me again. I could see his temper starting to rise. He pushed himself off the lab counter and paced in front of me. "I'm sorry, I'm so sorry. Can't you see I'm bending over backward to try and make it up to you? Can't you see I want you more than anything?"

"What about what I want? Isn't that important?"

"What do you want, then?" He stopped pacing and stood in front of me, crossing his arms and raising his brows. "Tell me. *Honestly.*"

I felt like bursting into tears. My heart was so heavy I was sure it had turned to lead in my chest. With every ounce of my being, I wanted to scream that I wanted him, that I *needed* him. That he made me so illogical, yet made so much sense to me.

"You are Micah Moore—"

"So you admit it?" he cut me off, his voice rising. He pointed at me like he was accusing me of something. "You admit you want me? You admit you still have feelings for me too?"

"You're Micah Moore," I said again.

"Stop!" He moved towards me, trapping me between the counter and his body again. "Stop pretending that I'm any different from you. Stop calling me Micah Moore. I'm just Micah. I came back, and I'm here—"

"But you're going to leave!" I shoved him away from me and tore my goggles off. "You're never going to stay here. We are in high school. You can't promise to stay, and I can't promise to follow you." I stopped, breathing heavily. "You're going to have to leave again." The last statement came out sounding like I was admitting defeat.

I was, after all.

He stared at me, his eyes flicking between mine, his chest heaving up and down with frustration. And then he closed the space between us, reaching out to pull me towards him. This time I was too weak to stop him, to keep up my resolve and stay away from him. I couldn't say no, not anymore. I wanted this. I wanted him.

He slipped his hand behind my head, tangling his fingers in my curls, and slowly lowered his mouth to mine.

My goggles fell, hitting the linoleum floor with a clap as I wrapped my arms around his waist, pulling him closer even though his whole body was already pressed up against mine. I was suddenly unable to recall my own name, but could feel every cell in my body vibrating as if to signal that there was no going back.

"Navy Blue," he sighed, resting his forehead on mine, our breaths still mingling.

"Kiss me again," I whispered softly.

And he did. This time, there was nothing slow about his kisses. He kissed me hard, and then let go, and turned his head, and kissed me again. He kissed me like he'd never get enough of me. I certainly knew I would never get enough of him. He moved his hands to my waist, running them up my back and then down it again. My hands went to his face, running my fingers up his neck into his thick dark hair.

His tongue traced my lower lip, sending shivers up my spine. He wrapped his arms so tight around me I was certain the magnets in our hearts had finally connected and there was nothing, *nothing* we could do to pull them apart.

The door to the lab clicked loudly behind me and I spun out of our kiss, facing Mr. Thompson.

If he had seen what we had been doing, he didn't let on. He looked over his reading glasses at Micah and me, said, "Remember your goggles, Miss Monroe, Mr. Moore," and walked into his office.

NEEDLESS TO SAY, Micah and I didn't finish our lab before my call time despite our best efforts. I left him to finish the report while I hurried into the dressing room to get ready for opening night. As I sat in front of the vanity applying heavy stage makeup, I had butterflies for a whole new reason. Suddenly I didn't feel inadequate anymore, and the thought of performing in front of hundreds of people was exhilarating. This was, after all, what we'd been working so hard for, wasn't it?

Despite what everyone told me about expecting several things to go wrong on opening night, the show was nearly perfect. James and I even nailed the final dance.

After the show, I joined the rest of the cast and audience in the auditorium foyer. My parents, Max, and Becca were the first to search me out, thrusting a bouquet of roses into my arms and wrapping me in congratulatory hugs. I spent the next 15 minutes taking pictures, saying "Thank you" so many times it didn't even sound like English anymore and smiling so much my cheeks hurt. I kept scanning the crowd for Micah, but I couldn't find him. Surely he'd come to the show. It was his aunt's hard work that made it possible, after all.

After snapping one last picture with a group of friends, Melanie grabbed my elbow, steering me away from the crowd.

"Micah's on the stage. He wants to see you."

"Okay," I nodded, slipping nonchalantly back into the auditorium before anyone could stop me for more pictures and congratulations.

Micah stood in the center of the stage, another bouquet cradled in his arms as he clapped slowly.

"Well done, Navy Blue, well done." He beamed at me as I walked through the auditorium and up onto the stage to meet him.

"Thank you, thank you," I said, giving him a dramatic curtsy once I was standing in front of him.

I took the flowers he offered me and set both of my bouquets on the floor next to my feet. I reached up, framing his face in my hands. "Micah, I'm sorry. I'm sorry I never called while you were away, and I never answered any of your calls. I'm sorry I was so stubborn and wouldn't let you explain when you came back."

He shook his head, "Let's not be sorry anymore."

I swallowed, feeling like crying happy tears, "Okay."

"Tell me about Paris," I said, lacing my fingers through his and motioning him to sit with me on the edge of the stage.

He started from the moment he got off the plane and filled me in on every detail about how beautiful Paris was, where all their filming locations were, the parties, and the long days on set.

"Navy, about what you said earlier in the chem lab, about me leaving, "

"Yeah?" I looked up at him.

"I will have to leave again, but I want us to work. I want you to be mine. I want to fly here for long weekends, and I want you to come visit me in Malibu. I want you to be with me on every red carpet."

I smiled, leaning into him. "I want you too, all of you, everything."

"I never want to lose you again." He kissed the top of my head.

"Don't worry, Micah," I whispered, "You're not going to lose me."

We sat in silence for a few moments before Micah spoke again.

"Navy Blue, I love you. I know we are only in high school, but I love you. I love you as much as I know how at this very moment."

"Micah," I sighed, tracing his bottom lip with my thumb before leaning in slowly, just brushing my lips against his before he pulled me all the way into him, one hand wrapped around my waist, the other holding my head.

This kiss was unlike anything I'd ever felt before. In it were all the things I had never been able to find words for; the inexplicable joy I felt with Micah, like being with him was more than fleeting happiness. In this kiss, I felt all the love and fear inside of me in the best possible way. I was reminded then, as I had been many times before, that my heart didn't belong to me anymore. It was Micah's to take or break.

"Micah," I said again, resting my forehead on his. "I love you, too."

Nothing we could say or do would make this moment, perhaps our last memory on this stage, any more beautiful. So we sat there for a little longer, wrapped around each other.

"We'd better get back out there," Micah said finally. "I know a million people want to see you."

"We probably should," I sighed, trying not to sound too disappointed.

"But promise me something," Micah said as he helped me up and wrapped his arms around me one more time.

"Anything." I looked up at him.

"Promise me you'll never let go," he whispered in my ear.

"I promise," I whispered back before giving him one more kiss.

And that was the last time I was on that stage with Micah, but the first time in a while I wasn't afraid, because I knew that Micah and I had a million marvelous memories yet to make.

**Want to read Max & Melanie's love story?**
Turn the page for a sneak peak at the next book in the Moore
Family Series, *Unforgettable.*

∾

**Loved this book?** Tell everyone now by leaving a review. It
helps more than you know!

∾

**Want a FREE Short Story?**
Follow me on Instagram (@authormadisonbailey), click the
link in my bio and sign up for my newsletter to be the first to
learn about new releases from Madison Bailey. As a thank you,
I'll send you my newsletter-exclusive short story, "Truth
Universally Acknowledged."

# UNFORGETTABLE

The Moore Family Series Book 2

# 1

## MELANIE

Micah Moore is the sun. And that makes me the moon. I'm not mad about it. When you're twins, one of you is bound to be the more dominant one. The thing is, everyone's heard Micah's story. This one's mine.

"Melanie," I heard my name, but it sounded distant. I was faintly aware of someone shaking me awake. "Melanie."

I opened my eyes slowly and saw my mom standing above me. "Hmmm?" I mumbled, still feeling groggy and trying to orient myself.

The room was dark, so it must have been the middle of the night.

"Micah was in a car accident. Your dad and I are going to the hospital." That snapped me awake. I sat up.

"I'm coming, too," I said, my heart racing as I whipped the

blankets off of me and bounded over to my dresser, pulling out a pair of leggings and an oversized tee shirt.

"What happened?" I asked, pulling my PJ shirt over my head.

"It sounds like he and Logan were driving, and they hit a cement barrier. Logan was probably drunk."

My heart sank. Just a few hours ago, I caught my twin brother sneaking out. I should have stopped him. I should have put up a bigger fight and made him stay home, or told my parents he was leaving.

"Is he going to die?" I asked. I still didn't feel completely alert, and panic was setting in. I felt my room start to tilt around me, and I thought I might fall. My mom rushed to me and gripped my shoulders, stabilizing me.

"No, no, I think he'll be okay. But we've got to get going. Are you sure you want to come?"

"Yes, absolutely," I said, nodding. I couldn't stay here all alone. I wanted to see, with my own eyes, if Micah was okay.

We met my dad in the garage, where he had our black Audi running.

My parents didn't talk as we sped to the hospital. My dad gripped the steering wheel, his knuckles white and his jaw clenched. My mom reached across the center console, resting her hand on his leg. I stared out the window, bouncing my leg and trying to take deep breaths and stay calm. My hands shook, my heart beat so hard and so fast I was sure it would give out.

What if it was more serious than we thought? What if Micah did die? There wasn't a single thing in this life I had done without him. How would I go on without my twin brother?

We pulled up to the hospital door, which was swarming

with members of the press and paparazzi decked in all black, their cameras hanging around their necks. News traveled fast, I guess. Their attention had been on the doors of the hospital, but now they turned to the car. The paparazzi lifted their cameras to their eyes, and the reporters readied their microphones and recorders.

"Go on in. See if he's there yet," Dad said, stopping in front of the doors and looking out at the press we'd have to wade through. "I'll go park the car."

I'd learned a long time ago to ignore the camera flashes and the mics shoved in my face. Privacy was not a luxury my family enjoyed, even in moments like this. Dad was one of Hollywood's most revered directors, and even the critics considered him "one of the most brilliant screenwriters of our day." Mom had studied film in college and wasn't officially a director, but often worked on projects with Dad. Wherever Dad was, Mom was sure to be, and their 25-year relationship was, as tabloids had written numerous times, "ultimate couple goals." And now Micah was the media's current obsession because the first film where he'd been given top billing was the summer's biggest box office hit.

I jumped out of the car, my head down as I pushed through the wave of camera flashes and ran through the automatic doors.

I slammed into the receptionist desk. "Micah Moore," I said, breathless, "Is he here yet?"

Mom was behind me now, and she wrapped an arm around me as we waited for the receptionist to flip through something on her computer.

She looked back up at us. "Yes, they just checked him into the emergency room." She stood up and motioned for us to follow her. "Mrs. Moore, we have a private waiting room if you'd like to wait there. We'll let you know when you can see him."

"Thank you," Mom said as the receptionist led us into a tiny room lined with chairs. "When my husband comes, will you tell him where to find us?"

"Of course," she nodded before closing the door.

I sat down, but Mom walked in circles around the room. I buried my face in my hands and my whole body shook, wracked with guilt.

"Mom, I could have stopped this," I said, my eyes watering and my voice cracking. "I caught him sneaking out, and I didn't even do anything. He's so stubborn, and he insisted on going."

Mom dropped into the chair beside me and rubbed my back. "Hey, this is Micah's fault, not yours." Her voice was soothing.

"But I should have told you and Dad. Maybe you could have stopped him." I sat up straight and faced her.

Dad opened the door and slipped into the waiting room, but didn't sit down. He paced back and forth, running a hand through his greying hair.

"Will he ever learn?" Dad said, after my mom repeated to him what the receptionist had told us. "Did you know he'd snuck out?" He stopped and looked down at me, his hands on his hips.

"Yes," the tears spilled out of my eyes now, and I swiped them away. "I did. I'm sorry."

He started pacing again, pinching the bridge of his nose. "Why didn't you say anything?"

"Andrew," Mom said, standing up. "This is not her fault, and you know it."

We were in the waiting room for an hour before an African-American doctor in pale blue scrubs and a long white lab coat came in. "Mr. and Mrs. Moore, I'm Dr. Smith," he said, shaking their hands. "Micah is stable, but he's still unconscious. His right leg is fractured in two places, and he has quite a few cuts and scrapes. We're certain he has a concussion, but we won't know the extent of it until he wakes up and we can do a few more tests."

"Can we see him?" Dad asked, gripping Mom's hand.

"Of course." He nodded, and turned on his heels, motioning for us to follow him.

Dr. Smith led us to an elevator. As we rode up to the fourth floor, the only noise was the little beep that indicated each level we passed. The silver doors slid open and we walked down a long white hall. Micah's room was a few doors down on our right. Dr. Smith held the door open and I held my breath as I followed my parents in, afraid of what I'd see.

The light in Micah's room was dim, and he looked almost peaceful laying in the hospital bed. His dark hair, usually styled to perfection, was swept back from his forehead, and the right side of his face was covered with cuts. Some of them had been sutured and some of them were just red, but none of them were bleeding anymore. I could see, even in the dim light, the beginnings of green and purple bruises. There was an IV in his left arm, and a little plastic clip on his finger, feeding information to the machine sitting next to his bed. A blue blanket covered his leg, but his right one looked more bulky where I was sure they'd put a cast on his broken leg.

I wasn't sure how I'd react to seeing my brother, unconscious and scarred, but relief flooded over me as I watched the steady rise and fall of his chest.

"The boy that he was with, Logan Miller, how is he?" Dad asked, after looking over Micah.

"He regained consciousness soon after he arrived. He has a concussion and a broken arm, but he'll make a full recovery. His room is a few doors down, if you'd like to visit him at any time." Dr. Smith walked over to a whiteboard that was hanging on the wall across from Micah's bed and wrote Logan's room number on it.

I was so angry with my brother's good-for-nothing friends, I would not be going down the hall to check in on him. Logan was the whole reason we were in this mess. He was the stupid one; the one who had decided to get behind the wheel even though he was drunk. Granted Micah was dumb enough to get in the car with him, but still. He would have a lot of explaining to do when he finally woke up.

"I have to go check in with a few other patients, but nurses will be in and out periodically. If you have any questions, don't hesitate to ask, or call for me." Dr. Smith said, nodding to my parents before turning to leave.

There was a couch situated under the window that my parents settled down in, and I dragged a chair over to the side of Micah's bed. I was relieved to see with my own eyes that Micah wasn't on death's doorstep, but still felt on edge. I didn't want to be far from him.

Dad let out a sigh, but we didn't talk. We didn't really know what to say, and until Micah woke up, we had a lot of unanswered questions.

Pretty soon there was another knock on the door, and Winston, Micah's talent agent, opened it and stepped inside, closing it quietly behind him.

"Hey," Dad stood up and walked over to him, shaking his hand. "Thanks for coming. Sorry it's so early."

It occurred to me that I hadn't checked the time at all since Mom woke me up. I pulled out my phone. It was 4:43 in the morning.

Winston chuckled, "No worries, my man. How is he?" He nodded towards Micah.

Dad scrubbed his face. "He'll be fine, but it was a real bone-headed move."

Winston and my parents continued to talk, working on a statement they could give the press. I slipped my hand into Micah's and turned to stare out the window. I was still coming off all that adrenaline and it was grounding to feel Micah's hand in mine, to know that he was alive and would be okay. As I listened to my parents talk and the machines beep around us, I started dozing off. I don't know how much time passed, but I was vaguely aware of my parents leaving the room with Winston before Micah's hand moved in mine, squeezing it. I snapped awake and stood up.

I was torn between slapping him and grabbing him up in a hug—both options I was sure would cause discomfort given his state.

"Why didn't you call me, you idiot?" Thinking back, the first thing that came out of my mouth should have been something kinder. After all, a few hours ago, I was thinking he might be dead. But now I was just upset at the panic he'd given us.

"Gee, I love you, too," he joked.

"No, I'm serious," I leaned over the bed so I could look him in the eye. His pupils were dilated and one of them was blood-shot. "You could have died. What were you thinking? I need you, Micah."

"I know, I'm sorry. It was a stupid decision. The paparazzi surprised us coming out of the bar and Logan was just trying to help me get away."

"Never, *never,* do that again, do you understand?" I was still gripping his hand, afraid he would slip into unconsciousness again.

"I won't Mel, I promise. Where's Logan? Is he okay?"

"He's a few doors down," I said, settling back in my chair. "He woke up about an hour ago, and aside from a concussion and a few broken bones, he'll be fine. How are you feeling?"

"Sore. I have a huge headache. How long was I out?"

"A few hours. It was a pretty bad crash."

"Did I die? Did they have to revive me? Did we hit anyone else?"

"No, you didn't die," I rolled my eyes. Maybe he thought a brush with death would mean Dad would go easier on him. "And thankfully all you hit was a cement barrier blocking off a construction zone."

"Oh good." Micah started to move, but stopped. The color draining from his face and he clenched his jaw together.

"Oh yeah, and you broke your leg."

"Yeah, I noticed," he said through his teeth, breathing so deeply it sounded like he was giving birth. So dramatic. "Where are Mom and Dad?"

"They're walking Winston out. They should be back any minute."

"Is Dad mad?"

"You snuck out while you were grounded, got drunk even though you're only 17 and got in a car accident that could have killed you. Mad is an understatement."

I knew Dad was furious, but even I wasn't prepared for the bomb he was about to drop when they came back to the room.

When Mom saw that Micah was conscious, she rushed to his side, looking him over. "Oh Micah, I'm so glad you're awake. How do you feel?"

"Okay. My head hurts," Micah said, rubbing his forehead. "And I moved my leg, so now that hurts too."

"Don't you ever drive drunk again, and don't you ever drink again. Do you understand?"

"I'm sorry, Mom."

"I'm just glad you're okay," she said, her voice cracking and tears brimming her eyes. "It's a miracle you escaped with just a broken leg."

Dad had yet to say anything. His lips were pressed into a thin line, and it looked as if he might explode at any minute. He'd never been one to yell, but Micah's teenage years had been trying for both of my parents, and this crash was the final straw.

"Dad, I'm so sorry," Micah said, finally looking at my dad. "I really am. I was stupid."

He still didn't talk. He let out a loud breath, pacing in front of Micah's bed as if he was doing his best to calm down before speaking to my brother.

"Micah, how could you be so foolish?" Dad finally said. "I understand you are going to make mistakes, I do. But these kinds of mistakes are unacceptable. You could have killed yourself, or someone else. Something has got to change."

"I know. It will." Micah sounded sincere, but I understood my parents skepticism. He'd been breaking rules all his life, and he was getting more brazen the older we got.

"I just don't trust you. You say you're going to change, but I fear that once you're better, you'll forget that you could have died tonight. I'm not willing to let that happen again, and I think it's time for a little reality check." Dad was gripping the end of Micah's bed, and he dropped his head, filling his cheeks with air and letting out a huge breath before he looked back up at Micah. "I'm sending you to live with my sister in Utah for your senior year. No more drinking, no more partying, no more girls."

Panic set in for the second time that night. Micah and I had never been apart for more than a couple of days, and I wasn't ready to face that change right this moment. I thought we still had at least a year together.

A few days ago, Dad discovered that Micah had started drinking, and threatened to send him away if he didn't start making better choices. I thought it had been an empty threat in an effort to get Micah to rein it in, but apparently he'd made his contingency plan.

Dad's sister, Aunt Juliet, was our "cool aunt." She was quite a bit younger than my dad, but still about 10 years older than Micah and me. She'd spent her teenage years babysitting us, taking us to the beach or to the movies. She was a high school teacher, and had just gotten a job to teach theater in a little town called Park City, Utah. When she moved at the beginning of summer, she told us we were welcome to visit any time we wanted, but I wasn't sure this was what she had in mind.

"What?" Micah struggled to sit up, the color draining from his face. Whether that was because he was still woozy from his accident, or terrified of moving to Utah, I wasn't sure. "But my life is here."

"And how, exactly, is that going for you?"

"Dad, please," I said. "Don't send him away."

"You're going, too," he said, looking at me.

I wasn't sure which was worse: facing a year without my brother in the same state or being shipped off with him and having to leave home. I mean, sure, I knew he was sneaking out and that it definitely wasn't soda pop he was drinking, but did that really warrant punishing me too? I wasn't the one who had spent most of my summer breaking the rules, and most of my life before this summer pushing them to their limits.

"I'm sorry, what?" I'd never talked back to my parents, but it had been a weird night.

"Yes," was all he said in response.

I wanted to kick and scream and demand to know why I was being exiled too. Okay, maybe exiled is a bit dramatic. But why was my life being uprooted because Micah was like Icarus, *always* flying too close to the sun?

Dad said something about precautionary measures, and although Micah tried to charm his way out of it, my parents remained determined. We were heading to Utah whether we liked it or not. And boy, we did not.

Dad left the room, leaving Mom asking Micah a million questions about how he was feeling. I stood up and followed him out into the hall.

"Dad," I called after him.

He stopped and turned, facing me. He opened his mouth like he was about to say something, but I put my hand up, "Look, I know there's no changing your mind," I said, "But I'm not a little girl anymore. I deserve to know why I have to go with him, when the only thing I did wrong was going to bed instead of telling you about Micah."

"You're right," Dad nodded, sighing and scrubbing his face again. I'd never seen him like this. He was usually so confident and authoritative, but it struck me that the decision to send us to Utah was just as hard on him and Mom as it was on us. I even felt a little guilty for being upset with him.

"Your mom and I weren't raised in the spotlight, and I think that was a really good thing for us," he said. "We've talked a lot about this, and believe me, we don't want to send you away. But after this summer, with the changes we've seen in Micah after his movie premier, we think it's something both of you need, too. Kids need a chance to be normal, to grow up in a place where their every move isn't scrutinized. It may be past the point where that's possible, but I think it's worth a try. I know it will take Micah a little bit to understand, but I hope you both know we're doing this because we love you."

"I get it, Dad," I nodded. I didn't want to, but it was hard to argue with reason.

"I know I've made a lot of mistakes as a dad," he said, "I'm just trying to do right by you and Micah. You guys and your mom are the most important things in my life."

I wrapped my arms around him. "I think you're the greatest, Dad." I said, "I'm lucky to be your daughter."

He kissed the top of my head. "I'm the lucky one."

"When do we leave?" I asked.

"We'll consult the doctor and wait for him to give Micah the go-ahead. Then we'll head out there."

*Dying to find out how Max & Melanie's love story really played out? Buy Unforgettable now!*

# ACKNOWLEDGMENTS

At our wedding, my husband and I had a beautiful sparkler send-off. I think my husband, and our guests, expected us to get in the car and leave, but after we'd walked down the steps and the sparklers all went out, we stuck around for another 20 minutes because I felt like there were so many people I needed to thank. I'd just had the most beautiful and perfect wedding day, and I couldn't leave without thanking my parents, my new in-laws, the wedding planner, the caterers, my bridesmaids and my husband's groomsmen, and all of our friends and family who had come to celebrate us. My husband teases me all the time about taking so long to leave our reception, and I worry these acknowledgements might end up the same way our send-off did, so I'll try to keep this brief.

To Zach, my wonderful husband, thank you for your undying support of my dreams. Thank you for staying up until 2 AM talking about my ideas. Thank you for believing in me. Thank you for loving me on the hard writing days, and reminding me that I can do this. Thank you for being the love story that changed my life forever.

To my incredible parents, Stephen and Wendy Swensen, thank you for showing me what a true love story looks like. You guys are the reason I'm a romantic. Thank you for unconditionally loving me, supporting me, and cheering for me. Thank you for instilling a love of books and storytelling in me from a young age, and for teaching me that I can do anything.

To my sisters, MarKay and Emilee, and my brother, Taylor, thank you for being my dearest friends. I hope you know how grateful I am to be your big sister, and how much my relationships with each of you have enriched my life.

To my father-in-law, mother-in-law, sisters-in-law, and brothers-in-law, thank you so much for loving me as much as my own family does, and for being excited with me about my books.

To my amazing editor, Djinji, thank you for your invaluable help, support, and encouragement in getting this story ready to publish. Your edits and suggestions made this book far better than I could have made it on my own. Every writer needs someone as amazing as you in their corner.

And finally, thank YOU, my dear reader, for picking up this book and seeing it through to the end. You make this dream possible.

# ABOUT THE AUTHOR

Madison Bailey read Pride & Prejudice for the first time when she was 14, and she hasn't put the romance novels down since. A Jane Austen fanatic, and hopeful romantic, Madison writes clean and wholesome romances with guaranteed "Happily Ever Afters." When she's not writing, she loves reading, drinking hot chocolate, watching old Disney movies or reruns of The Office, and taking long naps and even longer bubble baths. She lives in Utah with her wonderful husband and their adorable puppy dog.

instagram.com/authormadisonbailey